GUARDIANS OF PORTHAVEN

/// SHANE ARBUTHNOTT ///

ORCA BOOK PUBLISHERS

Published in Canada and the United States in 2021 by Orca Book Publishers.
orcabook.com

Library and Archives Canada Cataloguing in Publication
Title: Guardians of Porthaven / Shane Arbuthnott.
Names: Arbuthnott, Shane, author.
Identifiers: Canadiana (print) 20210105321 |
Canadiana (ebook) 20210105356 | ISBN 9781459827042 (softcover) |
ISBN 9781459827059 (PDF) | ISBN 9781459827066 (EPUB)
Classification: LCC PS8601.R363 G83 2021 | DDC jc813/.6—dc23

Library of Congress Control Number: 2020951471

Summary: In this science-fiction novel for middle readers, just as
fifteen-year-old Malcolm prepares to take on the traditional role of
Guardian of his city, he learns some shocking truths about his family.

Orca Book Publishers is committed to reducing the consumption
of nonrenewable resources in the making of our books. We make
every effort to use materials that support a sustainable future.

Orca Book Publishers gratefully acknowledges the support for its publishing
programs provided by the following agencies: the Government of Canada,
the Canada Council for the Arts and the Province of British Columbia
through the BC Arts Council and the Book Publishing Tax Credit.

Design by Dahlia Yuen
Edited by Tanya Trafford
Cover artwork adapted from illustration by Malchev/Getty Images
Author photo by Erin Elizabeth Hoos Photography

Printed and bound in Canada.

24 23 22 21 • 1 2 3 4

To the rebellious superheroes in my life: my children,
Avery, Lachlan and Leah. You make the world a better place.

||||||||||||||||||

ONE

"Ladies and gentlemen, please welcome your newest Guardian, Malcolm Gravenhurst!"

Malcolm tugged at the knot of his tie and blew out sharply. A few feet in front of him his uncle Felix stood at the balcony railing, announcing him to the world. Felix turned, smiling at Malcolm and motioning for him to come forward. Malcolm forced himself to step up beside his uncle. He looked down at the ballroom full of people below them. Most were in finely tailored suits and gowns. Above their heads a flock of camera drones hovered, lights flashing in staccato bursts as they took pictures of him. He could identify the reporters in the crowd because they were the only ones not applauding. Instead they were fiddling with their bulky control bracelets, trying to maneuver their drones for the best angle.

The rest of the crowd was made up of politicians, shareholders in the Gravenhurst family's businesses, and other prominent citizens of Porthaven. Many of the faces were familiar to him, though he knew hardly any of their names. These people had their own drones as well, of course—

but they were the personal sylf models, like the one Malcolm had waiting back in his bedroom. He wished he had it now. He always found it reassuring to have the small silver orb hanging over his shoulder.

Beyond the crowd, through the floor-to-ceiling windows that ringed the entire room, Malcolm could see the city, the lights of its skyscrapers glimmering across the glass, crowding close to Gravenhurst Tower like a throng of supplicants.

Malcolm reluctantly turned his attention to the crowd. He half raised his hand to wave, but Felix's long fingers came down on his, pushing his hand back onto the railing.

"Don't wave," his uncle said softly without looking at Malcolm. "Just stand, and smile if you can manage."

"How long do we have to stand here?"

"An uncomfortably long time."

As cameras flashed and the crowd applauded, Malcolm attempted a smile. It felt as stiff and uncomfortable as his tie, so he dropped it.

"Today marks Malcolm's fifteenth birthday," Felix announced to the room, "and the beginning of his larger responsibilities as a member of the Gravenhurst family. We are here today to honor him as he takes on the mantle of Guardian of the city of Porthaven, as his mother and grandparents did before him."

More applause from the people below. Malcolm felt his knees wobble a little and gripped the railing tighter.

After what felt like an hour, the applause faded and Felix finally stepped back from the railing. Malcolm went with him, letting out a long breath as he turned to face his uncle. Felix adjusted the handkerchief in Malcolm's pocket.

"There. That's the worst part over."

"I thought it was all the worst part," Malcolm said softly.

His uncle shrugged. "Well, this next part could be fun, don't you think? Showing off a little bit?" He smiled down at Malcolm, and Malcolm found himself returning the smile despite the nervous energy tying knots in his muscles. "They'll love you. Now, let's show them what a Gravenhurst can do," Felix said, putting a hand on Malcolm's shoulder and guiding him to the curving stairway down to the lower floor.

Malcolm could feel sweat running down the insides of his arms and hoped the dark jacket would hide it.

The crowd parted before him, revealing the gleaming walnut dance floor at the center of the room. On one side of the floor sat three concrete blocks, each four feet cubed. Malcolm stepped onto the wooden floorboards. People and camera drones immediately filled the area behind him, cutting him off from his uncle. Tall as Felix was, Malcolm couldn't see him through the crowd. But then, as if he knew Malcolm was searching for him, Felix stepped back up onto the stairway. He gave Malcolm a reassuring nod.

Malcolm took his place in the center of the room and stared around. The sheer number of people was paralyzing. He closed his eyes, trying to focus on something besides the crowd. *We practiced it a million times. And after this you can finally do real hero work.*

He raised his arms and started. There were gasps from the audience as Malcolm's armor unfolded from his skin, darkly glittering facets passing outward through his clothes and then snapping into place. Malcolm still wasn't sure how it worked—the armor could pass through whatever he wore like it was intangible, but once it was in place it was as hard as steel.

The armor fully encased him. To the people around him, it would look like he'd been shrouded in gray glass, obscuring his features and smoothing out his edges until he looked like a crude sculpture. From Malcolm's perspective, the room just dimmed a little, like he'd put on shades.

It felt strange to use his powers in front of all these people. Ever since they had manifested five years ago, he had only been allowed to use them around his family. Not that he hadn't known this was coming—he'd trained for this moment his whole life, even before his powers came in, practicing combat and acrobatics alongside basic geometry. He'd known since birth that he would become a Guardian and use his powers to protect the citizens of Porthaven. It was what the Gravenhursts did. But his powers still felt private to him. Intimate. His armor put another layer between him and the crowd, but somehow he felt like he was stripping naked in front of the cameras.

All eyes were fixed on him. He sought out familiar faces in the crowd. There was Felix on the stairway, smiling proudly. His aunt Aleid stood nearby, wearing a broad-shouldered suit that looked almost military on her. She wasn't smiling—but that was normal for her. Malcolm's cousin Melissa, dressed in an immaculate navy suit, stood near the back wall next to someone Malcolm thought might be the mayor. And up on the balcony where Malcolm had been a moment before was Malcolm's grandfather, Hendrik. He looked out over the room, stony-faced. When his eyes met Malcolm's, his expression didn't change in the slightest.

Fingers snapped in the crowd, and Malcolm turned. His cousin Eric had wedged himself between two of the reporters. He raised one eyebrow at Malcolm and twirled his hand, signaling him to get on with it.

Malcolm nodded and flexed his arms a few times. The armor was no impediment—it moved and flexed with him as easily as his skin—but the same couldn't be said for his suit. He'd always trained in looser clothes.

I guess I could have just taken the jacket off. Too late now though.

He dropped into a crouch, then leapt straight into the air. With the enhanced strength his armor lent him, he soared several yards up, almost to the roof of the huge room. He flipped in the air then landed with a thud.

Oh crap. I think I cracked the floor. He was used to working in the gymnasium, with its more durable maple flooring. He glanced at his grandfather and saw him frown.

He jumped again, this time doing a backflip and landing more softly. He then went into a series of flips and tumbles he had trained long and hard to be able to do. It wasn't the high jumps that were tough—he was pretty sure he could jump straight through the roof if he wanted to. The hard part was keeping control, using just enough force. If he went into the crowd at the speeds he was moving right now, he would break bones. He stumbled on his last landing but stayed on his feet. As he made his way to the concrete blocks, applause rippled through the room.

He bent his legs and wrapped his arms around the first block. There was another gasp from the crowd as Malcolm lifted the concrete into his arms and placed it on the block next to it.

Then he lifted both of those blocks onto the third. Finally he gripped the third block and lifted the full stack of three.

The crowd applauded loudly again, and the cameras flashed. The blocks each weighed more than a car, but for Malcolm, with his armor up, they felt about as heavy as a stack of textbooks. He started to relax, to enjoy the crowd's obvious wonder. This was nerve-racking, but it felt good too. It felt free.

And then an image of the blocks tumbling from his arms popped into his head—if he leaned too far forward, the top block could slide off and crush that reporter with the paisley tie. He put the blocks down.

He leapt to the top of the cement blocks and paused for a moment, checking to make sure no one was close enough to be hit. Then he raised his fist and brought it down.

The force of the blow cracked the concrete, and he dropped down onto the next block. He struck twice more, breaking through each block in turn until he stood on the dance floor again, chunks of concrete in a ring around him.

While he waited for the dust to settle—for pictures, as he'd been coached—he glanced up at his grandfather. There was a grim smile on his face. Malcolm exhaled.

As the cameras began snapping again, Malcolm dropped the armor. The facets folded in on themselves and disappeared through his suit and into his skin. He forced a smile as he turned to make sure he showed his face to the cameras on all sides. Eric stood just behind one of the cameras, giving Malcolm a thumbs-up.

Felix stepped smoothly through the crowd to join Malcolm, putting a hand on his shoulder.

"As you can see, Malcolm promises to be an excellent asset in our battle against the klek. We are proud to have him join the rest of the Gravenhurst family in keeping Porthaven and its people safe." There was another burst of applause, which quickly died down. "We will take five minutes of questions," Felix said, and then everyone was surging forward, shouting, drones humming over Malcolm's head to record his every word.

"When did your powers manifest?" "Tell us more about your powers. How strong are you?" "Are you scared to fight the klek?"

Malcolm's ears rang under the constant questions. "Um…I first got my powers a few years ago. And the armor protects me pretty well, so I'm not too scared. Maybe just, like, a little nervous."

"So the armor is durable? Enough to protect you from the klek?"

"Well, it can stand up to gunshots. With the klek…I guess we'll have to see."

"And what about outside the klek?" one reporter shouted, physically pushing his drone so close that Malcolm flinched backward. "You won't be fighting aliens all day, after all."

"Well, um, I'm responsible for keeping the city safe now, and that's where I'd like to focus. I've only ever fought the klek in simulations before now, right? So I'll have to get used to the real thing, I guess. And I have this idea about—"

Felix's hand came down hard on Malcolm's shoulder. He looked up at his uncle, who smiled at him and shook his head subtly. Malcolm turned back to the reporter. "I've still got lessons and everything too. School stuff."

"And socially? Anyone special?"

"Any…oh, you mean am I dating anyone? No, no, not right now." Between his training and his lessons with private tutors, Malcolm didn't really spend time with people his age. Even when he was at one of the Gravenhursts' charity events, he spent more time with adults than other teens. He knew Eric's romantic relationships got a lot of press, and there were always one or two camera drones following him wherever he went. The thought made Malcolm start to sweat again. "Um, maybe later?"

"Are you worried about dying in the line of duty, given what happened to your parents? Your grandmother?"

The room seemed to go silent—even the drones stilled. Everyone looked at the journalist who had spoken as if he'd just slapped Malcolm in the face. Malcolm scowled, but not at the journalist. He could see the old familiar pity in the eyes of the crowd around him, the pity that told him that when they looked at him they saw a tragedy, not a person.

"Well, Malcolm?" Felix said at his side. Malcolm looked up at his uncle and saw no pity, only wry amusement, like he was embarrassed for the reporters. "Want to answer the question?"

Malcolm nodded. "I don't really remember my parents," he said. "I was only two when they died. And I mean, yeah, the klek might kill me too. They're dangerous, I know that. But I'm a Gravenhurst. We've got powers that no one else has, and that means we've got the best chance against the klek. We're the only ones who can really fight them, right?"

"But aren't you a little young to be a Guardian?" the reporter persisted. "Your cousins didn't take up the mantle until they were eighteen, I believe."

"I'm young, yeah, but my powers are strong. My aunt and cousins have been doing this alone for a long time, since my grandfather retired to run the business. I want to help." Malcolm looked up at Felix. Felix smiled and nodded.

"Is that really all you want though?" another reporter said—Malcolm noticed it was the one with the paisley tie. "Your cousins have other ambitions. Might you follow Melissa's footsteps into the business side of things? Or take up acting, like Eric?"

"Um…I don't know. Honestly, all I ever wanted to be was a superhero." Malcolm paused, realizing what he had just said. "I mean, not a superhero, a Guardian." Chuckles rumbled through the crowd. "Sorry. That wasn't what I meant. I—"

"Malcolm has always been determined to live up to his role as a Guardian," Felix said, stepping forward. "Even more so than my own son and daughter, who of course bear the mantle admirably but have interests that lie elsewhere." He smiled out at Eric, who looked back blandly. "From a very early age, Malcolm was aware of the responsibilities that come with being born a Gravenhurst, being born with these extraordinary powers. And he has prepared to shoulder those responsibilities with a determination that reminds me very much of my sister, Aleid, or our parents. I think what Malcolm is trying to say is that he loves this city, and his sole interest in these early days is to protect it, to earn the trust and respect of its citizens." He looked down at Malcolm with an easy smile.

"Um, yeah. Yeah," Malcolm said, nodding gratefully.

"And with that, the time for questions is over," Felix said. "Members of the press, thank you for coming to celebrate with us. Malcolm will make himself available for interviews at a later date. If you could make your way to the doors, our valets will see you out."

There was another round of flashes, which caught Malcolm off guard and left him blinking lights out of his eyes, and then the reporters and the camera drones were all heading for the door, ushered along by Felix's long arms.

"Like a deer in the headlights," a voice said behind Malcolm.

He turned. His cousin Eric was standing there, a drink in his hand.

"But don't worry about it. You're young enough to pull off the doe-eyed thing. The press will eat it up."

"You think?"

"Sure. As long as you don't—"

"Malcolm," his grandfather said beside them, and both Malcolm and Eric stopped moving. In the hubbub of the party they hadn't heard him approach. Now he loomed over them both, wide shoulders stooped slightly forward. Malcolm wanted to step back, but he didn't dare.

"*Superhero*, Malcolm?" he said with a frown. "I thought you took your role as a Guardian seriously."

"I...I do, sir. I take it very seriously."

His grandfather rubbed his chin, stubble scraping against his rough fingers. "I suppose little harm is done. The public may enjoy it. Humanizing, perhaps. But I think we should look into getting you a new tutor for media relations. Melissa can write up some talking points for you in the meantime."

"Oh. Um, yes. Sir."

His grandfather nodded. "Speaking of Melissa, she is over there waving rather emphatically for you. Happy birthday," he added and then nodded to Eric before walking away.

Malcolm looked at Eric, who stared after their grandfather. "Not the best reaction," Eric said. He turned to Malcolm and saw the expression on his face. Eric shrugged. "But hey, you should have heard what he said about *my* debut." He shivered. "And with that fond memory, I'm going to go get another drink." He put his empty glass down on one of the chunks of concrete and headed for the bar.

Malcolm stood alone for a moment. People had arrived to clean up the mess of concrete, and someone was swiftly nailing down the board Malcolm had split with his first jump. He watched them work while he pulled at his tie, trying to settle it somewhere it wouldn't press against his Adam's apple. Then he scanned the crowd until he found Melissa, who was indeed gesturing for him to join her. Malcolm made his way over.

She gave him a tight-lipped smile as she wrapped her hand around his arm and turned him to face the man beside her. "Malcolm, this is Mr. Jacoby, the head of our merchandising department."

The rail-thin man stuck out his hand, and Malcolm shook it. "Very impressive, the way you moved in the air. Do you perhaps share some of your aunt Aleid's talent for flight?"

"No. Just, like, high jumps."

"Ah." The man deflated a little. "Still, your power has a nice visual impact, and I think enhanced strength will be a big seller. I can see several opportunities…"

Malcolm nodded, trying to listen while the lights of the city winked through the window at him.

Hours later, when he had shaken the hand of every shareholder and influencer Melissa could find for him, Malcolm was finally released to wander the ballroom on his own. The crowd had continued to thin, and Malcolm found a quiet corner under the curving stairs, beside the catering table. He noticed an obliterated cake, which still bore a few smeared letters in blue icing: *HAPP BI*. He hadn't even known there was a cake.

He turned to look out the window. Up close to the glass, Porthaven was more than just glittering lights. He could see the clustered skyscrapers of downtown. Some were built in improbable shapes, like the double helix of the Salvas Dynamics Tower, or the Coleworth Financial building that curled over the city like a shepherd's crook. Hover tech and ultralight materials, invented by Gravenhurst R&D, made otherwise unstable configurations possible.

Other buildings were more traditional—tall rectangular towers of gleaming glass or gray concrete. But even they were capped with fanciful green-light projections—glowing minarets, swirling clouds or surreal landscapes. Back when the company had released the projection technology—before Malcolm was old enough to remember—the Gravenhursts had successfully campaigned for laws to make sure architectural projections could only be used aesthetically, not for advertising. Down at street level, things got more garish, but up here the result was this gleaming dream city, half real and half illusory. It was probably the thing he was most proud of about his family—aside from the way they protected Porthaven from a perpetual alien threat, that is.

And there were possibilities for even greater things. Now that everything in Porthaven ran off the ambient energy grid—cars, lights, personal devices, everything—their emissions were down to zero. Once they got that tech working outside of Porthaven, his family could solve climate change overnight. But so far, for some reason, their technology wouldn't play nice with the rest of the world. Something about the alien tech having landed here first, he supposed.

Malcolm heard footsteps behind him. Felix stepped up to the window, his smiling face reflected in the glass.

"A bit much, isn't it?" Felix said. "All these people here for you, but not really for you precisely."

"Yeah." Malcolm looked around the room and was happy to see that it was mostly empty now.

"You did us proud, Malcolm," Felix said. "And, to answer the question you're too polite to ask, yes, you can leave whenever you wish."

Malcolm smiled sheepishly. "That obvious?"

"Only for those who know you well," Felix said.

Malcolm nodded and turned to leave. Then he paused. "Is it hard, being here for this? I mean, because you're…"

"Powerless? It's okay to say it, Malcolm. I'm not sensitive about it."

"I know, just with the whole big debut, showing off my powers, and you being the only one in the family..."

Felix shrugged. "There are things to be envied, certainly. But I don't think the debut night is one of them. From the outside, it doesn't look like much fun."

"It's not. But still—"

"I'm fine, I assure you."

Malcolm studied his uncle. Felix didn't look upset, or left out, but he could be hard to read sometimes.

"Why did you cut me off? When I was talking to the reporters?" Malcolm asked.

Felix sighed. "Because I knew what you were going to say, and it would have been a mistake to speculate publicly about expanding our responsibilities as Guardians. It would have generated ill will toward the family."

"But we should—"

"No, Malcolm." His uncle put a hand on his shoulder and looked into his eyes. "Your job is to fight the klek, not fight crime. You are not a comic-book superhero, despite your hopes. Leave the rest to the police."

"But I could help people with more than just the klek. I could—"

"You could get involved in a lot of situations you don't understand and make them worse," he said. "Or you could get yourself killed and leave us with one less Guardian to fight the true threat. We have discussed this." His grip on Malcolm's shoulder relaxed. "I know you want to help people, Malcolm. And you will. You know Porthaven needs you. Now go to bed, before you're forced to spend time with your grandfather."

Malcolm nodded. He wanted to say more, but he couldn't think of the right words. So he did as his uncle suggested and left the party.

A dozen floors down, he stepped off the elevator and went into his bedroom. He walked past his tall bookshelves, past the wide window and into the alcove where his bed and dresser sat. His tie and collar had left deep grooves in the skin of his neck, and he probed them with one hand while he threw his jacket and tie onto the floor with the other. He picked up his sylf drone from the bedside table and thumbed it on. The small silver orb turned weightless in his hand, and glowing green readouts sprang into life in the air around the drone as it lifted off his palm.

"Did I miss anything?"

His sylf chimed and then projected a list of notices into the air in front of him. Malcolm swiped through them— mostly people tagging him in the media that had popped up about his debut. He wondered if he should respond, but the social media department would probably rather he left that to them. He dismissed the notices with a wave of his hand and looked out the window, the sylf returning to its familiar place just behind his right shoulder.

Things were still and silent this far up. But down below, the city was wide awake. Countless cars crawled the streets, while gleaming hoverpods zipped past them above. Late-night crowds gathered outside restaurants and bars, their drones flocking around them like curious birds. Even beyond the glimmer of downtown, the city stirred, innumerable lights piercing the darkness.

He'd been staring out this window at the city of Porthaven since before he could remember, but now it looked different. It was his city now, his responsibility. He'd been dreaming of this day since he knew what it meant to be a Gravenhurst, since he'd tied a blanket around his neck and his aunt Aleid took him flying.

He finished getting undressed, crawled into bed and dreamed of fighting monsters.

TWO

"So when do you think the klek will—"

Malcolm's question was interrupted by a kick to the back of his head. It didn't hurt through the armor, but it unbalanced him and sent him sprawling onto the floor of the gymnasium. He slid a fair way before stopping—Eric seemed to be hitting harder than usual today.

"Focus," Eric said, dancing around Malcolm. "The klek aren't going to stop to answer your questions."

Eric flipped over gracefully and brought his heel down toward Malcolm's head again. Malcolm rolled away, but Eric twisted himself in midair and landed on his hands, turning his dropkick into a spinning kick that took Malcolm's feet out from under him.

"Hey! Let me stand up at least!"

"The klek don't do that either." Eric jabbed the side of Malcolm's head with a punch before jumping away with a grin.

Malcolm pushed up hard with his hands, sending himself into the air and landing on his feet. He got into a proper stance, legs bent, arms up, and then feinted left with a kick before stepping right to try to grapple his cousin. But Eric planted his hand on Malcolm's armored head and deftly flipped himself over Malcolm before kicking him in the back and sending him to the floor again. Malcolm lashed out with a foot as he fell, hitting Eric's leg, but Eric calmly turned the new momentum into a somersault and rose again.

Malcolm grimaced. His cousin's power meant he never lost his balance—he moved with inhuman grace and agility at all times. Which had made him an amazing action hero in his film career, as well as the world's most frustrating sparring partner.

"Come on, Eric, seriously! When do I get to fight the klek?"

"How would I know?" Eric said, sauntering over to give Malcolm a hand up. "They're alien invaders. They don't send us a schedule or anything."

"But we're always ready for them. I just assumed we had some way of knowing—a special sensor or something—and that when I became a Guardian you would—"

Eric turned his hand on Malcolm's arm into a throw, and Malcolm went sailing across the room. Not for the first time, he wished his armor weren't so light. His cousin couldn't hurt him much, but he tended to toss Malcolm around like a rag doll. Malcolm managed to tuck and roll to his feet just in time to block Eric's next kick, but when he spun to retaliate he found Eric halfway up one of the ropes that dangled from the ceiling.

Malcolm dropped his armor. "Stop for a second, Eric!"

Eric swung on the rope, and for a moment Malcolm was certain he was going to hit him again, even without the armor.

He got into moods like this sometimes—got a look in his eye like he wasn't just practicing.

Malcolm flinched but held his ground as Eric swung closer and touched Malcolm lightly on the tip of his nose with a closed fist. "Boop."

"Please, Eric. Talk to me for a little bit, okay? No one else will answer my questions."

Eric sighed and sent himself into a graceful spin on the rope, hanging by one hand. When he stopped spinning, his face had softened. "Look, there's no special sensor. When an attack is happening, Aunt Aleid will send you a text and come pick you up."

"That's…that's honestly it?"

"It's not complicated. We show up, smash the alien robots and get back to our day."

"But, I mean, we're fighting a constant alien invasion. 'Aunt Aleid will send you a text'? That seems so basic."

"I don't make the rules."

"What about the secret hideout in the basement of the Tower? When do I get a key?"

Eric snorted, then slid down the rope to land lightly on his feet. "I'll tell you when I find out." He folded his legs and sat on the floor in one smooth motion.

"You don't have the key? But I thought it was, like, our base of operations."

"You think a lot of things, it sounds like. But that's not how it works. Only Grandpa Hendrik, Aleid and Felix go in the basement, and I'm pretty sure it's just where they keep the sketchy business records. There's no secret hand-shake either."

Malcolm sat next to his cousin. "Can you at least tell me more about the klek?"

Eric shrugged. "Tell me what you already know."

"I only know, like, the basic stuff. The stuff everyone knows."

Eric nodded and twirled his hand to indicate Malcolm should go on.

"I mean, the original klek gate fell to Earth and the klek started popping out. And our grandparents were close when it fell, and it did something weird to them and gave them their powers. They used those to destroy the gate. And that stopped most of the klek, but every few weeks, new ones teleport in even without the gate."

Eric nodded. Malcolm waited for him to say something, but Eric just smiled that lopsided smile the tabloids liked so much.

"So tell me the real stuff!" Malcolm finally said after a long silence. "Where do they come from? What the heck do they want? How do they get here even without their gate thing?"

Eric shrugged.

"Seriously? You don't know anything more than that?"

Eric shook his head. "Don't think too much about it. The klek are just a thing that happens, like a storm. The big ones can put up a fight, but otherwise?" He shrugged. "They invade, we stop them. Simple."

"Okay, well, what about the tech? I know we started using the klek technology to make new stuff, but the tech only works in Porthaven. Why?"

"Yeah, that is weird, isn't it?" Eric said. "And also, why don't they use the tech to invent anything cool, like jetpacks?

Or giant robots we could use to fight the klek? I've been asking for giant robots for ages, but Grandpa always gives me that look." He laughed. "But seriously, Malcolm, I can't answer any of these questions. I'm not sure anyone can."

Malcolm shook his head. "That can't be—"

Without even getting up from the floor, Eric reached out and grabbed Malcolm's wrists, twisting them until Malcolm was pressed face-first into the floor beside his cousin, shoulders aching. "Ow," he said into the cold, smooth wood.

"I can tell you this," Eric said, casually pinning Malcolm with a knee on his back. "The klek are metal right through. Just machines. No pilots or anything. I used to wonder if they might not even be intelligent, you know? They sure don't seem very smart. Maybe they're just programmed to invade. They're like tools that got away from their makers or something, and that's why they keep on coming even though we stop them every time. Like ants trying to get into someone's house."

"Used to wonder? What do you think now?"

"I try not to think about it at all, honestly. They're alien. They don't make sense. Find something better to do with your time, cuz." Eric stood, finally letting Malcolm get to his feet. "The klek are dumb, but they don't pull punches. Now spar with me, or I'm just going to start kicking your butt anyway." He raised his arms in a loose boxer's stance and gestured Malcolm forward.

Malcolm sighed and raised his armor. He knew already he wouldn't win—likely wouldn't even land a hit.

He lifted his fists and stepped forward. "Think you could go easy on me for once? As a birthday present?"

Eric smiled and kicked Malcolm in the face.

Sore and tired, Malcolm stepped into the shower in his room. The water jets on all sides scoured him with hot water, and he instantly felt better.

Once he was done, he toweled himself dry and pulled some more of his workout clothes from his closet—light cotton pants and a white T-shirt. His laundry from the night before had vanished from his room while he was training.

He checked his sylf. It was 2:00 p.m. on a Saturday, which meant he didn't have any tutoring this afternoon. And apparently he didn't have a battle with the klek coming up either.

Find something better to do with your time, Eric had said. Malcolm looked toward his bookshelves, at the rows of graphic-novel spines. Most of them were the fictionalized tales of his own family, which seemed to be relaunched each year. He hadn't read them all, but the publishers always sent him copies. The most worn books, on the lower shelves, weren't about the Gravenhursts. They were his own collection—Squirrel Girl, Ms. Marvel, the classic Claremont and Davis run of Excalibur that he'd worked hard to collect. Ones about heroes who didn't just do it as a job but tried to do every ounce of good they could in the world. He knew exactly what he wanted to do with his time. He pulled on his running shoes and left the room.

He stepped off the private family-only elevator eighty floors down, into the busy lobby of Gravenhurst Tower. People with blazers and briefcases moved in and out of the public elevators on the opposite wall, busy at work despite it being the weekend. Near the front doors, security guards with slim, silvery body armor sat at the wide front desk, watching people through the green visors that let them scan for weapons. People without clearance checked in their sylfs at another desk farther in. Malcolm wasn't sure what the point of all the security was. Who would commit a crime in the home of the only superpowered family in the world?

As he approached the front door, Orin—the doorman—nodded to him and tipped his hat, pulling his red jacket straighter. "Going out, are we, Mr. Gravenhurst?"

"Yeah. Just for a bit. It's not in the schedule."

"I'll call you a pod, shall I?"

"No, that's okay, Orin. I'm going for a run."

"Is there something amiss with the sim suites? Usually you take your runs there."

"No. Just…fresh air."

"Are you sure, sir? Have you mentioned this to anyone?"

"Yeah, Felix knows. See you later!" Malcolm dashed through the front door before Orin could call Felix to confirm. Outside he started running as he had said he would, his sylf whirring louder as it sped to keep up. People looked at him sideways as he passed, but he hurried away before they recognized him. He ran until he was out of sight of the Tower, then armored up and leapt skyward.

He came down on the balcony of a building a block away and looked around. Gravenhurst Tower loomed over him and the rest of the city, its silvered windows reflecting the blue sky perfectly, making it look like the framework of a building more than a full skyscraper. The Tower flared toward the top, like a giant scepter rising out of the ground.

It looked like it should fall over at any moment, but nothing would ever topple the Tower.

Malcolm turned his attention groundward. He wasn't sure what to look for. Was there a lot of crime here, in the richest part of the city? Probably, but mostly white-collar. The kind that armor and superstrength wouldn't help with. He needed to go somewhere with street crime.

After a moment his drone ascended to join him. It wasn't going to be able to keep up with him, he realized. He signaled it with a click of his tongue, and it flew immediately into his palm. "Hover off," he said, and its weight settled into his hand. He dropped his armor long enough to tuck it away in his pocket.

He looked down again. There were a few gawkers on the ground who had seen him jump. He leapt farther away, jumping from rooftop to rooftop until he had left them behind. It wasn't as easy as he had imagined, moving this way, and he almost went over the far side of a roof more than once. But slowly he found the rhythm of it. And then he started to enjoy himself. He'd never been able to jump like this before, full strength and free. He'd kept his powers inside the Tower, where he always had to worry about going through the walls. He jumped farther and farther with each leap, arcing high into the air, clearing multiple buildings with each stride. He left downtown behind, following Lockheed River south, toward the rail yard and the poorer areas of the city.

Malcolm had never been here before—he generally stuck close to home, since there was no family business to bring him this way. In fact, he generally didn't even leave the Tower unless he had to. Out here, Porthaven looked almost like any other city in the world. Square buildings, made solid to carry their own weight, marred by the grime of years without self-cleaning materials mixed into their stonework. Unfamiliar as this area was, he found it easy to keep his bearings as long as he stuck to the rooftops. There was the river, just to his left, splitting the city in two. And behind him Gravenhurst Tower stood tall above the rest of downtown. He began moving more slowly, scanning the streets for signs of people in distress, listening for the telltale whine of sirens.

"My first patrol," he whispered under his breath and grinned.

Hours later he wasn't grinning anymore. The sun had gone down as Malcolm crossed and recrossed the river. So far he had only found a man getting a speeding ticket and an ambulance loading a woman with a broken arm. It was shocking how hard it was to find someone he could help. His armor was getting stifling, and his already-sore legs complained more with each leap he took. He came to rest on top of a strip mall—one story, not much of a vantage, but there weren't many tall buildings nearby. He was contemplating giving up and returning home when he heard raised voices—some kind of genuine conflict.

"Finally," he whispered to himself, jumping down from the roof to the lane behind the mall.

He followed the angry voices to the right. In a smaller alley off the back lane, Malcolm could see three people. One held a gun, another a knife, and the third was digging into his pocket. A mugging.

"Stop!" said the man with the gun. "Get your hands where I can see them."

"I'm not messing with you," the other man said, putting his hands out to his sides. "I don't have a weapon. You can take my wallet." His voice was shaking as the woman with the knife moved forward. Malcolm prepared to leap in, aiming for the space between the robbers and their victim.

Something caught his eye. Malcolm froze. There was movement on the other side of the alley. A shadow was creeping along the wall, but there was nothing there to cast it. The sourceless shadow was moving toward the robbers.

Malcolm stared hard at the blob of darkness, trying to figure out what could be creating it. For a moment the shadow flickered, light flooding in, and Malcolm saw something. A person hiding inside the darkness. Their hands raised, pointed toward the man with the gun. And then the shadow deepened again, and Malcolm lost sight of the person.

At the same time, the nearby streetlamp flickered. The light it cast warped and focused like sunlight through a magnifying glass, a bright point forming on the barrel of the gun. The gunman noticed the shifting of the light too and looked from his gun to the lamp and back. After only a moment the gun began to glow red-hot. The man dropped it with a shout.

"Ho-ly crap," Malcolm whispered, staring at the shadow, trying to see the person it hid.

The man with the gun was shouting now, looking around wildly. He tried to pick up the heated gun but dropped it immediately. While he panicked, his partner with the knife simply looked angry. She turned on their victim, who still had his arms out. "What did you do?" she shouted at him as he stumbled backward. "Show me what you've got in your pocket. Is it some kind of Gravenhurst thing?"

"No, no, I swear!" the man sputtered.

The woman raised her knife.

Across the alley, the shadow dispersed and the person inside came running out, heading for the woman. Her victim backed against the wall of the alley, nowhere else to go.

Malcolm suddenly realized he shouldn't just be watching this. Whatever the other person was doing with the lights— *Using superpowers! Fighting crime!* Malcolm's thoughts screamed—Malcolm had come to help. He surged forward, armored feet thudding against the pavement.

The knife started coming down at the same time as the shadow-person slid into the woman, knocking her feet out from under her. The knife clattered onto the ground. She reached for it again, but her mysterious attacker kicked it away fast. And then Malcolm bowled into both of them.

The woman spun away into a wall. Malcolm and the shadow-person tumbled across the ground and landed right at the other robber's feet, Malcolm on top. The robber looked down at them, fists still raised.

"Um," he said, taking in Malcolm's gray armor. Then he turned and ran.

"What the hell?" said the person beneath Malcolm.

A man, Malcolm realized. Dark skin, short hair. Tall.

"Oh, uh, sorry. I was trying to help." Malcolm got up. "Sorry about that. But did you...the shadow and that light, were you—?"

He heard scuffling behind him and turned to see the woman running the other way with her knife, her victim left behind. "Hey!" Malcolm shouted after her. "Hey, you're under arrest! You—" But she was already around the corner. He thought about jumping after her, but instead turned back to the person he'd knocked over.

Only he wasn't there.

THREE

Malcolm stared all around, looking for suspicious shadows, hardly aware of the victim approaching him on shaking legs.

"My goodness! Thank you for intervening! Are you that Gravenhurst boy?" the man asked. "I saw you on the news."

"Yeah. Sorry I didn't get here sooner or help better. But that person, he—"

"I owe you my life! I—"

"No, you don't. I was too late. There was someone else here, and he—" Across the street a patch of shadow moved along a fence, and Malcolm started running. "Hey! Wait!" he shouted. The shadow only moved faster.

Malcolm gauged his distance and jumped, landing ahead of the shadow. "Just stop for a second," he said, extending his arms wide. The shadow continued moving straight toward him and then flowed over him. There was no one inside. "What the…?"

A block away he saw a slim figure running in the other direction, legs pumping. Malcolm jumped again, trying to get ahead of him, but misjudged. He was coming straight down on him.

"Heads! Look out!" he shouted. The man looked up, then dove sideways. Malcolm landed with a crash. The man was only a few feet away from him. Under the bright streetlight, Malcolm saw that he was young, maybe just a little older than Malcolm himself—a boy more than a man. His skin was dark and acne-scarred, his hair cropped close to his head. As he stared up at Malcolm the light bent again, away from them, and everything started dimming.

"Is that a power? Are you using a power right now?" Malcolm asked, standing and walking toward him. The boy scrambled back, the shadows following and starting to coalesce around him. "But you're not a Gravenhurst! How are you…I mean, I don't *think* you're a Gravenhurst. Maybe you are? I don't—holy crap, dude, this is awesome! What are you even doing to the lights?" He stared around him in wonder. The light was bending, visibly curving away from the boy. Malcolm clapped his hands together and laughed, then realized this probably looked ridiculous. He dropped his hands to his sides. He couldn't do anything about the grin stuck to his face though. "How do you do that?"

The boy stopped moving away, and the shadows dispersed. "You're…not going to kill me?" he said softly.

"*What?* No, of course I'm not! Oh, sorry, sorry, I figured you'd recognize me." He dropped the armor and stuck out his hand—to shake or to help him up, though he wasn't sure which. "I'm Malcolm. Gravenhurst."

"I know who you are." He didn't take Malcolm's hand as he stood. He was taller than Malcolm—but then, Malcolm was used to looking up at people, since everyone in his family was taller than him. "What are you doing here?"

"I was doing what you were doing, or what I think you were doing. Trying to stop a crime. Patrolling. But I'm kind of new, I guess. I'm sorry about the whole knocking-you-over thing. I've trained a lot, but it's really different being out here. But you saved that guy! What's your name?"

The boy just stared at Malcolm, eyes narrowed. "You were patrolling? Gravenhursts don't patrol."

"I know, but I think we should. I mean, we've got super-powers, right, so shouldn't we—hold on, that's not important right now. You've got powers too! That's incredible! Are you, like, a second cousin of mine or something?"

The boy's eyes narrowed further.

"I know you don't look like a Gravenhurst, but if you are a Gravenhurst, awesome! But if you're not, that's even bigger! Other people besides the Gravenhursts with powers? What would that even mean?" *Team-ups,* his brain suggested unhelpfully.

"You always talk this much?" the boy said.

"Oh. Um. I don't know. Not really? Just when I'm nervous, but my family usually cuts me off." He closed his mouth, but that made him feel like all that nervous energy was trapped inside him, rattling between his bones. "So…"

"This is weird. I don't know how to deal with this. With you."

"Sorry, I guess? What do you mean?"

"I have to go." The boy turned on his heel and started jogging away. The light around him dimmed, flickering in waves on either side of him as it shifted away. For a moment Malcolm just stared, fascinated, and then reason reasserted itself.

"Oh hey, wait up!" Malcolm armored his legs to enhance his speed so he could catch up, but kept his upper body unarmored so he didn't look threatening. The boy didn't even stop or look at him. "How does that work? You can control the direction of the light? Oh man, when I tell Felix, he's gonna flip—"

The boy's hand suddenly shot out and grabbed Malcolm's sleeve. They both stopped running. The boy looked down at his own hand as if surprised to find it there. He let go.

"Don't. Don't do that, please."

"What, talk so much? Sorry, I—"

"Don't tell your family about me."

"What are you talking about? Of course I'm going to tell my family! If the powers are spreading, this is huge! We could have teams to fight the…"

The boy hid his face in his hands for a second, and Malcolm trailed off. Then he uncovered his face and stared at Malcolm.

"You honestly don't know anything about this?" the boy said.

"About what?"

The boy huffed, looking around them. They were on an empty residential street, lit only by streetlamps. He stepped in closer and lowered his voice.

"Look, just please don't tell anyone about me, okay? Not your family, not anyone."

"I don't get it."

"And I do not want to be the one to explain it to you. Here." He reached into his pocket and pulled out a phone. "Give me your number, and I'll send you a text. We can talk later, okay?"

"A phone? Don't you have a sylf?"

The boy's lip curled. "Do you know how expensive those things are?"

"Umm…no, actually."

"Your sylf should have a number it uses to interact with old mobile networks," he said. "Do you know it?"

Malcolm shook his head.

The boy rolled his eyes and held his hand out. "Can I see your drone?"

Malcolm dropped his armor and pulled his sylf out of his pocket. It was vibrating for some reason, but the boy grabbed it from him before he could figure out why. The boy turned it over, looking at the engraved text on the bottom of the silver orb. With his other hand he tapped something into his phone.

"Got it," he said, tossing the sylf back to Malcolm. "I'll text you later. You won't tell?"

"No. But can you at least tell me your name?"

The boy narrowed his eyes, tightened his lips over his teeth. "Drew," he said, and this time when Malcolm stuck out his hand, he shook it.

"I promise I'll get better at this whole rescuing-people thing," Malcolm said. "Maybe next time I won't knock you over."

"Yeah. Sure," Drew said, then squinted at Malcolm again. "Why are you looking at me like that?"

"Could you…maybe show me the light thing again? Just a little bit?"

"No."

"Right. Sorry. It looks really cool is all."

Drew actually smiled, though he still looked confused. "I gotta run." He turned and did just that, without a backward glance.

Malcolm stood there for a moment, watching the lights on the cracked pavement. He was so excited he felt like he was shaking. *This is so cool.* And then he realized some part of him actually was shaking. It was his hand, still holding his sylf, which was vibrating to get his attention. *Did he text me already?* But no, it had been vibrating when he handed it over to Drew. He thumbed the sylf on and it immediately jumped into the air, projecting a green display in front of his eyes. His heart dropped. Two texts. Three missed calls.

Both texts and calls were from his aunt Aleid. The first text read, **Klek. Lobby in five minutes.** It had been sent fifteen minutes ago. And then another, ten minutes later. **Where are you?**

FOUR

Malcolm brought up his armor and leapt for the top of the nearest house. Then he realized he should text back, so he dropped his armor and said, "Message to Aleid. I'm…" He trailed off as he saw his drone appear over the edge of the roof, struggling to catch up to him. "Crap crap crap crap crap," he muttered as he ran across the roof and grabbed his drone roughly out of the air. "Message to Aleid. **I'm coming! Send!**" Then he shoved the drone into his pocket and got moving again. The sylf struggled for a moment before getting the idea and turning its hover engines off.

Malcolm aimed for the gleaming shape of Gravenhurst Tower, jumping as fast as he could. He was so frantic that he almost landed in the river, but he skidded to a halt on a paved trail, startling a man walking his dog. He muttered an apology and kept moving.

He was nearing downtown now, the buildings getting taller and taller around him. Maybe he could still make it in time. If he could figure out where the fight was. He gathered himself and leapt for the top of one of the skyscrapers.

As he flew through the air, there was a deafening boom to his right that rattled the windows of the building beside him. He turned his head and saw a fireball bloom just a few blocks away. And then he collided with the building he had been trying to jump onto.

He bounced off the corner of the building and hurtled through a green projection of immense flowers, then arced down toward the street. He was at least twenty stories up, with nothing but empty air around him. The armor would absorb the impact, he knew, but if he landed on someone, he would kill them. And the street below him was crowded with people, cars and pods.

"Incoming!" he shouted. Some of the people heard and looked around. "Up! Up! I'm falling!" A woman with a misshapen fedora looked up at him and stared mutely. She was still staring at him when he pinged off the side of a hoverpod and collided with the trunk of a car.

The car crumpled around him, and Malcolm felt it bounce on its wheels. He heard screams, followed by shocked silence. Malcolm pried his eyes open. He was embedded in the trunk. Above him he could see the pod he had hit. The side was buckled, but the pod was still stable in the air.

He had to fold the metal back to get himself out, and broken glass pattered on the ground as he stepped out onto the hood of the next car, which had stopped an inch away from the bumper. The middle-aged driver watched him in shock.

Malcolm turned and looked behind him. One woman in the car he had hit. And a dog, wagging his tail and barking out the window at Malcolm.

"I'm sorry," Malcolm said. "Are you okay?"

The woman nodded. Malcolm looked around. "Is anyone hurt?" he asked loudly. Traffic had stopped, but people were shaking their heads.

"I'm so sorry about the car. I can pay for it—"

Another boom echoed through the streets. Malcolm turned toward it. "Klek. Got to go! Anything I damaged, bring it to the Tower later. I'll get it fixed!"

He leapt—lower this time, keeping to street level as he moved east. He could hear the telltale sounds of battle— glass breaking, metal tearing, the basso *thud* of his aunt breaking the sound barrier. He rounded a corner running and then stopped.

There they were. Really there, in front of him, between two rows of tall glass-fronted buildings. Three klek. Two on the ground in front of him, and one climbing the building to his right, its feet embedded in glass and concrete.

He froze. He'd seen videos of them, of course, and the meticulous digital recreations in Eric's latest movie. But never for real. He'd studied so much about the klek that for a moment he couldn't process their actual presence. They were things on screens, not part of the actual world.

These were big ones. You never knew how big the klek would be when they showed up. Sometimes you got a swarm of klek the size of small dogs. Sometimes you got one gargantuan machine the size of a building. Always the same shape though. The silvery, bulbous bodies with no openings—no visible lenses or sensors of any type. The five multi-jointed legs, many times longer than the body itself.

These ones were about three stories high. As he watched, the one nearest to him lifted one of its legs, uncurled a vicious barb from its end and impaled a parked car. With each movement, the robot clicked and whirred, making the strange sound that had given them their name. *Klek klek klek* as it lifted the car. *Klek klek k k k* as it hurled the car down the street, away from Malcolm. The car was struck by a bright green beam of energy and exploded in fire.

That's Melissa, Malcolm thought. *That klek just threw a car at Melissa.* Still it didn't seem real.

One thing even the live footage couldn't convey was the unsettling way the klek moved. It was both fluid and abrupt, with the metal bending in ways metal shouldn't bend. Or maybe it wasn't metal, he supposed, but something alien. The way they walked, legs folding and unfolding, made him want to run the other way. The bizarre rhythm of their footsteps told him better than any of his lessons that these machines were not from Earth. They didn't belong here.

There was a thump above him, and Malcolm looked over to see his cousin Eric skidding down a wall, pushing off and landing lightly beside him. He wore his combat gear—black jacket and pants, lightly armored but not so much that it would slow him down—with his signature long-bladed daggers at his belt.

"You made it!" Eric said. "Aunt Aleid is gonna want to talk to you…"

Then he was gone again, running at the nearest klek. It brought its foot down toward him, but Eric dodged to the side and swung around the leg, clambering up until he reached the first joint. He turned to Malcolm and shouted something, pointing.

"What?" Malcolm shouted back.

"HIT IT HERE!" Eric said, hands cupped around his mouth. The klek snapped its leg up, trying to fling Eric off, but Eric swung around and landed on the klek's silvery body. He pulled the daggers from his belt and plunged one of them into the gap in the klek's metal shell, between its body and its leg. The klek reared and bucked, clicking wildly.

"Oh. Oh, right!" Malcolm shook his head, checked his armor—all fine—and leapt toward one of the klek's legs, aiming for the joint.

It raised its leg at the last moment, and Malcolm collided with a solid metal plate. His extended fists buckled the metal, or whatever it was, and he had to pull hard to dislodge himself. Then he wrapped his arms around the leg and climbed higher, to the joint.

It was awkward, holding himself in place on the wide leg and trying to strike it. His armor and the klek's metallic surface slipped against each other. He found a crevice between two segments of its shell where he could wedge a foot, and then raised his fist and brought it down. With a deafening *clang* the joint buckled. Malcolm whooped and tried to climb higher, but the now-broken leg came up fast, swinging around and slamming him into a wall. Glass and concrete shattered around him, and Malcolm fell to the street in a shower of rubble.

He was dizzy but unhurt as he rose to his feet and turned to face the klek. He bent his legs, getting ready to jump back into the fray, but the klek suddenly went limp and crashed down onto the street. A moment later he heard a supersonic boom. *Aunt Aleid!* She had collided with the klek so fast that all Malcolm had seen was a blue blur. As he watched, Aleid climbed out of the robot's body and flew straight up, only to come hurtling down again, tearing another chunk out of the klek. Its legs twitched. Malcolm grinned, watching his aunt work. She, more than anyone else in the family, looked like a real superhero in her rugged blue flight suit. She didn't have his enhanced strength, but with her flight and invincibility it didn't matter. She could throw herself through the klek like a missile. She was unstoppable. She was exactly what he hoped to be.

Malcolm got up and went to help her finish off the klek, but one of its twitching legs caught him and sent him hurtling through the air.

"Oh come on," he said as he slammed into another wall. By the time he got his feet under him again, Aleid had broken the huge robot into pieces. She'd defeated the giant alien robot while he'd been busy acting like a human billiard ball.

He began to turn, looking for a new target, and just had time to register the car hurtling through the air toward him before it struck.

It didn't hurt—not exactly. His armor absorbed the blow. But it knocked him back so fast that he felt nauseous and feared he might throw up in his armor. He wasn't sure what would happen if he did, but he felt certain it would be unpleasant.

The car landed on top of his legs. Malcolm bent to lift it off, but then one of the klek scuttled over the top of the car and put two legs down on it, pinning him to the ground again. The metal of the car and his glass-like armor both groaned under the weight. The klek lifted one leg and brought it down, punching a barb through the car and onto his right hip. Malcolm felt the blow. He wasn't sure how many hits like that his armor could take.

The klek began to bring its leg down for a second strike, but a blinding green light tore it apart. There was another flash, and the leg holding the car down on him was bisected, its foot falling across his chest with a clang. The klek stumbled and turned as Malcolm pushed leg and car off him and struggled to his feet.

Melissa ran up to him, her shirt untucked under her blazer but otherwise looking like she might have stepped out of a sales meeting. "You okay?" she shouted.

He nodded.

Melissa raised her hands, and green light curled around her fingers before blasting out toward the klek. The blast caught its body, lifting it slightly off the ground and leaving its silver surface charred. "You might want to step back!" Melissa shouted as she ran after the klek.

"Yeah, but…" Malcolm faltered. *Maybe I really should step back. It doesn't seem like I'm doing much good.*

He looked around. Aleid had joined Eric to handle the klek that was climbing the building on Malcolm's right. Eric was standing atop the klek, calmly dodging its barbed legs as he worked at it with his daggers. As Malcolm watched, Eric managed to separate one of the legs from the body, sending it crashing to the ground far below.

The klek struck again, and Eric leapt smoothly out of the way. But midjump he was caught by another leg and knocked sideways. He flew through the air, limp as a rag doll.

Malcolm had never seen his cousin get hit before. He didn't know how it had happened. *It looked like that leg came out of nowhere.* And it had, Malcolm realized a minute later. The leg that had hit Eric was sticking straight out of the building, and as Malcolm watched, a fourth klek pulled itself out through the broken windows. It had been hiding inside.

He looked for Aleid, to see if she would catch Eric, but she had already started her descent toward the other klek, and once she built up speed it was hard for her to change direction. She collided with the wall-climbing klek, smashing two of its legs off, as the new klek emerged behind her and leapt toward Eric. Eric still wasn't moving.

Malcolm checked his cousin's trajectory and jumped. As he drew close, he saw his cousin stir, head turning to take in the klek coming for him and Malcolm moving toward him from another direction.

Malcolm reached Eric first, but instead of catching him, he found Eric's feet pressed against his cheek. "Thanks, Mal," Eric said as he used Malcolm to springboard up toward the klek. Malcolm, thrown off his jump by his cousin, spun through the air, bounced off a window and crashed to the ground.

By the time the fourth klek landed, Eric had both of his knives dug into one of its joints, and Malcolm was pretty sure he was smiling.

Malcolm stood, thought about helping and then sat down on the ground. First the robbery, and now this. He felt exhausted. He felt tiny, ineffectual.

He looked up at his aunt, who had knocked the third klek off the wall of the building, sending it smashing to the ground. He looked at Eric gleefully dodging between the new klek's legs. He wasn't sure where Melissa had gone—maybe back to the boardroom this fight had pulled her out of.

He stood up. *I can do this. I want to do at least one worthwhile thing.* He watched his aunt smash down into her klek. *That's how to do it.*

Malcolm looked at the buildings on either side of them—both straight slabs of concrete and glass, no balconies, no handholds except the holes the klek had punched through. *But maybe,* he thought, *if I time it right...*

He jumped as high as he could.

He soared upward and hit the wall of the building on his right. He pressed his hand against it for balance, then pushed off with his armored legs, and he was moving upward. He hit the opposite building and jumped again, moving higher each time, past the klek, past his aunt Aleid, almost to the top of the high towers, light from their projections glittering off his armor. He looked down at the klek on the street far below, still thrashing its legs at the tiny figure of Eric. On his next jump, Malcolm let himself fall.

He began to pick up momentum, hurtling downward. He bent his knees, bringing them up to his chest.

Just before he collided with the klek, he kicked out with both feet. The klek's silvery shell split, and with a yelp Malcolm fell straight through it. He landed with a crash, ending up in a heap in the center of a ring of cracked concrete.

He looked up and saw stars through the hole he had made in the klek. It was still moving, but aimlessly now. Its legs flailed left and then right, until they didn't support the body's weight anymore and the robot toppled to the ground beside Malcolm.

One of the legs twitched in his direction. He caught it between his hands and smashed it to the ground, crumpling its plating. The klek lay still.

Someone whistled, and Malcolm turned to see Eric nimbly making his way over the wreckage of the klek. He was holding his side like it hurt but otherwise seemed unruffled by his near death. "Straight through. That was A-level, kid."

"Thanks," Malcolm said, looking around for the next threat. But there wasn't one. The other two remaining klek were in pieces on the ground, destroyed by Aleid and Melissa. "What about the building that klek came out of? Are there—"

"People?" Eric said. "Nah, we had these buildings evacuated two minutes after the first klek showed up. We know what we're doing."

Malcolm looked at the klek he had defeated, at the hole he'd punched through it, and he felt a surge of giddiness, like his adrenaline had just caught up with him. "Is it weird that that was kind of fun? I mean, not when I was getting chucked around, which was, like, 95 percent of it. But that last bit…"

Eric smiled at him. "Wait till you see the footage. All of the fun, none of the danger."

"The footage?"

Eric answered by pointing down the street. A few blocks away the pavement was packed with news vans and people. And was that a tour bus squeezed in on the sidewalk? He could hear faint cheering. A swarm of camera drones was already whirring toward them.

"Aren't they a little close? They could have gotten hurt."

Eric shook his head. "The klek don't really go for the civvies. They only fight things that attack them. Otherwise they just do a lot of property damage. And people know to stay far enough back to avoid flying rubble."

"Is it always like this?"

"Pretty much," Eric said. "I like fighting the little ones better. Faster, more exciting."

Wind whipped Malcolm's face, and suddenly his aunt Aleid was at his side. "Malcolm," she said. "I'm glad you made it. I thought we would be fighting this one without you."

"Yeah. Sorry. I didn't hear the texts."

"You were busy?"

He thought of Drew. "Out for a run. Had my sylf in my pocket."

She frowned and turned to look at the klek. "That was a good hit at the end," she said, rising slightly into the air. "We'll see if something can't be done about your sylf, to make its notifications louder." And then she flew away.

The crowds rushed forward, and at the same time a fleet of trucks swept in from alleys and side streets. People with Gravenhurst logos on their overalls flooded out and began sweeping up the klek pieces to be taken to the labs in the Tower. By the time the first camera drone reached Malcolm and Eric, half of the wreckage was already loaded into the trucks.

Malcolm took a step back from the crowd while Eric stepped forward. Malcolm could barely pick out the questions the reporters were shouting, their voices all crashing together, but Eric seemed to have no such problem.

"Yes, caught me off guard," he said. "Did you see the way it hid inside the building? Clever strategy." He spoke casually, smoothly—like this was a conversation with friends rather than the press. "No, nothing more than a few bruises. Of course, if my cousin hadn't caught me, it could have been much worse." He turned and winked at Malcolm, gesturing him forward. Malcolm hesitantly walked up, realizing at the last moment that his face was still hidden behind his armor. He dropped his armor down to neck level.

The reporters resumed their clamor. "I'm sorry, what?" Malcolm said. "Can you talk one at a time? I think my ears might be ringing from the fight."

"Were you injured?" one of them shouted.

"A little rattled, but I'm okay. They got a few good hits in."

"And how does it feel to take your place as a Guardian of the city so soon after your debut?" another asked.

"It…it feels pretty good, I guess," Malcolm said, smiling. "Very different from the sims. I'm, like, buzzing now. I think it's the adrenaline, probably. My face feels like—"

"I thought he did quite well for his first outing," Eric said. "Especially against monsters like those." He patted Malcolm on the shoulder.

Malcolm shut his mouth and nodded, taking the hint from his cousin to stop rambling.

Off to the side a black hoverpod dropped down from the sky, and Felix stepped out. He smiled at Malcolm and beckoned him.

"Um, excuse me," Malcolm said to the reporters. He left Eric to answer more questions.

"How are you? Your armor held?" his uncle asked as Malcolm reached him.

"Yeah. I think they chipped it at one point, but it's okay."

"Well, you should have plenty of time for your armor to regrow before the next attack. A few weeks, at the least." As they spoke, Felix drew Malcolm over to the other side of the pod, where the cameras couldn't see them. "Now, I'm about to be very busy organizing the cleanup, but before I start... Aleid mentioned that you arrived late."

"Yeah, I didn't get the text right away. I'm sorry."

Felix leaned down, clasped Malcolm by the arms and looked into his eyes. "And I heard from Orin that you were out for a run," Felix said. "A very long run, considering you went out just after two."

"Yeah, I...yeah." Malcolm squirmed.

"Is there anything you would like to tell me, Malcolm?"

"Umm..." Malcolm chewed his lip and huffed. "Okay. I was out patrolling."

Felix straightened, so he stood a foot taller than Malcolm. "Yes. I guessed as much as soon as Orin contacted me. And, of course, after the pictures appeared online."

"Pictures?"

"You are not used to being out in the world yet, I know. In the Tower you have your privacy, but when you are outside, wherever you go, people will be watching you. You are a Gravenhurst. Some saw you with your armor up, jumping between rooftops."

Malcolm winced.

"Luckily the camera drones couldn't keep pace with you. Where did you go?"

"South a ways. I don't know that part of the city very well, so I don't know what it's called."

"And did you find anything?"

"No. Nothing really."

His uncle squinted down at him, and then his face softened. "Good. Likely no harm done. We will have to talk about this again. For now, why don't you take my pod home and get some sleep?"

"Yeah. Yeah, that would be good."

Malcolm climbed into the pod. The door slid closed, blocking out the sounds of cameras and cleanup crews. Lights flickered across the dashboard, and a soft androgynous voice reverberated through the pod's cabin.

"Hello, Malcolm Gravenhurst. Where would you like to go?"

Malcolm watched through the pod's tinted windows for a moment. The repair crews had arrived, and they were scattering their mites everywhere—tiny robots, each only a few millimeters long, that could break down the fractured pavement and rebuild it. The mites crawled over the street in the thousands. From where Malcolm sat, they looked like gray sludge oozing along the ground, like some kind of chemical spill. But within minutes that sludge would have the pavement fully repaired. Within an hour it would be like the fight never happened.

"To the Tower, please," Malcolm said. The pod lifted off without the slightest bump. Malcolm leaned back in his chair, breathed deep and wondered why, even as adrenaline still coursed through his veins, he had such a sour feeling in the pit of his stomach.

FIVE

Malcolm woke to his sylf buzzing excitedly around his head. "What is it?" he asked muzzily. The drone responded by projecting a flurry of notifications into the air above his bed. He blinked the sleep from his eyes and focused. Hundreds of hits on social media about the klek fight. He tapped on one news feed and said, "Play."

The cloud of notifications turned into a wide playback of news footage. It had felt like the fight lasted an hour, but in reality it had taken a little less than six minutes. Malcolm watched himself get kicked around for five of those minutes—just another piece of shrapnel in the air. His final attack—leaping from building to building and smashing down—looked appropriately heroic. That is, until he rewound it and watched what was happening on the ground. He could see when Eric noticed what Malcolm was doing and began distracting the klek in order to keep it in position for Malcolm's blow. Malcolm had been falling for several seconds—plenty of time for the klek to step out of the way. Without Eric's help, he wouldn't have hit the klek at all.

The coverage, though, generally spoke well of his first fight, sometimes even glowingly. Malcolm clenched his teeth and flicked back to the social media notifications. But his account had already responded to some of the more positive messages—the social media team must have worked overnight. He swiped everything away and went to sit up, but his sylf chimed at him again and put a message in front of his eyes. A text from a private number.

You free this morning? Meet me at 11 on McKercher and 8th. Don't tell anyone!

Drew. Malcolm sat up. It was already ten thirty, according to his clock. He'd slept in after the battle yesterday—and, this being Sunday, no one woke him for tutoring or meetings. He still felt tired and bruised. But he'd had worse in training.

"Response: **I'll be there**. Send," he told his sylf. It chimed. He went into his closet and searched for something that wasn't formal wear or training gear—something an ordinary person might wear.

Malcolm spent too long debating what to do with his drone—he hated to tuck it away again after he had missed Aleid's texts. But the thing recorded passive video, and Malcolm didn't know enough about how it worked to know if his family could access that. Besides, the klek never came more than once a month. With a twisting feeling in his stomach, he turned it off and stuck it in his pocket.

He took a pod to his favorite lunch spot, Sigmund's, a little deli on the west side of downtown that made amazing calzones. He used the bustle of the midmorning crowd to slip out the back unnoticed and ran the rest of the way unpowered, hoping no one would recognize him. It was a couple of miles—McKercher and 8th was in the area where he'd first encountered Drew, just west of the rail yard. His family didn't do any business out here, so Malcolm didn't have an excuse to take a pod closer. The buildings around him grew shorter and dirtier as he moved south.

When he arrived at ten minutes after eleven, he was relieved to see Drew waiting. Drew raised his hand in greeting but kept glancing around. Malcolm did the same. There wasn't much traffic, just a few people hanging out at a corner store a couple of blocks away.

"You didn't tell anyone? No one followed you?" Drew asked before Malcolm could even speak.

"No. Just me."

Drew looked him up and down. "You planning on selling me something today?"

Malcolm was in a pair of slacks and a button-down. Drew was in jeans and a hoodie. "I told my family I was going to lunch. Thought it would look weird if I went in sweatpants, and I didn't have anything else," Malcolm said.

Drew shrugged. "Come on." He started walking, and Malcolm kept pace with him. He found himself staring at Drew's face, looking for something familiar there. His nose, maybe—it was arched kind of like his aunt Aleid's. But his skin was a deep black, and as far as Malcolm knew, his family was all white, back to when his grandparents emigrated from the Netherlands.

"Why are you looking at me like that?" Drew asked without turning his head.

"Sorry. Trying to figure out how you could be related to me."

"I'm not."

"Then how do you have powers?"

Drew shot him a look. "You seriously don't know anything about this?"

"You asked me that before, but I don't even know what you mean by 'this,'" Malcolm said.

Drew shook his head and gestured Malcolm into a nearby alley. They walked through a series of alleys and parking lots until they came to the back of a store—flat brick wall, a gray door without a handle. There was a ladder on one side, and Drew climbed it. When he reached the top, Drew gestured for Malcolm to follow.

"Try to keep quiet," he said softly.

Malcolm brought up his armor on his lower legs and jumped to the roof, landing lightly beside Drew. Drew watched Malcolm's armor fold down into his skin.

"How do you do that? Like, turn it on?"

"The armor? I don't know. I just kind of do it."

Drew nodded and then sat on the edge of the roof, legs hanging down. Malcolm joined him.

"So..." Malcolm said.

"Why didn't you tell them?" Drew asked without looking at him.

"You mean, why didn't I tell my family about you?"

Drew nodded.

"Because you asked me not to. Why didn't you—"

"Tell me about your armor," Drew said. "What's it made of? How tough is it?" He turned fully toward Malcolm.

Malcolm brought up the armor around his hand and held it out to Drew, who grabbed his wrist and pulled it closer to his face, carefully feeling the facets. His brow furrowed, and his mouth opened slightly as he concentrated all his attention on the armor.

"I don't know what it's made of exactly. Feels like glass, but it's a lot tougher and a lot lighter than glass."

"Have you tried to take a chip off it to study?"

"Well, no. When it breaks it dissolves, so there's nothing left to study. We tested how tough it is, how strong it makes me, but—"

Drew made a noise at the back of his throat.

"What?"

"That always bugged me about you. Your family, I mean. You don't seem very curious about any of this. Why aren't you being run through tests 24-7? You know if it had been a different family, if it had been my family, people would have forced—"

"We *are* curious. We've got labs to study the pieces of the klek."

"Repurpose them, you mean. That's what you do, right? Turn it into things like..." He suddenly got a hard look in his eyes. "Where's your drone?"

"In my pocket," he said. "It's off."

Drew nodded, his eyes softening slightly. "My point stands. You guys don't *study* the klek. You *harvest* them."

"We do study them. But some parts of them we can't figure out because they're, like, millennia beyond human tech. And if we can't learn from them, we can at least use them."

Drew shook his head and dropped Malcolm's hand.

Malcolm sighed. "Not that I'm not glad you called me, but why am I here? And why do you want to keep your powers a secret?"

Drew sighed. "That's complicated, and it's not really my responsibility to explain it to you."

"How am I supposed to understand if you don't—"

"They're your family, not mine. I have powers. I'm afraid of the Gravenhursts. Figure it out," Drew said.

"Okay, fine," Malcolm said, irritated. "Be cryptic shadow guy then. You shouldn't be afraid of my family though. My grandfather can be a bit scary, but he's just old. I bet you'd like my uncle Felix."

Drew turned his head, focusing elsewhere. It took a moment for the sound to register for Malcolm—there were people talking in the store below them. Raised voices. "Is that—"

"Did you see those guys outside the bodega when you met me?" Drew asked.

"Um…yeah, I think so."

"They're robbing it right now." Drew patted the roof of the building. Malcolm looked around. He hadn't realized they had circled back. "I've been tailing them."

"Oh. Oh! So we're here to—"

"I think they have guns. So, you know, shields up." As he spoke, he stood and started walking across the roof. He fanned his hands at his sides, and the light began to curve away from him, shadows creeping in. He sat down on the edge of the roof and then pushed off. Malcolm scrambled to his feet, brought up his armor and followed Drew off the roof.

Through the windows of the store, he could see three men at the counter. All of them held handguns, and one of them was pointed across the counter at the owner—a short woman in a sari, with her hands extended in the air. Drew—or the patch of shadow that held Drew—was beside the door. "Ready?" he whispered.

"I guess," Malcolm said, noticing how squeaky his voice sounded.

The shadow moved, and the door opened, and then they were both running inside.

All three men turned their heads toward the door, and suddenly there was a blinding flash of light just in front of them. Malcolm's armor shaded some of it, but it still left bright spots dancing across his eyes. The robbers flinched away, blinded.

Drew kept moving, and the nearest of the men was enveloped in shadow. Malcolm hurried toward one of the other men, then slowed to a stop.

How do I do this? he suddenly thought. He'd trained to fight robots—things you defeated by breaking them. His only experience with fighting people was against Eric and his combat instructors, and he never actually tried to hurt them. *How hard do I hit them? I mean, what if I—*

His train of thought was interrupted when one of the men raised his gun and pointed it at Drew's shadow. Malcolm ran forward, aiming himself at the end of the gun, stretching out his arm. The man pulled the trigger just as Malcolm thrust his hand in front of the muzzle.

The force of it spun him around and sent him sprawling to the floor. He looked up to see the man aiming the gun again, this time at him. He pushed himself to his feet and let his training kick in, slowing his thoughts.

Get off the line of attack. Direct the blow away from yourself while leaving yourself open to retaliate.

The gun leveled at his head, and Malcolm shifted right. He brought his left hand up against the man's wrist so he couldn't aim the gun at him again. And he brought his right hand down on the gun, full strength. He'd meant to disarm the man, but the gun shattered under the blow, pieces of it embedding in the floor between them. Malcolm kicked the man's legs—carefully. Just enough force to knock the man backward into a shelf.

The third robber was shouting, and Malcolm spun, expecting another bullet. But the man was shouting because Drew was focusing light on the gun, heating it as he had the mugger's gun the night before. This time Malcolm wasn't standing by. He stepped forward and grabbed the gun, the heated metal warping in his hand. Then he dropped it, grabbed the man and pinned him to the floor. He held him there with one hand and looked back.

Drew emerged from the shadows, letting the light in around him. The third robber was unarmed and unconscious behind him. Drew walked over and knelt by the man Malcolm had knocked into a shelf.

"Don't…don't…" the man muttered, trying to back away.

"I don't know you," Drew said. "And I don't know what your problems are. But stealing from innocent people won't fix them. This neighborhood is under my protection.

You come here again or try robbing another store, and I call the cops. Understand?"

The man nodded vigorously.

"Wait," Malcolm said. "You're going to let them go? They tried to rob a store. They threatened someone with guns!"

Drew stayed focused on the robber. "Take your friend and get out. Don't come back."

The man stood, and Malcolm uncertainly released the one he had pinned. The two of them picked up their unconscious friend and carried him out of the store, starting to run as soon as they were outside.

"What the hell!" Malcolm said, dropping his armor. "We should have called the cops! They should have been arrested!"

Drew glanced at him but didn't say anything. "You okay, Mrs. Jindal?"

"Yes," said the woman in the sari. "Thank you once again." She hugged him across the counter. "And thank you to your friend as well," she said. "I do not believe we have met." She looked over at Malcolm, and Malcolm smiled, waiting for recognition to dawn. But it didn't. Malcolm stood, smiling awkwardly, until he couldn't take it anymore.

"Um, no, we haven't. Mal—Malcolm."

"Sorry about the damage," Drew said, looking around the store. "Hey, do you think you could get that stuff out of the floor?" he asked Malcolm.

Malcolm walked over and armored up his arms to pull out the fragments of the gun he'd broken. Once he had gathered them all, he looked down at the pieces in his hands. He'd seen plenty of guns before, and had them fired at him to test his armor, but encountering them out in the world like this felt different. He put his other hand over the fragments and pressed until they were an indistinguishable blob of metal.

"Would you like a drink? A snack?" the owner asked.

"No, thanks, Mrs. Jindal. Let me or one of the girls know if you see them around here again, okay?"

She nodded, and Drew gestured for Malcolm to follow him out of the store. They walked out and down the street toward the spot where they had met.

"That was awesome," Malcolm said. "But I still don't get it. You let the robbers go with a warning? They could have shot someone, and now they're—"

"It's not perfect. But calling the cops doesn't work the same for everyone. And this is the first time I've seen these guys, so I at least want to give them a chance to wise up before I do something drastic. Besides, I don't want to start showing up on the news."

"So this is something you do regularly? I mean, stopping crimes, or patrolling, like—"

"I've got the powers, right? And this neighborhood needs more people looking out for it."

"Yeah. Yeah, for sure. Hey, why didn't that woman recognize me?"

Drew smirked. "Mrs. Jindal doesn't watch the news, read newspapers, anything. Like, ever. She probably knows the name Gravenhurst, but if a klek walked into her store I think she'd ask if it wanted a samosa."

They reached the intersection where Drew had waited for him, then stopped. Malcolm stood silent, a million thoughts buzzing through his head. He picked one.

"How do you see when you've got the shadows around you?" he asked. "I mean, if all the light is steering away, how does that work?"

Drew looked puzzled for a second, then smiled. "I let just a little through at my eyes. I can't see too well, and I've kind of got tunnel vision. But it works." He squinted at Malcolm. "That's really the first question you wanted to ask me?"

"It was one I figured you might actually answer."

Drew nodded. "Fair point."

"Can we do this again? I mean, do you want to do this again? Was this some sort of audition?"

"Sort of," Drew said. "And I'll text you." He started walking away.

"Okay," Malcolm said to his back. "Thanks and everything."

"Yeah," Drew said without turning. "Thanks for helping. That was good."

Malcolm watched him go. He was in the middle of an ordinary intersection, no one around him, no cameras, no tour buses. And for the first time in his life, he felt like a superhero.

SIX

Malcolm returned to Sigmund's. The pod was still parked in its spot on the roof, and when he whistled, it descended to the street. Malcolm was glad the pods were self-piloted—a real chauffeur probably would have commented on the fact that Malcolm had somehow managed to drench his shirt with sweat during lunch.

By the time they got back to the Tower, it was midafternoon. Malcolm showered and changed, then spent a little while with his sylf, catching up on messages. One of the admin managers had sent him proposed timetables for media interviews. Felix had already responded on his behalf, confirming the schedule. Malcolm still had some time before dinner. He considered pulling one of the comics off his shelf, but instead he went down to one of the sim suites on the fifty-second floor and spent a while knocking alien spaceships out of the air. The game wasn't that good. Sim games in general were pretty basic—probably because the sims only worked in Porthaven, being built on klek tech, and no major developer wanted to make a game that would only play in one city.

When it was time for dinner, he took the stairs up to the eighty-seventh floor. This floor was dominated by a large dining hall. Unlike the rest of the Tower, this room was decidedly old-fashioned. A long oak table surrounded by high-backed chairs. Glass-and-iron wall sconces along the walls, and a crystal chandelier hung from the high ceiling. No visible tech, save the small drone that Malcolm himself brought in.

Malcolm knew the room was used for some business meetings and visits from important guests. He himself only saw the room on Sundays, when the family had their weekly dinner together, presided over by his grandfather. The room had seen so much uncomfortable silence that it seemed etched into the walls—like the sconces were watching him disapprovingly, wishing he would tuck in his shirt and show some ambition.

Today when Malcolm entered, only his grandfather sat at the table. Malcolm slowed just inside the door and glanced at his sylf. When it detected his attention, it flashed the time. It was exactly 6:00 p.m.

"I've asked the others to find their own meals," his grandfather said, his voice echoing in the large room.

"Oh," Malcolm said. "So it's just—"

"I needed to speak with you," he said and gestured for Malcolm to approach. Malcolm hesitated, but his grandfather's glare got him moving. When he took his usual seat near the foot of the table, his grandfather shook his head. "Up here. Next to me," he said.

Malcolm forced himself to stand and walk to the other end of the table.

Their dinner was already laid out, but his grandfather was ignoring it, so Malcolm sat with his hands in his lap.

"Did you have a chance to see the media coverage of your battle with the klek yesterday?" his grandfather asked.

"Yes. Some," Malcolm said.

His grandfather nodded. "Took you some time to find your feet. You should keep moving. You will not be hit so much if you do not stand still."

"Yeah. Thanks, I'll do that."

His grandfather stared at him. Malcolm stared down at the table.

"Did you perhaps see the other coverage from yesterday?"

"Other…um, no."

His grandfather slid a newspaper across the table. On the front page there was a man with a familiar face. It took Malcolm a moment to recognize him from the mugging in the alley—the victim. SAVED BY A GRAVENHURST, the headline said. Malcolm tried to stifle his groan.

"This man in the picture here claims you saved him from criminals yesterday evening. Is this true?"

"Um…" Malcolm's mind raced, trying to find an excuse. "I didn't really save him. It was—" He realized where that sentence was heading and clamped his mouth shut.

"Oh?" his grandfather said, drawing the newspaper back. "He is under the impression that you did. 'He came in all armored up, just like on the news,' the man says. 'Is this a new direction for the Gravenhursts?' the newspaper wonders."

His grandfather stared at him. Malcolm tried to swallow, but his throat wasn't working anymore.

"You understand your role?" Malcolm's grandfather said, his voice low and gravelly. "You understand the trust we are placing in you when we make you a Guardian?"

"Yes, sir," Malcolm said.

His grandfather sighed—a sound so deep and heavy that it felt like a weight settling on Malcolm's shoulders.

"I am…disappointed, Malcolm. I know Felix has spoken to you about this matter and made it clear that such vigilantism is unacceptable. We are not the superheroes you find in those juvenile comics. This is reality. Felix and I both expected better of you. And while you were pursuing *this*"— he waved the newspaper through the air—"our city was under attack. Our family was fighting, and you were nowhere to be found."

"I know. But I—" He stopped himself. He already knew it was useless arguing with his grandfather.

"But?"

"Nothing. Sorry."

"Over the next week you will be conducting your first interviews since you took on your new responsibilities. I expect you to remember that you represent our family. What you say and do reflects on us all. We will prepare a statement for you, making clear that this incident was mere happenstance and not a new direction. And that it will not happen again." His grandfather went on, outlining every moment of his next week.

Malcolm simply nodded. *I didn't even save him. Drew did that.* He finally noticed that his grandfather had fallen silent. Malcolm looked up into his eyes.

"Is everything clear?" his grandfather asked.

"Um, yes. Yes, sir."

"Good." His grandfather leaned back in his chair. "Now, if I'm not mistaken, I believe our chef has prepared us a cassoulet with duck confit. We should not let it go to waste." He reached across the table and served himself dinner. Malcolm did the same, though he felt anything but hungry. He settled himself in for a long, silent meal.

When he finally returned to his room, he felt more exhausted than he had after fighting the klek. He fell onto his bed fully clothed and considered not moving until the next morning. But his belt was pressing into a bruise on his hip.

Halfway through changing, he realized something was different in his room. It had been cleaned, which wasn't a surprise. His clothes and towel were gone from the floor. His shoes sat neatly by the door. And his shelves were half-empty.

He went to the shelves and ran his hands along them, as if he might feel something there even though he could clearly see that all his comics and graphic novels had been cleared away. His textbooks remained, but his personal books were gone.

He sat down on the floor and wondered if it would be okay to cry. His grandfather wouldn't approve. Gravenhursts didn't cry. Gravenhursts stood strong and unwavering.

He wasn't even sure why this stung so much—he had digital copies of most of the comics, and he doubted his grandfather would have thought to clear those out. This just felt so petty. The only possible reason for it was to hurt him.

There was a tap at his window. He looked up, startled—his window was eighty stories above the ground, with no balcony. His aunt Aleid hung in the air on the other side of the glass, squinting to see him in the dimly lit room. He stood and walked over to her. She simply pointed up. He nodded and left his room.

A minute later he stepped out of the elevator onto the landing pad at the top of the Tower. His aunt was already standing there, beside the parked hoverpods. Malcolm walked over to her.

"Felix said you were having a private dinner tonight," she said. "And he suggested that I check in on you after."

Malcolm nodded. "Did you know he was going to take my collection?"

She raised her chin. "Felix mentioned something about that. Your grandfather thought they might be giving you the wrong ideas, he said."

"They're not! I'm not—I don't think I'm living in a comic book or something. They're just..." He could feel his breath growing ragged, and he didn't want to cry in front of his aunt, so he stopped talking. He looked out at the city far below them. Out past the gleaming silhouettes of downtown to where the streetlights were fewer and farther between, and the lights of windows were pinpricks in the darkness.

"You went out looking for trouble last night though," she said. "Human trouble."

He looked up at her, ready to defend himself, but she didn't look angry. She was simply watching him. If anything, she looked sad.

"I just wanted to help people. And taking my comics is so...And now I have to give a statement or something. Why is he—"

Malcolm stopped dead. Someone else's words had suddenly flashed into his mind. *I'm afraid of the Gravenhursts. Figure it out.*

"Why is he what?" his aunt asked him.

"Nothing. You know how he is."

Aleid nodded and walked up to Malcolm. She didn't touch him, simply stood at his side. The most noticeable things about his aunt were often the things she didn't do. She didn't smile. Didn't hug. If Felix were here, he would find the perfect words to comfort Malcolm or make him see his grandfather's point of view. Aleid didn't do any of that. Malcolm was glad, because he didn't want to be comforted now. He wanted to be angry. Aleid let him be angry and just stood with him.

After a while Malcolm felt himself slow down—his breathing, his heart, his thoughts. He stared out at the city, his aunt beside him, steady and solid as stone.

"Want to go out for a bit?" Aleid asked.

"Out? Like *out* out?" He extended his hands upward in a Superman pose. Aleid smirked but nodded. "It's been a while. I didn't know we could do that anymore."

"Helps me think sometimes." She turned, bending her knees and offering her back to him. He wrapped his arms tightly around her neck and let her lift him up. It felt awkward—his aunt wasn't a touchy-feely person, and he could feel her muscles stiffening. But her back was warm and strong, just as it had been years ago when she used to take him flying every weekend.

As he rose into the air, his thoughts seemed to fall away behind them. She started slowly, curving out and around the Tower, then picked up speed as they moved out over the river. Malcolm could feel the wind pulling at his skin. Aleid's hair tangled with his own, got between his teeth. His stomach was somewhere miles behind them.

"Too fast?" she shouted.

"No," he said in her ear.

When he was jumping, even in the wide-open spaces of Porthaven's rooftops, it felt like falling. Like the ground had a grip on him, and it was already drawing him down the moment he leapt. This was different. Up here, it was like they could outrace gravity, like they could just decide to never land.

"Think you can go faster?" his aunt said.

"Yes," he breathed. He thought he heard her chuckle, and then they were moving so fast the lights of Porthaven beneath them blurred. He tightened his grip and forced his eyes to stay open even as the wind dried them out. They circled the city once, twice, and on until he forgot to count, and all he could feel was the air around them and his aunt beneath him.

"Gonna slow down now," she said finally, and the lights separated back out into windows and streetlamps below them. They flew along the river, slowing as they moved north, then banked left and circled around Gravenhurst Tower, coming for a landing on the roof again. Malcolm's stomach caught up with him, and he realized he was panting like he'd just run a marathon, and he felt so dizzy that he sat down on the tarmac.

"Did it help?" she asked.

"I don't know. But it was nice. Thanks."

She nodded. She sat down beside him, a few feet away, and took deep breaths. He straightened and copied her, letting his body get used to gravity again.

"I like it up here," he said. "I should come here more."

"It's best at night," she replied.

SEVEN

When he showed up for his math-tutoring session on Monday morning, he found his cousin Melissa sitting in the room.

"Oh. Sorry, I thought this was my—wait, this *is* my tutoring room." All Malcolm's lessons took place in one of the company meeting rooms—dark wood table, rolling chairs, bland walls and carpet to keep distractions down. His tutor wasn't there, and he didn't see a note left for him. "Are you using this room?"

"Yes," Melissa said. "I'm here to teach you."

"Oh, okay. You're teaching me math?"

"No, Malcolm," she said as she snapped open a briefcase. "Change of schedule. Grandfather asked me to spare a couple of hours to walk you through some media-relations basics. You've got a round of interviews this week, and clearly your tutoring thus far hasn't been up to snuff." She pulled something out of her briefcase—a small round device that looked like some kind of compass. She slapped it on the wall, where it stuck, and waved her hand in front of it. Light streamed out of the thing, throwing up a projection display just behind Melissa. Malcolm hadn't seen one of these before, but then, R&D was always coming out with new things he hadn't heard about.

"We've got to talk about brand identity," Melissa said, still not looking at him as she took a pile of papers out of her briefcase and closed it. The display had a jumble of words on it. **Reassuring. Undaunted. In Control.**

"So, Malcolm," Melissa continued, "what image would you say you've projected to the media thus far?"

Malcolm blew air out between his lips and flicked quickly through his math textbook, then set it aside and sat down at the table. "I don't know. I've just, like, tried to answer their questions."

Melissa nodded. "And it hasn't been bad. Personable, mostly. Young. That's fine for some, but it doesn't really fit with the brand we've cultivated for the family."

"The brand?"

She dropped her papers on the table and moved to the display. "When we focus-grouped this, these were the identifiers people wanted from the Guardians. And we've tried to hew closely to them. People want to see us as an immovable wall between them and the klek." She gestured to the lower edge of the screen, and sure enough, there was the word *Immovable* in the jumble. "It's how they can live here in Porthaven without fear despite this city's unique dangers. So we need to figure out where you fit into this."

"I don't know," Malcolm said. "I don't really feel immovable. I mean, I want to protect people."

Melissa nodded. "That's come across, yes. And I think we can build on that."

Malcolm frowned up at the screen. "I don't think I get it. Some of these words might fit me, maybe. Does that say 'powerful'? I think I'm powerful. Usually. Sometimes."

"We're not talking about you," Melissa said. "We're talking about your *image* here. How the concept of Malcolm can fit into the wider umbrella of the Gravenhurst brand. Strengthen it rather than dilute it."

Malcolm frowned at Melissa, and she frowned back at him. He felt like they were having two different conversations. He wasn't exactly surprised. Being a Gravenhurst was sometimes more like being part of a business than part of a family, but he'd managed to mostly ignore that stuff so far.

Melissa walked closer, and now she was looking directly at him. Her habitual frown had softened a bit. "This is part of being a Guardian, Malcolm. Comes with the job. I know maybe you hadn't thought about that, but you've got to get up to speed."

"Yeah. Yeah, I guess that makes sense."

"So where do you see yourself in here?" She returned to the screen.

Malcolm scanned the words, looking for himself. None of them were really him—he wanted to be a Guardian, but he couldn't say he felt undaunted by it. And he definitely didn't feel in control. "It would be good to be reassuring, I guess? I mean, I want people to trust me to protect them."

"Good. Good, okay." Melissa sat down. "We'll put a pin in that for now, circle back to it later. The next thing we should do is develop a key script for you—talking points you can rely on without the stutters and hesitation you've shown in your interviews thus far. I've written up a proposed list…"

She went on. The words on the screen and the page seemed to swim around the room. All the things his family was. All the things Malcolm was not. He took a deep breath, blinked hard and tried to focus on what his cousin was saying.

The next three days disappeared into that cloud of words. His regular lessons and training were canceled as he prepped and conducted his first proper interviews. Melissa and various PR staff fussed over him, with Felix occasionally showing up to straighten his lapels or point out that his hair had gone askew. He sat for hours on different soundstages, all a blur of spotlights and cameras. Everything was a mess of power cables, which felt bizarre and alien to Malcolm since he was used to everything running on the ambient grid. But these were cameras from the national networks, ones outside Porthaven, so they couldn't connect to the grid. He tried not to embarrass himself—or, rather, tried not to embarrass the family, he supposed. It wasn't about him.

Despite the flurry of activity, the stress, Malcolm somehow felt he was only half there. His mind was stuck on Drew, on a message that might come at any moment or might not come at all. Every spare minute he checked his drone. He turned off his social media notices, which were getting out of control and weren't handled by him anyway. He wanted to see texts as soon as he got them. But the only texts that came were snide comments from Eric on his interview performance.

When the last of the interviews was finally over late on Wednesday night, he collapsed into his bed. It was nearly midnight. He was almost asleep when his sylf picked itself up off his nightstand and chirruped.

Malcolm's eyes snapped open, and the drone projected its display.

Done being famous yet? There are some people I want you to meet.

From an unlisted number.

"Finally," Malcolm said, sitting up. "Response: **Yes, yes, yes. When can**—no, wait, stop response and delete. New response: **Sure. I can do something tomorrow night.** Send."

He stared at his drone, which hovered passively in the air. He tapped it, sending it back a few inches and letting it return before tapping it away again. When its display lit up with a new message, Malcolm's hand went right through it. He moved his fingers quickly out of the way and read.

I was thinking more like now. South end of the rail yard.

Now? "Response: **Okay. I'll come.** Send." He was already moving. Once the sylf chimed that his message was sent, Malcolm flicked it off and put it in his pocket—or tried to before realizing his pyjama pants didn't have pockets. He changed into sweats.

He snuck out of his room and took the stairs upward, stepping lightly past the floors where the rest of his family slept. He was happy to discover that the door to the roof was unlocked—he didn't know why anyone would lock it, but then, he'd never tried coming out here in the middle of the night before.

He brought up his armor. Against the night sky, his gray armor would be good camouflage. There was still a risk that someone would see him, and then he'd have to talk to his grandfather about news coverage again. But he didn't have the patience to find a subtler way. He leapt down to the next-tallest building, and then to the next.

As he went, he made a conscious effort to look around at where he was, to try to learn the city better. Beside him was Morningside Avenue, flanked by tall buildings and running through the city like a spine. The river was like a black scar on the city's face. But Kingsgate Bridge spanned the darkness, lit by dozens of spotlights perched on its steel beams.

It took only a few jumps before Malcolm didn't recognize any of the streets around him anymore. He paused atop a dark roof and pulled out his drone, flicking it on.

"Do you have maps?" he asked. It immediately projected a map into the air, his location marked with a small black dot. Old Cross, this neighborhood was called. He'd never heard that name before. Was there a New Cross? He'd lived in Porthaven his whole life. He'd even thought of it as *his* city the night of his debut. So why didn't he know it?

From here the rail yard would be southwest. He tucked the sylf away again, and as he leapt he got a clear view of the yard. The north end was well lit and moderately busy. Sleek grav trains hung weightless above their single silver tracks as their cargo was moved over to the older wheeled trains that could move freely in and out of the city. But in the south end there were no lights, only old railcars perched on even older tracks, weeds growing up around them.

He moved across the rooftops around the rail yard and landed on the ground in the shadowed south.

He dropped his armor and looked around. He didn't see anyone, so he moved farther into the yard. It was hard to see in the dim light, but the railcars on either side of him were a riot of color. Some were covered in layer after layer of tags, others held single large murals. He stopped to admire a shipping container painted to look like a flatbed with a dragon asleep atop it. It was brilliant, right down to the texture details on each scale. He pulled out his drone, thinking he should take a picture, before realizing he didn't want to turn on his drone right now. As he was about to put it back in his pocket, he noticed light flashing across his shoes.

He wondered if it might be a broken streetlight flickering, but this light pulsed, fading in and out smoothly. It was coming from under one of the trains. Malcolm lay down on the ground and looked. There, two tracks over, was a pair of legs, light all around them.

He hurried to the end of the railcar and clambered over the coupling. His feet scuffed in the dirt as he moved, and the light suddenly stopped. He moved forward in the dark between two more cars.

"Drew?" he said softly. "That you?"

He heard a sigh, and the area around him brightened. He could see Drew's silhouette against one of the cars. "Just you, Malcolm?"

"Yeah. Of course just me." He walked closer to Drew, and his eyes adjusted to the light until he could make out Drew's face.

"That thing off?" Drew asked, and Malcolm realized he was still holding his sylf in his hand.

"Uh, yeah." He double-checked that he had turned it off after consulting its maps.

"Good. Come on."

Drew turned and tapped on the railcar behind him. It was a basic red boxcar with a latched door in the middle and the word *JEST* spray-painted across it for some reason. "He's here," he said through the door and then turned back to Malcolm. "Before we go in, I should warn you. They're nervous about this. Just…keep your cool, okay? Try not to geek out too much."

"Who's in there?"

Drew took a deep breath. "Let's go in and I'll make the introductions." He lifted the latch and pulled the door open, climbing in and beckoning Malcolm to follow.

There was furniture inside the small space—a ratty couch on one side, a folding chair and a lamp. On the far side of the room sat a table with a computer on it. The projected display looked pinkish to Malcolm, which made him think it was probably a couple of generations out of date. Sitting in front of the computer were two girls. One turned to look at Malcolm and gave him an uneasy smile as she stood up. She was a bit taller than him, and broader, with dark skin like Drew's. He could clearly read the anxiety on her face, but she still looked friendly. The other girl didn't turn away from the screen.

"Malcolm, these are my friends. Blair…" Drew gestured to the girl who had stood. She waved to Malcolm. "…and Kaz."

"Kazue," the girl at the computer said without turning around. "He doesn't get to call me Kaz." With her back to him, all Malcolm could see of her was short black hair and the thin fingers of one hand, shifting between the keyboard and the display.

"Okay. Um, hi," Malcolm said. "You probably already know my name—" Kazue snorted, and Blair nodded slightly. "You two are Drew's friends? You know about his, like, powers?"

"Friends and teammates, sort of," Drew said, putting his hands in his pockets. "They have powers too, Malcolm."

Malcolm's jaw dropped. "You...really? Both of you?"

Blair nodded slightly. Malcolm noticed for the first time that she was holding Kazue's hand—awkwardly, given that they were facing different directions. But they had a tight grip on each other. *They're not just nervous. They're afraid of me.*

"Sorry. I'm not trying to be weird about it. It's just that Drew's the first person I've met besides my family who has powers, and I always thought it was only Gravenhursts who had them. This is all kind of a big deal to me. It's—ah, crap, I'm talking too much. Drew pointed out that I do that. Usually my family cuts me off when I get going, so you can— and now I'm talking too much about talking too much." Malcolm closed his mouth and tried to keep it closed. But Blair kept watching him nervously, and Drew looked on with a half smile, like he was waiting for something, and Malcolm felt like his lips were a tiny, cracking dam and all the words he wanted to say were a tidal wave. "The three of you, like, fight crime?" he finally asked.

"In the poorer neighborhoods. Nothing that will get us on the news," Drew said. But he was still watching Malcolm expectantly.

"Okay, um…I know you probably think I'm an idiot, but can I see? I mean, your powers? Say no if you want to, that's totally cool, I'm just…" He shrugged. "You don't have to. Is it rude to ask?"

Blair's nervous smile softened a little. She let go of Kazue's hand. "I make, um, walls, I guess? Here." She put her fingers together and drew them slowly apart. Between them a blue line of light sparked and then spread along with her hands. It formed a small rectangle, and when Blair pulled her hands away it stayed there, hanging in midair.

Malcolm stepped forward and examined it. It shone blue at the edges but was mostly transparent in the center. "Can I touch it?"

Blair nodded, and he put his hands against it. It felt smooth, kind of like his own armor, but it thrummed with energy. He pressed hard, but it didn't move. He giggled. "It's like a force field! That's really, really cool."

"If I concentrate, I can put up more than one." She gestured, and the rectangle blinked out, leaving only empty space.

"And Kazue, you—"

"Nope. Don't know you," Kazue said, and he realized that she had turned to face him for the first time. Her dark eyes were narrowed, and her lips pressed tightly together as she watched him. She was short and slight, but despite her size she gave the impression of being much older than anyone else there. Malcolm didn't think she actually was older—it was just something about the knowing, wary look in her eyes.

Blair sat down, and her hand found Kazue's again. Kazue never took her eyes off Malcolm.

"Okay. That's okay," Malcolm said. "Do you guys want me to keep this a secret from my family too?"

"Yeah, Malcolm," Drew said from the couch. Malcolm backed up and sat next to him. "And you should ask the question you really want to ask. The big one."

Malcolm took a breath. "Yeah, okay. How? How do you guys have powers and I never knew about it? Were your families close to the klek gate when it fell, like mine were?"

Drew and Blair shook their heads. "My family moved here when I was three," Drew said. "So no chance of that. And Blair—"

"Lived here my whole life," she said. "Me and my mom. But she's normal. No powers or anything."

"And, um, Kazue? Were you—"

"Parents didn't have powers. At least, they didn't last time I talked to them."

"So...how?"

"We don't know," Drew said. "We can't answer the first part of your question—how we have powers. But why you don't know about it? You might actually be able to answer that better than we can." For a moment Drew looked nervous, which Malcolm hadn't seen from him before. He usually seemed so composed. "There used to be more of us," he said. "My friend Ibrahim. A couple more we knew."

"Used to? What happened?"

"That's actually why I invited you here," Drew said. "We thought you might help us find out. Because they all disappeared when your family found out about their powers."

"They…my family…" Malcolm felt like the conversation had left his brain behind. It caught up with a lurch. "Hold on. Are you saying my family *did something* to them?"

Drew took a long breath. "We don't really know—"

"'Course we do," Kazue cut in. "Only thing we don't know is if the Gravenhursts killed them or not. I think they probably killed them."

"Kaz, please," Drew said. "Look, Malcolm, we know the Gravenhursts—your family—were sniffing around some of these people."

"How do you know that?"

"I watched people from your company go into Ibrahim's house, and the next day he was gone. Completely, I mean. His whole family. Not in his house. Phone out of service. His social media disappeared. Like he never existed."

"Other ones too," Kazue said. "Gravenhurst pod shows up, people disappear."

"No. No way." Malcolm stood, and so did Drew. "You're wrong. Maybe you misunderstood. We're the good guys! We fight the klek!"

Kazue scoffed. "Still think this was a good idea, Drew?"

"Come on," Malcolm said. "There are other explanations. I mean, people from our companies might have been investigating or something. We do that—investigate places where the klek appear. Or maybe it was someone using a company car, but not from the family. Or the klek! What if it's the klek doing it?"

"We don't really see the klek this far south," Blair said. "They stay mostly within the downtown area."

"Sure, mostly, but—"

"No, not mostly," Kazue said. "Always. The klek always appear within five miles of Gravenhurst Tower. Never farther."

"What? That can't…really?" Malcolm said.

Kazue nodded.

"Okay, fine, but we still don't even know how the klek teleport themselves into the city, right? What if they're, like, teleporting people *out* of Porthaven, and my family was—"

"All right, Malcolm. We don't know what happened to them for sure," Drew said. "But you have to admit it seems odd, and we're freaked out. You might be able to find out more for us. If it's something the Gravenhursts are doing, or someone inside the company, or the klek, or I don't know what else. Would you look around? Not ask any questions or anything, but just see what you can see?"

Malcolm watched them all. He didn't believe it for a second, but looking at their pleading eyes…even Kazue was watching him with something that might have been hope. He nodded slowly. "Your friend's name was Ibrahim?"

"Ibrahim Khoury. He could make things, um, float. Not like flying, but—"

"Klek," Kazue said.

"He made the klek float?" Malcolm asked, turning to Kazue.

But she was staring at the computer screen again. "No, I'm saying right now, klek in the city."

"What?"

Kazue tapped her display, and the projection expanded to fill the far wall. Malcolm still had to move closer to see—it was a small space, and Blair's big frame filled much of it. Onscreen was a newsfeed showing what looked like a café on the ground floor of a taller building. It was overrun by klek—human-sized ones this time, not the big ones. They were bursting through the windows and spilling out into the street, people running everywhere. Kazue turned on the sound, but all they could hear was screaming.

"This is now? Where?"

"Downtown. Two-point-five miles north of the Tower," Kazue said with a smirk.

"They shouldn't be here already. It hasn't even been a week! Oh crap, I have to—"

"Go, go," Drew said, opening the door for him.

Malcolm jumped out of the boxcar. "I'll talk to you later," he said as he leapt away. Once he was clear of the rail yard, he pulled out his sylf and turned it on. There were no texts waiting.

"Message to Aunt Aleid," he said. "There are klek! Meet you there!" Then he pocketed the drone, brought his armor back up and hurried northward.

———○———

It wasn't hard to find the klek—the screams could be heard from several blocks away. He landed on the building across from the café. Klek lined the road below him, and people were scattering everywhere. The klek weren't chasing them, but there were so many people running in every direction. They collided with the robots, fell under their feet. And no one else from his family was here yet.

Malcolm's sylf finally buzzed in his pocket. "Read out message," he said without taking the drone out of his pocket.

"Aunt Aleid: There in two minutes. Wait for us," the sylf said in its buzzy voice, muffled by Malcolm's clothes and armor. Malcolm looked toward the Tower, then back to the road below him.

Someone was getting into a car, despite the klek running across its hood. "No, don't do that," Malcolm muttered. The person started the car and hit the gas. The street was too crowded—he was going to hit someone, or one of the klek. And if he hit the klek, they might take that as an attack.

The car collided with one of the robots within a few yards. The klek picked itself up, clicking angrily, and jumped at the car, barbed legs tearing into the motor and stopping it dead. Other klek started to move in on the car from behind.

"Crap," Malcolm said, stepping off the edge of the building.

The klek was moving across the hood. With a flick, it put one of its legs through the windshield and was reaching for the driver when Malcolm landed on it.

His momentum crushed the robot—and the hood of the car beneath it. But the klek's barbed leg was still twitching inches away from the driver. Malcolm grabbed the limb and pulled, wrenching it off the body.

"Go!" Malcolm shouted at the driver. The driver looked down and turned the key in the ignition. "Not in the car!" Malcolm shouted, throwing the still-twitching leg at the klek advancing on them. "Get out! Run!"

As the driver opened the door, one of the klek jumped for him, but Malcolm met it midair. Its barbed feet slashed at his face, the attacks sliding off his armor. He managed to get his arms around the klek's body and squeezed until the silvery metal crumpled.

He turned back to the car. The driver was out now and running for the far end of the street. Three of the klek were on the car, tearing at it savagely. Thankfully, they seemed focused on the car that hit them rather than the driver.

I always wanted to try this. Malcolm put his hands under the side of the car and lifted. The car came off the ground. He almost lost his balance and fell backward, but he managed to keep his feet under him and threw the vehicle. It hit the ground and rolled, slamming into the crowd of klek and crashing into the building on the other side of the street.

Every klek on the block—dozens of them—stopped in their tracks. Then they all scuttled in Malcolm's direction.

He looked skyward. The crown of Gravenhurst Tower was visible between the tall buildings, but he saw no sign of his aunt. "Okay then," Malcolm said, and he jumped to meet the nearest klek.

It swerved at the last moment, and Malcolm slid across the ground. Instantly several of the klek were on him, blades hammering his armor. He caught one of their legs and swung, using the klek as a cudgel to clear the others away. Then he slammed it onto the ground, where it broke into pieces.

He heard a scream. Half a block away he saw a man in a trench coat lying on the ground. The klek weren't attacking him, but he looked injured, and the klek rushing toward Malcolm didn't seem to care that they were trampling him. Malcolm ran. The klek rushed him, attacking, but his armor turned away the blows and Malcolm kept moving forward, knocking the robots aside. As he reached the man he grabbed two of the klek and threw them forward, knocking them and several others off their feet. Malcolm knelt quickly.

"Can you run?" he asked the man.

"I don't think so."

"Okay. This is probably going to be pretty uncomfortable," he said. He picked the man up and leapt.

Klek jumped after him, but he'd used his full strength, and he flew clear of the swarming robots, landing a couple of blocks away. The man in his arms promptly vomited across the front of Malcolm's armor. Malcolm put him down and paused only long enough to check that he was still breathing. He hated to leave him lying there in the street, unable to move, but the klek were already coming after him—fast. The clatter of their feet on the pavement was overwhelming.

He leapt back toward the swarm.

There were so many klek, crowded so close together, that not all of them could get out of his way as he landed. He slammed into two, punching them into the ground. Then something hit him from behind, and he toppled forward on his face. Dozens of legs came down on his back, hitting so hard and fast it felt like jackhammers. He heard a crack. *Was that my armor?*

He rolled over quickly and kicked out. He knocked away a few of the klek, but they were immediately replaced by others. He tried to grab one of their legs, but it bent away from his hand and then shot around his arm, multiple joints flexing until its leg was wrapped around him like a tentacle. He shook but couldn't untangle himself, and the klek was wrapping another leg around his other arm now. Below him the other klek were striking at the armor over his stomach, multiple legs hammering down on a single point, and his armor was definitely cracking now. With a cry he lifted the klek wrapped around his arms and brought it down on the others surrounding him. Metal crumpled, pieces came apart, and Malcolm's hands were free. But other klek were moving in, more of them wrapping themselves around him, piling on top of each other until he couldn't lift them all. And still they were chipping away at his armor, opening cracks wider and wider. He kicked out wildly, but he couldn't see anything, and he couldn't connect with his attackers. He felt something sharp prick against his skin, trying to worm its way deeper.

There was a clatter, and suddenly the weight on his arms lessened. He pushed, and the klek scattered. He struggled to his feet, lashing out to keep the klek from gathering on him again. Once he had his feet under him he went on the attack. But the klek he was aiming at came apart before he could even hit it—legs falling away, body suddenly unsupported and crashing to the ground. A shape spun past and several more klek lost limbs, skittering away with furious clicks. It took Malcolm a moment to recognize the blur of flashing blades as his cousin Eric.

Once he'd dismembered several of the robots, Eric came to a stop for a moment, and he smiled at Malcolm. "Told you the little ones were more fun," he said. And then he was off again, his long-bladed knives flashing. Beyond him a blue streak shot across the street, plowing through the klek dozens at a time—Aunt Aleid had arrived. Malcolm breathed deep and checked his armor. There was a large gouge out of it just above his navel.

He spun slowly, looking for approaching klek. But between Eric and Aleid, they were falling fast. Malcolm concentrated on the ones his aunt knocked down, finishing them off with a few good hits before they could get up again. It felt like only moments before the street was still, the pavement buried under a blanket of shattered metal.

"That was pretty awesome, with the car," Eric said.

"What? You weren't here. How did you—"

Eric gestured upward, and Malcolm realized the sky above them was crowded with camera drones. "But I have to ask," Eric said, "what have you got against cars lately?"

Malcolm smiled sheepishly, but his reply was cut off by a crash to his right. He turned and saw Aleid rooting through the broken pieces of the klek. Eric headed toward her, and Malcolm trailed after.

"You didn't wait," Aleid said, picking up a klek leg that was still twitching, its blade almost grazing her cheek. She put one end of the leg under her foot and pulled until it came apart, her impressive arms flexing.

"I couldn't," Malcolm said. "Some guy hit one of the klek with a car, and they were going after him. And there were people on the ground. Did they—"

"No casualties, as far as we can tell," Aleid said, stomping on a klek body that was still whirring with energy. "But a fair number of injuries. Did you jump with a civilian?"

"Yeah," Malcolm said.

"You know what kind of damage that amount of force can do to someone?"

"Again, didn't have much choice," he said.

Aleid squinted at him but nodded. "Well, it could have been a lot worse. Probably would have been a lot worse if you hadn't stepped in. People owe you their lives."

A warm glow started below Malcolm's ribs and spread out until he felt it tingling in his lips and fingers. "Thanks." But the warmth was replaced just as quickly by a bone-deep chill. He stared around at the wreckage. There were no crowds this time, no applause. The repair and salvage crews were nowhere to be seen. The last klek attack had felt more like a public performance than a battle. This was different.

"We weren't ready for this, were we? Does anyone know how long it's been since—"

"Four days," Aleid said without hesitation. "It's been four days since the last klek attack."

"But they never come again this fast. Isn't it usually at least—"

"Average thirty-nine days between attacks. Thirty-two was the record."

"What does it mean?" Malcolm asked. He looked from his aunt to his cousin, but neither of them met his eyes.

"I don't know. Yet," Aleid said, and she flew off without another word, leaving Malcolm and Eric to walk home. Malcolm watched her go until he was distracted by a series of grunts from his cousin.

Eric was huffing and raising his arms above his head. Malcolm watched, baffled, until he realized his cousin was miming lifting a car, imitating Malcolm. Eric roared and threw the imaginary car. He ended his performance with an explosion sound and then grinned at Malcolm. "Seriously, dude, just because you're too young to have a license doesn't mean you have to wreck the cars for everyone else."

EIGHT

Back in his bedroom, Malcolm checked the stitches on his midriff. One of the klek blades had taken a chunk out of him, and the infirmary had stitched him up. It was still red and swollen, and the local anesthetic they'd given him was wearing off.

He checked the damage to his armor. The gouge in the middle was still there. If he concentrated, he could close it by moving the armor from another part of his body, putting the gap in his defenses somewhere less vital. But that seemed unnecessary. A good night's sleep should recharge this level of damage. He lay down.

But sleep wouldn't come. He tried for an hour before he finally got out of bed and grabbed his sylf. "Computer mode," he told it, and it immediately projected a display and a small keyboard. A real computer would have been better—the projection keyboard was pretty laggy, even on the newest models—but this would do.

He checked the news first. The klek attack was the headline, even on national news sites. He scanned a few articles and found the numbers he was looking for. Eighteen injured, all told. Two in critical condition. None dead so far. No one had been this badly injured in a klek attack in seven years. No one had been killed by the klek since…

He typed a date into the search bar. A date he knew well. A date that was never far from his mind, because it was the day his parents had died.

He found the report he had been looking for in the *Porthaven Herald*. The too-familiar picture of a giant klek, bigger than any before or since, looming over downtown. They didn't have camera drones back then, and no one had been crazy enough to approach the thing for a picture. So the only images they had were grainy ones taken from dozens of blocks away. Though he had read the article many times already, he found himself reading it all again. The giant klek destroyed the Porthaven Symphony Hall, where Heleen and Cole Gravenhurst, Malcolm's parents, had been spending their evening. His mother had used her telekinetic powers to hold up the collapsing roof while his all-too-human father helped people who couldn't get out on their own. One hundred and twenty-five people had died in that attack, but only two had died when the symphony hall collapsed: Malcolm's mother and father.

Malcolm had been only a few blocks away, sitting in the nursery of Gravenhurst Tower with his nanny. The attack would have been audible from the Tower—visible, even, with a klek of that size. Malcolm had no memory of it.

What he did remember was his grandmother, Sandra, coming into the nursery. It was the only memory he had of her—and he sometimes wondered if it was real, since he had only been two at the time. But he thought he remembered her drawn face. The fierce hug she'd given him.

She had been the one to take out the giant klek. Her powers turned her into pure energy, like a star in human form. She'd powered herself up as high as she could go, destroying the giant klek and herself in the process. It was, by most accounts, the most famous moment in the entire, incredible history of the Gravenhurst family. They made movies about that fight between Sandra and the giant klek. Novels, both graphic and prose. An image from that fight had become a meme that never seemed to disappear, the words *Better to burn bright than fade away* imposed over her glowing body as she tackled the giant robot.

After that there wasn't another klek attack for months. People thought perhaps they had given up. But they came back eventually, and the remaining Gravenhursts fought them off, month after month, year after year.

Malcolm left the *Herald* site and found his way to one of the Gravenhurst fan pages, one with a list of dates of all the klek attacks. He ran through the list. There had never been two attacks anywhere near this close together He stared at the list, wanting answers he knew weren't there.

He scrolled back to the beginning. The gate had fallen to Earth more than fifty years ago, and that marked the beginning of a long assault by the klek, with the robots appearing in new locations a dozen times a day. His grandparents—and Aleid, who was only eight at the time—had finally destroyed the gate four months after it landed. And then the next attack hadn't happened for another three months. It fluctuated for a while after that. Two months until the next attack. Only one month until the next—and that had been a big one, with dozens of klek appearing at the same time. After one more attack, four months later, his grandparents had made their new roles official, leaving their previous lives to become the full-time Guardians of Porthaven, dedicated to stopping the klek. And then the frequency seemed to settle into a pattern. The attacks had continued about once every three months for some years. But over time the interval between attacks had shortened, until they were only a few weeks apart. The lull thirteen years ago, after the attack when Malcolm's parents and grandmother had died, was the only blip in that timeline. Malcolm had believed that the frequency of the attacks had been stable since the gate was first destroyed. But what he was reading now showed clearly that it had been accelerating for decades.

He sat back from the computer. He had no idea what all of this meant.

One thought kept popping into his head: *We could use some help.* If klek attacks were going to become a weekly event, he wasn't sure his family could handle Porthaven's defense alone anymore. Drew and his friends might be needed.

If only Drew weren't terrified of his family. If only he could figure out a way to get them working together.

Malcolm stared down at his keyboard for several minutes, watching the projection flicker subtly, the way the light played over his blankets like sunlight through waves. Finally he reached out and typed *Ibrahim Koory*. When nothing came up in the search, he played with the spelling of the last name until finally, with *Khoury*, he got a hit.

A report on the website of a high school. Ibrahim had won a medal at a regional science fair two years ago. And Malcolm knew it was the right Ibrahim because standing beside him in the picture was Drew, his hand on the trophy, a big smile on his face. They'd done something about observing gravity waves the story said—the science of it was over Malcolm's head and seemed to be over the reporter's head too. Malcolm dug around but couldn't find anything more recent about Ibrahim. He didn't even seem to exist online anymore.

"Can you search the family servers?" Malcolm whispered to his sylf. An ellipse appeared on the face of the drone, indicating it was working on something. Guilt roiled in Malcolm's stomach. *You're not doing anything wrong,* he assured himself silently. *Just looking for some information. Information you won't find anyway, because there's no way we're involved with Ibrahim's disappearance.* The ellipse rotated slowly around the silver orb of the drone until the sylf beeped cheerily and displayed a green check mark. A generic search bar appeared, and Malcolm's fingers hesitated over the keys.

"Search…employee records for the Tower, I guess?" he told his sylf, and typed Ibrahim's last name into the search bar.

Files are encrypted. Please enter password, the display read. Malcolm sighed. "Now what?"

As he stared mutely at the password screen, a second smaller display popped up in front of the first, showing five words: **What are you looking for?**

"What is this?" Malcolm asked his sylf. "Is this a text?"

The sylf didn't respond in any way. It didn't look like the display that usually popped up for text messages though.

Hesitantly Malcolm tapped at the keyboard, and letters appeared beneath the five words. *Crap*, he thought. *It's a live chat—probably with security.*

This is Malcolm Gravenhurst, he typed, hoping his name might get him off the hook. **Sorry if I'm looking in the wrong files or something. I'll get off the server.**

The reply came: *I already know who you are. Tell me what you want.*

Malcolm looked at it for a moment. He imagined his grandfather on the other side of the chat, and his heart lurched. **I'll just get off**, he typed.

He shut down his sylf and plunked it onto his covers. He lay back on the bed and then almost fell out when the drone chimed again. He was sure he had put it in sleep mode, and only priority messages from his family were supposed to come through then—and the only reason they would send a priority message would be for another klek attack.

The drone was blinking with the small envelope icon that indicated a new email. To his private account, rather than the public one the family's PR team handled. He turned his drone on and opened it.

The message wasn't from family. It was from someone called Gatekeeper. No subject. The text of the message was short and looked like it had been copied from a larger spreadsheet. *Ibrahim Khoury. Gravitational effects. Parents negotiable. Employee transfer to Gravenhurst Investment Group, Toronto. Full nondisclosure. Digital wipe. Moderate alteration.* There was a date and a few other details, worded so vaguely that Malcolm didn't understand what they meant. But two words kept drawing his eyes: *Gravitational effects.*

He heard Drew's voice in his head. *He could make things, um, float. Not like flying, but…*

"Reply," Malcolm said to his drone, but it buzzed unhappily at him. The message from Gatekeeper somehow didn't have a return address attached to it. He switched the drone off.

The guilt in his stomach had been replaced by pure confusion. Malcolm lay down, rolling his drone between his fingers, and stared at the ceiling.

He felt ragged during combat training the next day. He went through the paces, armored and unarmored, and spent more than half the lesson flat on his back. His instructor, a burly but surprisingly gentle kickboxer named Kuan-yu, kept asking if he needed a break, but Malcolm shook his head and kept going until he was drenched in sweat and every muscle in his body ached. He was pretty sure Kuan-yu was pulling his punches.

As Malcolm toweled himself down, Melissa banged through the door. Malcolm jumped to his feet. He didn't usually see her in the gymnasium—as far as he knew, she didn't train—which meant she was probably there for him.

"Something up?" he asked.

"We'll have to cancel your tutoring for the afternoon," she said. "Family meeting."

"Okay. Do I have time to shower?"

Melissa looked down at his sweat-soaked shirt and wrinkled her nose. "I think we'd better make time for that. Be quick though."

Twenty minutes later Malcolm hurried through the door of the dining hall. Everyone else was already there—Aleid and Felix had taken the chairs on either side of his grandfather, Malcolm noted thankfully. He took his usual spot farther down, beside Eric.

"Good. We can begin," his grandfather said. "First of all, Malcolm. Though I'm not sure about your tendency to rush in, your aunt tells me that without your intervention lives might have been lost. Good work." He nodded to Malcolm, and Malcolm nodded back hesitantly. "Now on to business. What does the coverage look like so far?"

"Up more than 500 percent and largely focused on injuries sustained as well as the unusual timetable, as one might expect," Melissa said. Her sylf was buzzing as she flicked through screens showing graphs and data.

"And inquiries to us?"

"High volume. We have not yet responded."

Malcolm's grandfather nodded. "I think it best to respond without concern. Remind them of our long, successful history of defending the city. Assure them that this is not a new pattern."

"We could call it a fluctuation," Felix suggested. "We've certainly had those before. And I've seen to it that we will assist with any medical bills incurred by the injured," he added. "Our labs could even contribute some of the new high-end prostheses, with your approval."

"That should go over well," Malcolm's grandfather said.

"Prostheses?" Malcolm burst out and then grimaced as everyone turned to look at him. "Oh. Sorry, just…did someone lose an arm or something?"

"Some of the injuries were fairly severe, yes," Felix said. He watched Malcolm from across the table as the others turned back to their grandfather.

"Eric, do you think you could arrange a set tour on your latest film for some of the press? It would be good to have something positive in the media, to counterbalance…"

His grandfather's words faded into white noise. Malcolm blinked repeatedly. He was having trouble focusing on all the business-speak, and he wondered if it was exhaustion from his poor sleep. But his heart was hammering in his chest, and his hands were clenched. He didn't feel tired. He felt furious.

"Wait," Malcolm said softly, but the conversation went on around the table over top of him. His breath was coming in short gasps, and he could hear his blood rushing in his ears.

"A moment please," Felix said softly, raising his hand to gather the others' attention. Once everyone was quiet, he turned to Malcolm. "Is something bothering you?" he asked.

"No," he said. "Yes. I just—I didn't—" He breathed deep, tried to steady himself and failed miserably. "Is this what the meeting is about?"

"Of course," his grandfather said. "We need to talk about the unexpected attack last night."

"Yeah, but we're not," Malcolm said. "We're not talking about the attack. We're talking about the press."

"There are things you do not yet grasp about our role as Guardians," his grandfather said, leaning forward. "If we do not act quickly, guide the public reaction, there will be panic."

"But shouldn't they panic? I kind of feel panicked. I mean, what happened? Why did the klek come again so soon?"

Aunt Aleid turned toward their grandfather, but he just scowled down the table at Malcolm. "We do not know that," he said.

"Do you know something? Anything?" Malcolm asked. No one answered. "Then how do we know it won't happen again? In another four days? Today? I mean, how do we—"

His grandfather slammed his hands down on the table, making the whole thing jump. He turned his deepening scowl on Felix. "I told you it was not a good idea to have him here."

Felix pursed his lips.

"What do you mean? How is that any answer?" Malcolm was surprised to find himself on his feet. "We're supposed to be Guardians, right? What are we doing to… to guard?"

"Leave the room, Malcolm," his grandfather said. "We will finish this meeting without you."

"I just want to know h—"

"GET. OUT." His grandfather rose to his feet now too.

Malcolm took a deep, shuddering breath and walked out of the room. He could feel eyes on his back.

The doors closed behind him. He stood in the hallway, digging his feet into the carpet, trying to stop his shaking. His blood was racing through his veins like he was in the middle of a fight with the klek.

He got on the elevator and pressed the button for the gymnasium. He hoped his instructor had cleared out already, because Malcolm planned to break a few things, and he didn't want anyone to get hurt by the shrapnel.

Half an hour later Felix stepped into the gymnasium. Malcolm sat in the middle of what had been a punching bag until he'd used it to bludgeon a high-bar frame into small, twisted pieces, spilling the bag's sand all over the floor in the process.

"Sorry," he said sourly.

Felix shrugged. "It's just equipment. We can have it replaced easily enough. Remember when you were thirteen and you managed to knock out most of the west wall?"

Malcolm nodded. His uncle walked over and sat down with him, his dark slacks immediately covered in sand. Malcolm clicked his tongue, and when his sylf came down from the air and set itself in his hand, he passed it to Felix.

"Why are you giving me your drone?" Felix said.

"I figured Grandfather would want you to take something else away from me. And I don't actually have that much stuff that's mine, so…"

"Ah." Felix pressed the drone back into Malcolm's hand.

"How mad is he?" Malcolm asked.

"Quite."

Malcolm knew what was coming, but his uncle didn't say anything right away. Malcolm appreciated the silence.

"In the meeting…that was uncharacteristic behavior, Malcolm. Challenging your grandfather. Raising your voice."

"Did I raise my voice?" He couldn't remember.

"You were clearly agitated. Quite clearly," he said, gesturing to the wreckage around them.

"I'm—"

"I didn't come here to scold you, Malcolm. I just wanted to ask if you're all right."

"How do you mean?"

"I mean, it has been quite a week. Your first public demonstration, followed by two major engagements with the klek. When I agreed to let you join active duty as a Guardian, this was not what I expected. I wouldn't wonder if you felt overwhelmed."

"I'm not overwhelmed. Or not…I mean, yeah, it all feels a little, um, bigger and more confusing than I expected." His uncle kept watching him, and Malcolm found himself rooting around for the right words. "Has it really only been a week?"

Felix nodded.

"I don't know. I don't want to stop or anything."

"I didn't imagine you would. You have handled yourself astoundingly against the klek so far, but remember that you do not have to handle everything." He turned to face Malcolm and put a hand on his shoulder. Malcolm was drenched in sweat again, but Felix didn't flinch away. "Do you trust me?"

"Of course, Uncle Felix. I trust you."

"Then trust that we are doing everything we can to safeguard the city. As we have always done."

"But can't you tell me more than that? *What* are we doing?"

"What we have always done. Preparing for the next time we are needed."

Malcolm sighed but nodded. With a pat on Malcolm's shoulder, Felix rose and wiped the sand off his pants. "Perhaps we could have supper together this evening?"

"Umm, thanks, but I think maybe I could just use some space for now."

"Of course." Felix smiled down at Malcolm. "Send me a message if you change your mind."

"Yeah."

Felix left the gym. Malcolm sat there, turning his sylf over and over in his hands, running his fingers along the subtle seams in its metal shell. He knew the sylfs had been created based on klek technology, but he'd never noticed before how like the klek they were. The silvery metal of the drone's shell could have been taken directly from the shells of one of the klek. He wondered if it actually was.

"Hover on," he said to it. He checked that the door had closed behind Felix. "Open email."

His mail opened, and at the top was the message from Gatekeeper. He sucked in air through clenched teeth and tapped his hands against his knees as he read it again. He did trust his uncle—that much was true. But he couldn't do nothing. Breaking the equipment hadn't actually made him feel better, and neither had his talk with Felix. He felt like if he sat in the Tower another minute, he would explode. He had to do something.

NINE

Kazue stared at the email on the sylf's display and tried to scroll it up and down. "Gravenhurst Investment Group?" With a few quick gestures, she was suddenly scrolling through the rest of Malcolm's email.

"Hey, don't—"

But she shut the program without opening any of his other emails and sent his drone flying back to him with a swat. "That's seriously all the info you got?"

"That's all I got, and I have no idea what it means," Malcolm said.

Kazue returned to her own computer and brought up a map. Malcolm joined Blair on the battered couch at the other end of the railcar.

"Do you have to go home soon?" Blair asked pointedly.

When he had arrived at the railcar, it had been just the two of them there, and Malcolm suspected he had interrupted something.

"I think maybe I should wait for Drew. Sorry."

"There's, like, nothing online about this company," Kazue said. "I mean, I know they exist, I can see the front of the building on Street View, but their website is pretty much a blank page. No employee directory, no job listings. Just some boilerplate company credo and a logo."

Suddenly the door of the boxcar clanged open, and Drew came inside. He was out of breath. "Kaz, did he—is that a map of Toronto? So Malcolm really found Ibrahim?"

"Not exactly," Kazue said. "He brought something. I still don't know if it's worth anything."

Drew looked down at Malcolm. Malcolm nodded to him, but Drew hardly seemed to see him. He was chewing the inside of his cheek.

"Can I see what you got?" Drew asked.

Malcolm tossed his sylf over to Drew.

Drew stared blankly at it. "What do I do?"

"Open last email," Malcolm said to his drone.

Drew flinched as the display opened a few inches in front of his face, then leaned in close as he read the email. "I don't even know what most of this means. 'Parents negotiable'? How did you get this, Malcolm?"

"I don't really know. I did a search for Ibrahim's name on the family server, got stopped by a password, and suddenly I was on a live chat and getting this email from someone named Gatekeeper, who doesn't even have a return address, so—"

"Whoa, whoa, whoa," Kazue said, spinning her chair around. "Did you say *Gatekeeper*?" She rolled forward and snatched the drone away from Drew.

"Uh, yeah. Does that mean something to you?"

She stared at the display for a few seconds, then gave it back to Drew. "Gatekeeper is the profile name of, like, the best source of info on the klek. The *only* source of info on the klek. Every once in a while she shows up on subreddits and old forums and drops new details. Like, that they're not exactly inorganic. Or that they radiate different wavelengths depending on their size. Then she disappears again."

"The klek are radioactive?" Malcolm said, sitting up.

Kazue glanced over at him. "Not make-you-glow radiation, rich boy. They send out ultra-low-frequency electromagnetic emissions. Radio waves."

"Oh. Okay." He sat back. "So who is she? And how do you know it's a she?"

"I don't, actually, but no reason to assume she's not. You wouldn't have asked that question if I'd said *he*, would you? You need to look at that internalized misogyny you've got going on. As for who she is, I have no idea. From what you said, she must have access to the Gravenhurst private servers. I wonder if she actually works in the Tower. That would explain how she knows about the klek when no one but Gravenhurst employees has access to klek parts."

"Can we talk about Gatekeeper later?" Drew asked. "I'd really like to know if my friend's alive or not."

"Yeah, 'course," Kazue said, turning to her computer. "It's just hard. The company was the best lead, and that's a bust. I can't find any trace of his family online by name. I'm gonna dig around in places I'm not supposed to go."

Malcolm turned to Blair and smiled awkwardly at her. "I'm sorry," he muttered.

She sighed. "Kaz is distracted now anyway. I won't have her attention until she's done."

"How, uh, how did you guys find this place?"

"Kaz. She lives here."

"She what? Here? Doesn't it get cold in the winter?"

Blair nodded.

"I, um, I don't exactly have my own money, but I'm sure I could get something to help if—"

"Don't say that to Kaz or she will kick your ass. We don't want your money."

"Oh. Yeah, right, of course. Sorry, that was pretentious. If you need something from me, you can ask."

Blair watched him for a while, eyes narrowed like he was something mildly interesting that she was examining. Malcolm tried not to squirm.

"What's it like? Growing up with the Gravenhursts?" she asked.

"Umm...I don't really know, I guess. I don't have anything to compare it to."

"Do teachers give you perfect marks because of your family?"

"Oh, I never went to school," Malcolm said. "They get in tutors and things."

"You have a private tutor?"

"Lots of them. A few at a time, and they change them up every few months."

"So if you don't go to school, where do you go to see your friends?"

"Friends? Umm..."

Blair waited a few moments for him to answer and then just said, "Oh."

The way she was looking at him had changed. She was looking at him the way people did when they talked about his dead parents. "It's not like I was lonely," he said. "I had my family."

"Who hired tutors rather than teach you themselves."

If anything, the look of pity was getting worse.

"My family is busy. But really, you don't have to feel sorry for me or anything."

"I don't," she said. "But you make a little more sense now."

"Oh. Okay." He watched her watching him. "What, um, what's it like growing up with your family?"

"I'll let you know when I'm done."

"Got it!" Kazue said, raising her fist in victory. "Phone."

Drew handed over his phone, and Kazue tapped at the screen and handed it back. Drew took it and just stared at it sitting in his hand.

"Drew, I had to pull some serious digital hijinks to get that number," Kazue said. "Call him."

Drew nodded. "Screw it." He pressed the call button on his phone and held it to his ear. Everyone else sat silently. After a few moments, Drew's eyes widened. "Ibrahim? Is that you?"

The door to the boxcar squeaked open. Blair was at the door—Malcolm hadn't realized someone that big could move so quietly. She motioned for Malcolm and Kazue to follow her. Once they were outside, Blair closed the door again. Kazue turned to Malcolm.

"Just so we're clear," she said softly, "I still don't trust you. But…this is good. Drew hated not knowing what happened to him."

"Okay," Malcolm said. They stood in the silent rail yard, half lit by streetlights several tracks away, silence spread all around them for miles.

After a few minutes Drew came to the door and hopped down onto the gravel. Malcolm could barely see his eyes in the semidarkness, but he thought they were glistening.

"It was him," he said. "He's alive." He scuffed the ground with the toe of his shoe. "Thanks, Malcolm. Thanks for bringing that to us."

Malcolm nodded, then realized Drew probably couldn't see that in the dark. "Of course. Is he okay?"

"Mostly. No one hurt him, it sounds like. But he doesn't remember having powers."

"What?" Kazue said.

"Why?" Malcolm added. "How can he not remember? I mean, he still has powers, right?"

All three of them turned and squinted at him. "You've never been out of Porthaven, have you?" Blair said.

"Um, no. Why is that important?"

"Powers don't work outside the city," Drew said.

"What? That can't be true. Are you talking about the klek tech? 'Cause I know *that* doesn't—" Three heads shook around him. "But they're our powers. They're *us*. Of course they work outside the city."

"Have you ever been out of Porthaven?" Drew said slowly and clearly.

"No. I just told you—"

"Then stop telling us what happens when you leave the city. Believe what we're telling you."

Malcolm fell silent for a moment. But there was more he needed to know. "What, um, what *did* he remember? About why he left. Did my family do something?"

"He doesn't remember. Says his dad was transferred, that was all."

"But that means maybe it wasn't us—the Gravenhursts. What if it really was just his family moving away?"

"No, Malcolm."

"How do you know it's not, like—"

"Because he doesn't remember *me*, okay? He remembers that he went to school with me, but he doesn't remember the years we spent together figuring out our powers. He doesn't remember being my best friend. He doesn't remember *any* of it." The hurt, the loss, in Drew's voice was so palpable Malcolm could feel it in his chest. "Someone made him forget. I don't know how, or who, but if it wasn't the Gravenhursts, then who the hell did that?"

By the end he was shouting. Kazue moved in beside him and put her hand on his arm. "Drew, cool it," she said. "Not so loud."

Drew took a deep breath and nodded to her. "Sorry," he said to Malcolm. "That was—I'm really, really pissed off right now, and it's not really at you, but it's kind of at you. Do you think you could go?"

"Um, yeah. Right. Yeah." He backed away as he spoke, moving a railcar's length away before he stopped. And then he stood there, watching the three of them. He realized he was waiting for one of them to say something more—to him, about him, he didn't know. But they were just waiting for him to leave. So he armored up and jumped away.

The first jump took him west, out of the rail yard. He turned north, toward the Tower, and then paused.

Where am I going?

He jumped west. As high and as far as he could go. The sun was out ahead of him, racing him toward the horizon. It was getting late. He should go home. He kept moving west.

When he reached the edge of the city, he slowed. He brought his jumps down until they were soft enough that he was moving just above a run. He kept moving along a road he didn't know the name of. The shadows were getting too long for him to read the signs. Pavement gave way to hard-packed dirt. The road was bordered by windbreak trees on the edges of wide farm fields. He kept moving, jumping forward.

Powers still work, he thought. *They were wro—*

His armor crumpled midjump, and he fell to the road. His legs buckled on impact, sending him rolling across the unforgiving dirt.

He lay on the ground for a moment. A rock pressed into his cheek. He tried to roll over, but it felt strangely difficult. His body didn't want to move. Finally he struggled up onto his knees and took quick stock of himself. He'd scraped his elbow in the fall, and it was bleeding. He got to his feet.

He tried to bring up his armor, but nothing happened. For a moment he thought he might vomit, it was so disorienting—it was like trying to speak and discovering you didn't have a voice anymore. He tried again. And again.

It wasn't just that the armor wouldn't work, either. He still felt heavy. Heavier than he had ever felt. Like his body was a lead weight. His muscles were beginning to tremble with the effort of holding him up. He sank back to his knees and slumped forward.

Something splashed on his hands, and he realized he was crying. "Oh great," he said. "This is…" He took a deep breath, but the tears kept coming. When he closed his eyes, he saw Drew, angry, shouting. He saw three faces, waiting for him to leave. He felt the crushing weight of everything he didn't know—why the klek had come twice in a week, why the klek came at all, how people who weren't his family had powers, what had happened to Drew's friend. His mind felt like it was skidding on ice, trying to find something it could grip and failing time and time again.

He forced his eyes up to look back at Porthaven. His city. It was like nowhere else in the world—a fragment of the future, a place where the laws of physics didn't always apply. He'd never wanted to leave. But suddenly, looking at it from this empty dirt road, it felt different. Stifling. Even if he wanted to leave, he couldn't. Not if it made him feel like this.

He took another deep breath and blinked hard, trying everything he had learned during his childhood to master his emotions, to stop tears when he felt them coming. Techniques he'd used to avoid the scorn of his grandfather, who never wanted to see him cry.

Why do I care what he thinks?

The question came in the wake of another wave of tears— raw, ragged, angry tears. And he couldn't find an answer. He didn't know why he cared, but he did. He didn't want to care though. His grandfather was more worried about the press than the klek. Whatever his grandfather wanted him to be, he didn't want to be that.

So he stopped fighting the tears. He let them flow, long and messy, out onto the dirt below him. His hands, still trembling from holding up his weight, curled into the wet dirt, mud streaking his fingers.

"It wasn't supposed to be like this," he said to the road, to the trees, to the lengthening shadows. They didn't hear.

But Malcolm heard, and the words felt right. His tears trailed off, and he could breathe again. He stood on shaking legs and began dragging himself back to Porthaven. After only a few steps, the weight lifted from him as he crossed whatever invisible border gave him access to his powers again. He called his armor and it responded like it had never gone. He leapt off the dirt road, over the windbreak trees. Back toward the Tower at the heart of the city.

TEN

Waiting sucked.

Not that Malcolm's days weren't full. His life was just as rigidly structured as before: lessons, training, meetings with marketing—apparently he had his own publicist now. One evening he even did a photo shoot, because his image was going to be on a T-shirt. He did all these things on autopilot.

What he was really doing was waiting. Waiting for the next klek attack. Waiting to hear from Drew, Blair or Kazue. Of course, he realized, they had never said they would contact him. And he didn't know if he should reach out. What if they just vanished from his life?

On Sunday, four days after the last klek attack, he spent the entire day jumping at shadows. And since Sunday was his only unscheduled day, he had a lot of time for jumping. He ended up spending hours in a sim suite, running through hyperborean forests until his legs burned and he couldn't run any farther, even armored. Trying, failing, to distract himself.

The entire day came and went, and there were no klek. No texts. He kept waiting.

On Tuesday morning when his sylf chimed in the middle of his science tutoring, and it was Aunt Aleid telling him there was another attack, he actually sighed with relief. It was only six days since the last attack, but at least the waiting was over.

And then the second text came through. **Be quick. Attack is near a school. Leaving from the roof in one minute.** Guilt washed through him. People were in danger, and some part of him was glad about it.

"Gotta go," he told his tutor, leaving his books on the table as he ran to the elevator.

Moments later he and Melissa were dangling in their aunt's grip, flying east. Eric hadn't made it in time. "Klek showed up just outside Gilchrist High School," Aunt Aleid said.

"Are there still people inside?" Malcolm asked.

"I don't know, so let's assume there are."

"What are we going to see?" Melissa asked. She'd taken off her blazer, which made Malcolm think this might be a serious fight.

"Smaller klek this time. Hundreds."

"Eric would have been useful."

"I know," Aleid said. "You can tell your brother a hangover is not an excuse."

"You think he'd listen to me?" Melissa said scornfully.

The school came into view, and Malcolm gasped. It looked like someone had kicked an anthill. Klek the size of dogs swarmed over the roof and in and out of the windows. The entire east wing of the L-shaped building teemed with klek.

"Melissa, you stay outside and see if you can clear some of this out. Malcolm and I will go in."

"Got it," Mel said. Aleid flew in low over the school fields and dropped Melissa onto the grass. She stumbled as she landed, but a moment later green energy was blooming from her hands, tearing into the mass of klek. They started moving toward her.

Then Malcolm lost sight of her as Aleid flew them through the school's main doors. The hallways were crowded with small klek, crawling over each other. Their clicking was deafening. Malcolm brought his armor up as Aleid set him down.

"Get to the north wing," Aleid said. "Hopefully the students have made their way there."

"What about you?" Malcolm asked.

"I'm going to try to keep these ones here," she said, and without another word she jumped into the middle of the swarm, kicking and punching. Her blows didn't do a lot of damage to the metallic klek, but they certainly drew attention. The klek surged toward her, climbing over one another until they covered her up to the shoulders. She stood unconcerned in the middle of the pile, occasionally swatting robots away. "Go!" she shouted to Malcolm.

He ran toward the north wing, peeking into classrooms as he went. All he could see were klek, covering desks, walls, windows. As he moved farther down the hallway, the klek thinned out. A few lost sylfs buzzed around near the ceiling, chiming unhappily to try to draw their owners back. Somewhere up ahead he heard screaming.

He hurried around the corner into the north wing and saw two people backed against the wall there, several klek around them. One of the two—a teacher, it looked like—had a broom and was swinging it at the robots to try to keep them at bay.

"Don't hit them!" Malcolm shouted. "They won't attack if—"

The broom connected with one of the klek and sent it into the far wall. The other four klek in the hallway made angry clicking noises.

"—if you don't do that," Malcolm finished. With a sigh he jumped forward and stomped on the klek nearest him. The others turned their attention to him. One leapt for his face, and he caught it, crushing it between his hands. The others clambered up his legs. He tried to get a grip on them, but they moved quickly and evaded his attempts, climbing to his shoulders and striking ineffectually at his armor. He gave up on grabbing them and just fell backward. He had to wiggle a bit to crush the klek against the floor. Not his most elegant move— Eric would probably say it wouldn't play for the cameras. But there were no more klek going for the teacher and student.

Malcolm got to his feet and checked the nearest classroom. It was full of students. Malcolm beckoned the pair from the hallway to follow him. They entered the room, and he smashed one of the far windows. "You can get out this way. Don't head east unless you want more klek."

The students all started climbing out the window. The teacher, to his credit, waited for the others to leave. A few klek seemed drawn to the sound, so Malcolm stood at the doorway and kicked them back as they tried to enter.

But he noticed that most weren't trying to get into this room. They were hurrying past it, farther down the north hallway. Once everyone was out of the room, Malcolm left to see where the klek were running to. There was a mass of them pressed up against a door at the end of the hall. It didn't look like they were milling aimlessly—something inside that room had their attention.

Malcolm ran down to the door and saw that it wasn't closed. The klek appeared to be pressed against open air. No, not open air. There was a telltale blue glimmer in the doorway.

A force field, Malcolm realized. He looked past it. Dozens of students were crammed into the single room—several classrooms' worth of students, all shoulder to shoulder. At the far side of the room a woman in a floral dress pushed a window open and started moving people through it one by one. And in the middle of the crowd of students, standing taller than the others, was Blair. Her face was taut, arms outstretched. She made a series of gestures in the air, and a second force field winked into existence just behind the pile of klek. This second field slid into the first, crushing the klek between them. When the second field winked out, the remaining klek rushed forward against the original force field, over the still-twitching wreckage of their kin.

Malcolm laughed in spite of the situation. It was a brilliant idea, using the force fields as weapons. This was the kind of help his family could use. He looked over his shoulder, wondering if Aleid might have seen, might be interested in recruiting Blair. But she was still out of sight.

Something pinged off Malcolm's armor. He refocused on the klek and saw that they weren't trying to dig through the force field anymore. Instead they were hammering at the walls on either side of it. Chips of concrete flew everywhere. The hinges of the metal door gave way, and it fell to the floor with a deafening clang.

Malcolm ran forward, laying into the small klek and momentarily clearing them away from the door and wall. He paused and looked in at Blair, whose eyes widened at the sight of him. And suddenly Malcolm heard Drew's voice again. *I'm afraid of the Gravenhursts.* The look on Blair's face wasn't relief—it was fear. Would she want Aleid to see her power? Even if Malcolm was excited by the possibility, this wasn't a decision he should make for her.

"The Guardians are here!" he shouted into the room, partly to reassure the students and partly to warn Blair.

Blair nodded, and the force field winked out.

Malcolm stepped into the doorway, blocking it with his thick, armored form. He struck at any klek who tried to squeeze past, crushing the small robots easily. He looked over his shoulder. The students were still escaping one by one through the open window. He looked down the hallway. A wave of klek was coming toward him.

There was no way he could stop them all. And the students wouldn't get out in time, not through one open window. He reached down and grabbed the door off the floor, shaking klek from it. "Heads down, please!" he shouted into the classroom. The students listened, ducking low as Malcolm heaved the door over their heads. It crashed through the far wall, taking two windows and the space between them with it. "Go, fast!" he said. The instruction was unnecessary. They were already pouring through the hole in the wall.

Malcolm dug his feet in—literally. He stomped them down until he was embedded in the floor, and then he braced himself. A moment later the surge of klek hit him. The first ones were crushed between his armor and the force of the swarm behind them. Malcolm reached up and tried to keep klek from crawling over his head, but there were too many. They surged between his arms, clinging to the doorframe and clambering in along the ceiling. Malcolm looked over his shoulder just in time to see the last of the students, including Blair, jump out onto the grass as the klek rushed toward them.

One of the klek jumped at a fleeing boy, but it was stopped in midair by one of Blair's force fields. At the same time, a shape swept down from the sky. His aunt Aleid caught two of the klek and smashed them against the wall of the school, then swept back around to catch the few remaining stragglers. Blair dropped her field as quickly as she could and took off with her classmates.

Aleid came to a stop on the grass and watched the crowd flee across the field.

Did she see? Malcolm didn't have time to figure it out. The mass of klek was still pressing against him, and he pressed them back, destroying several with each swing of his arms. It felt like it took forever for the force of the swarm to abate. By the time it was over, he was buried up to his waist in pieces of klek.

He turned to look out the window. Aleid was still standing there. Somewhere off to the left Malcolm saw flashes of green—Melissa, finishing off more robots.

"Aunt Aleid?" he called. She didn't turn. "Aunt Aleid?" he said again.

She turned to him, her eyes narrowed and her jaw set.

"Is everyone out?" she asked.

"I think so," Malcolm said. "But we should check the classrooms again."

"Yes," she said. "Yes, of course." Her eyes had drifted to the fleeing students, and she turned reluctantly and flew in through the hole Malcolm had made in the wall. "You take the classrooms on this side of the hall," she said, striding past him and moving off.

Malcolm took a quick glance outside. He could just make out Blair at the edge of the crowd. He thought she was looking at him, but she was too far away for him to be certain.

Hours later Malcolm sat on his bed, tossing his sylf from hand to hand. Between each throw its hover engines engaged, and it slowed a little. He stopped and then tossed it straight in the air, where it stayed. "Display on," he whispered, and its projections flickered to life. It showed the previous messages he had exchanged with Drew, still labeled only *Private Number*. A short message sat, unsent, at the bottom: **My family might have seen Blair use her power.** He opened his mouth to say, "Send," then closed it again. He plucked the sylf out of the air and resumed tossing as its display winked out.

They don't need my help, Malcolm thought. *Probably don't even want it. They can take care of themselves. Aleid might not have seen her. And even if she did, this is my family, right? Drew and the others don't need to be afraid of them. We save people.*

He sighed and put his head down into his hands, letting his sylf drift away. He felt so confused that it made his stomach clench. *What the hell am I supposed to do?*

His head snapped up. "Computer mode," he said, and his drone flew in close and cast out its display and projected keyboard. "Connect to the family server. Search employee records," he said. Once the search opened, he typed in *Ibrahim Khoury*. The password screen popped up. He waited.

The same small chat window appeared in front of the main display. *Again?* it said.

Gatekeeper? he wrote back.

What are you doing? came the reply. Which wasn't a denial.

Malcolm kept typing. **I wanted to ask you something. That info you sent me on Ibrahim. It came from a spreadsheet or something, right? Can I have that file?**

What did you do with the info I already sent you?

Malcolm gritted his teeth. He knew what kind of trouble this could bring down on his head. But he was in the dark, and he didn't see any other way forward. **Gave it to a friend of Ibrahim's**, he wrote. There was a pause, and Malcolm wondered how badly he had screwed up.

Finally, after a painful minute of waiting, a reply appeared. *Do you want the full 152?*

Malcolm stared at the screen. **What?** he typed, and then deleted it. Then **152 what?** and deleted it again.

Have to go. What do you want? the chat window asked.

He huffed. **The full 152**, he typed.

Okay. It'll take me a while to send it without being traced.

The chat window closed. "Discard message draft and close current activity," Malcolm said. "Drone mode." The sylf chirped and closed its display and keyboard. Malcolm lay down and watched it circle through the air above him.

ELEVEN

When Malcolm opened his eyes, the drone was still there, but now there were green lights swirling around it, blinking eagerly—an incoming call. "Answer," he tried to say, but a yawn slurred the word and his sylf buzzed quizzically. "Answer," he said again.

He waited for the display to pop up, but it didn't. It was an audio call. "Hello? Malcolm?" said an uncertain voice.

The voice cut through Malcolm's fog of sleep. "Drew?"

"Yeah. I have an emergency."

Malcolm pulled his blankets off and stood, already heading for his closet. "What is it?" His drone fell in above his shoulder.

"Blair's gone."

Malcolm stopped. A black hole opened in the middle of his stomach. "What?"

"It happened last night. Just like the others. We don't know where she is. Her mom is gone too."

"No," Malcolm said.

"What do you mean, no?" Drew asked.

They couldn't have. But it can't be a coincidence.

"I—I don't understand," Malcolm said.

"Well, I need you to understand. Fast. If someone connected to your family took her, you might still be able to find her. Can you look? Around the Tower or anywhere else you think she might be?"

"It was…" Malcolm sank down to the floor and dropped his head into his hands, holding it tight as if he could grip his spinning thoughts and make them stop. "My aunt. She—I was going to text."

"What are you talking about, Malcolm?"

"I, she…at the klek attack yesterday. Blair was there. She used her power, and my aunt might have seen it."

There was a long, long silence. The blood roared in Malcolm's ears.

"She *saw* her?" Drew said.

"I don't know. I…" His head felt like it was bursting. "Probably."

"And you didn't tell us?"

"I didn't think she would do anything. This is my family. I was going to text you, but I…"

He could hear Drew breathing on the other end of the phone. Breathing hard.

"Listen, I'll do what you said. I'll go search."

"Nah. Don't do that. Don't try to help." His voice was so soft now Malcolm struggled to hear him.

"What do you mean? Of course I'm gonna—"

"I shouldn't be surprised," Drew said. "I am, but I shouldn't be."

"I'll find her. I'll find her and—"

"Don't come here. I honestly think Kaz'll kill you if you do." His sylf beeped, and the green lights all winked out. Drew had hung up.

Malcolm stared at the blank silver surface of the drone, the abyss in his stomach gaping wider and wider, until he thought it might swallow him whole. He pictured Blair's round, kind face watching him from the other end of the couch. His aunt watching Blair flee from the high school.

Malcolm walked swiftly to his door, realizing at the last minute that he was only wearing a pair of pyjama pants. He got dressed as quickly as he could—in loose training gear, something he could move in. He strode out of his room and stopped.

"Where am I going?" he asked himself out loud. His drone bleeped in confusion. He took a deep breath. *Where would she be?*

He stepped into the elevator, went to press the ground-floor button and froze. His finger moved down.

The bottom button. The basement. Where he and even Eric and Melissa weren't allowed to go.

There was a sensor beside the button—a fingerprint scanner, he thought. He put his finger against it and was rewarded with an angry red light. The elevator didn't move.

He checked his sylf. Its clock blinked on, showing him it was only six thirty-three. Security would be in the lobby, but most of the office floors would still be empty. He took the elevator down to the fifth floor—which he thought was for accounting, but he wasn't sure—and then pressed the button for the roof before stepping out onto a floor full of beige cubicles. Automatic lights flickered on, but Malcolm turned away and faced the elevator. He listened to the elevator car move upward as he pocketed his drone and brought up his armor, then pressed the tips of his fingers between the doors and forced them apart. The metal crumpled. He looked down at the dark shaft stretching away below him. He didn't know how far below ground the basement was. It was pitch-black down there. He couldn't see anything.

He jumped.

He landed on his back, but his armor absorbed the impact easily enough. He dropped it so he could feel his way to the doors. They were on the wall behind him at shoulder level. He armored up and pried them open.

He pulled himself out and almost tripped over a bundle of cables. There were cables running everywhere, across the floor of a wide-open room, wanly lit and shadowed by ranks of concrete columns. Half of the cables ran toward the outer edge of the room, where Malcolm saw a ring of computer stations, screens blinking with numbers and graphs. The other half of the cables ran toward the center of the room, where there was a series of lights.

Why is everything plugged in? Malcolm felt momentarily disoriented. *Why isn't it using the ambient grid?*

One of the lights in the center of the room blinked on, and Malcolm scrambled backward. But a moment later it blinked off again. He heard something to his right. The sound of fingers on a keyboard. Malcolm crept forward.

Sitting at one of the computer stations was a short woman with gray, frizzy hair. He watched her for a moment as she typed something in and then turned to look at the cluster of lights in the middle of the room. Another one of the lights blinked on, this time for only a split second, and the woman leaned closer to her screen, clicking her tongue against her teeth.

"Have to wait," she said suddenly, without looking up. "In the middle of a cycle."

Malcolm stepped away from the column he had been crouched behind. "Are...are you talking to—"

"I said wait. Have to focus." She kept typing.

Malcolm frowned, bewildered. He went closer to one of the screens and squinted at it. It was drawing a jagged line from left to right, almost like a heartbeat monitor. He looked back to the woman, but she was still working intently. Lights were blinking off and on behind her as she worked. Malcolm turned around.

The flashing lights were set in a circle around something—big square lights that gave off a pure-white glow. Some were set on telescopic stands, while others sat directly on the floor. It was hard to see through them, but between the boxy lights Malcolm caught sight of something jagged and silvery. It looked vaguely familiar. He stepped closer.

One of the lights came on and blinded him. He shut his eyes and crouched, waiting for the stars in his vision to fade, and then opened his eyes again. He stepped forward, right into the thicket of lights.

In the middle of the ring sat the klek gate.

Malcolm's breath caught. He recognized it immediately from the pictures taken when the gate had first landed in Porthaven. Five silver spurs stretched upward from a multifaceted base. Glimmering filaments of metal stretched between the spurs in a pattern his eyes couldn't follow. It made a slow clicking sound—deeper and more resonant than the klek themselves, but unmistakably similar.

The filaments and spurs seemed to twitch and flex, but whenever Malcolm looked straight at them, they were still.

He blinked hard, willing the gate to disappear, but when he opened his eyes, there it was. Five silver spikes, reflecting his own distorted face back at him.

"How is this here?" he said, turning to the woman, who still wasn't looking at him. "What is going on? The gate was destroyed! It was—"

The woman suddenly spun around, eyes fixing on him for the first time. "Malcolm. Didn't realize it was you." As she spoke, one of her hands was still on the computer, typing. She turned away again.

"What?" he said. "What's happening? What is this? Who are you?"

"Be quiet right now," she said.

He looked behind him at the gate. *The gate...*

"Gatekeeper?" he said.

"Yes. Shut up."

For a few moments he stared back and forth between the woman and the gate. He felt dizzy, nauseous. *Focus*, he told himself. *You came here for something.*

"Where's Blair?" he asked. "What did you do with her?"

The woman turned her head just slightly. "One fifty-three?"

"What? Blair! She—"

There was a clunk from the elevator behind him, and his grandfather's voice roared across the concrete room. "What in the blazes!"

Malcolm groaned as his grandfather stepped off the elevator, fists clenched, teeth bared, coming toward

Malcolm like an avalanche. The crags of his face hid his eyes in shadow.

"What are you doing here?" he said, his voice as soft and threatening as distant thunder.

"I...I'm sorry, I..."

Felix stepped out of the elevator and strode swiftly forward. He took in each one of them, his face as calm as if he were entering a boardroom. "Malcolm. That would explain the broken doors on the fifth floor, I suppose."

Malcolm looked at his uncle's calm face, and suddenly he felt like thunder himself. "What is this? Why is the klek gate here?" He looked up at his grandfather. "You destroyed the gate decades ago!"

"It is none of your concern!" his grandfather shouted.

Malcolm almost flinched. But he didn't.

Felix held up a hand. "This is complicated. Still, it would appear we have no choice but to explain. We should leave Darla to her work—it would be dangerous to disturb her now."

"Dangerous?" Malcolm said. "How?"

"You could have damn well flooded the city with giant klek. That's how," his grandfather growled.

"Why don't we go upstairs?" Felix said. "I promise, Malcolm. It will all make sense."

"It's not an invasion."

Malcolm stared at Felix blankly from an uncomfortably deep armchair. They were sitting in a room Malcolm had never been in—a corner office on the twenty-third floor, with tinted windows. The brown leather chairs and dark wood furniture drank up what little light there was. From the way his grandfather settled into the chair on the other side of the desk, Malcolm guessed this was his grandfather's office. But the door had been unmarked, and he'd always thought his grandfather's office was somewhere higher.

"Did you hear me, Malcolm?" Felix asked.

"Yeah," Malcolm said. "But that doesn't make any sense. Of course it's an invasion. There are alien robots attacking the city, like, pretty often."

"Why the hell are we having this conversation?" Malcolm's grandfather growled.

"Father, please," Felix said. "Now that he's seen it, we really have no other choice."

Malcolm's grandfather settled deeper into his chair, glowering. "Fine. Say what needs to be said, Felix."

"Think about it, Malcolm," Felix said. "The klek don't actually attempt to take the city from us." When Malcolm opened his mouth to object, Felix held up a hand. "They are dangerous, yes. Self-defensive. But they don't actively seek to harm people. Most of the damage they do is simply collateral in the process of doing…" He wiggled his hands in the air. "…whatever they are doing."

"So the alien robots that invade Porthaven aren't an alien invasion is what you're saying."

Felix chuckled. "Yes. Our best guess is that the gate, the klek, all of it, is lost alien technology—something never intended to be here. Automated, built for some function we don't understand that has nothing to do with us or our planet. A function it continues to blindly carry out here. Heaven knows how it ended up on Earth, but the more we studied it, the less it seemed like an attack."

"So what is it then?"

"An opportunity."

Malcolm didn't think his jaw could drop farther, but it did. "A what? The klek have killed thousands of people!"

"Yes, yes. As I said, the danger isn't disputed. But there is a difference between something dangerous and something malicious. The gate, the entire alien system, doesn't care that we're here. We are not its enemy. And so we have been able to find ways to mitigate the damage and, what's more, to work *with* it."

"He won't understand," Malcolm's grandfather said. "This is a waste of time."

"I just…how can something that kills people, that sets monsters loose in the city, be an opportunity?" Malcolm said.

Felix pursed his lips. "There are aspects to the gate that you don't comprehend. This isn't widely known, but the gate isn't the entirety of the technology that fell to Earth. The gate is more like the heart—or, rather, the brain and the battery—of a broader system."

"A system of what?"

"Nanotechnology." Felix watched Malcolm's shocked expression. "In lay terms, microscopic robots—nanites—that reproduce themselves and—"

"I know what nanotech is," Malcolm said. "I read comics. So you're saying that it's not just the klek? There's alien nanotech too?"

"No, not klek *and* nanotech. It's all nanotech. Where do you think the klek come from?"

"I thought they, like, teleported in. *Everyone* thinks—"

"The nanites build the klek. They gather molecules from the environment—pieces so tiny no one ever notices them missing—and construct the klek from those. And they work so fast, the klek seem to appear out of nowhere. We saw no way to reveal this information publicly without causing a panic. So, yes, we have allowed the broader public to believe the klek teleport into Porthaven. But without the nanites, there would be no klek."

Malcolm blew out a long breath. "Where are these nanites? Can you track them?"

"Doing so would be pointless. They are everywhere by now," Felix said, gesturing vaguely around him. "At least, everywhere in Porthaven. Since they first landed they have steadily reproduced. They are omnipresent within the city now." He leaned forward. "Don't look so horrified. The nanites are programmed to build klek, yes, and we cannot reprogram them. But we've also found ways to turn them to our own purposes. How do you think we created an ambient energy grid? We learned how to tap into the power the gate sends to the nanites—we accessed it *through* the nanites. It's how all of Porthaven's technology continues to function. The drones, the hoverpods, the repair mites. The reason they work in the first place is because of the nanites. And every time we bring more pieces of the klek into our labs, we understand more. We've already come close to building our own version of nanites with the repair mites. Soon we might be able to create our own nanotech system, one without the drawbacks."

"The *drawbacks*? The killer-robot drawbacks?" Malcolm clenched his eyes shut. "So why is the gate still here? We destroyed it, didn't we?" He looked to his grandfather. "You destroyed it."

"That is what the public believes," said Felix. "But it is nigh indestructible. And as you saw—"

Malcolm's grandfather cut Felix off with a growl. "Where do you think your damn powers come from?" he said.

Malcolm was getting tired of gaping, so he tried clenching his jaw for a change. "What, so our powers are—"

"It's *all* nanotech. Your armor. Your strength. All of it is nanotech that feeds off the gate," his grandfather said. "You shut down the gate, you shut down your own powers. That's what we did, at the beginning. We tried to destroy it. When we couldn't do that, we buried it. Without light to power the gate, the klek went away. Powers went away."

"And then…you turned it back on?"

His grandfather looked at him like he had asked the most foolish question he'd ever heard. "Wouldn't you?"

"We didn't just start feeding it light, Malcolm. We—or rather, your grandparents—learned how to control it. To feed the gate enough energy to keep the system flowing and keep the appearance of new klek at a controllable level."

Malcolm sat silent for a long time. In his pocket he felt his sylf buzz with an incoming message. His fingers itched to take it out, if only to distract himself. But he needed his entire attention to get through this. "Okay. Okay. So let me go back a bit here, because this is…a lot. So the gate wasn't destroyed. And we've been keeping it in our basement for decades and, like, drip-feeding it with light. And it powers nanites, which build klek, but it now powers pretty much the whole city too, including our superpowers." With each statement, Felix nodded and Malcolm's grandfather frowned. "And there are nanites, like, crawling around under my skin? Under the skin of everyone with powers?"

"Not just in you or the family. In every person in the city. Likely in every person who has ever set foot in Porthaven, though they fall dormant once they are out of range of the gate. But in most people the nanites have no effect. They seem to have a unique impact on our family—we think because of our proximity to the gate and the nanotech when it first fell, or possibly because of some unique aspect of our DNA."

Malcolm closed his eyes and let his head reel. He felt stuffed full. This was almost how he had pictured his fifteenth birthday. When he'd taken on his role as a Guardian, he'd thought he would be let in on all the secrets. And now he was, but the truth looked nothing like he'd expected.

And he knew they still weren't telling him everything.

"Why are there more klek now if we have the gate under our control?"

"The technology is complicated, and much of it is still beyond us. It can be unpredictable at times," Felix said.

"So you really don't know?"

"Not yet."

"We will soon," his grandfather said, in a tone that suggested this was the last word on the subject.

"Who is the woman? Downstairs?"

"Darla," Felix said. "She is in charge of the maintenance of the gate."

"Is she, like, some kind of supergenius or something?"

Felix looked hesitant. "Why do you ask that?"

"She was talking to me and typing at the same time. Which, I'm pretty sure, is not something human brains are supposed to be able to do. Also, the whole big bank of computers with one person running them all is, like, classic supergenius stuff."

Felix glanced at Malcolm's grandfather, who only responded with a deeper frown. "Darla is something of a unique case. She was nearby when the gate fell, just like your grandparents and Aleid were. She has been changed by the nanites too. Her particular alteration makes her well suited to the task of keeping the gate in line."

"So other people besides Gravenhursts can get powers from the nanites?"

Malcolm's grandfather sat forward in his chair. Malcolm forced himself not to look at him. Felix narrowed his eyes.

"Us and Darla, yes," he said. "It's something about our DNA. We haven't been able to figure out the specifics, but the nanites respond to something in our genetic patterns and attach themselves to us in particular ways that correspond to those patterns."

Malcolm sat rigid in his seat. He felt he was on the edge of a rooftop, about to jump off. But not the fun armored, superstrength kind of jumping.

"So if..." He tried to sit forward, but the big chair wouldn't let him. He hadn't imagined doing it this way. Saving Blair was one thing. Confronting his grandfather was another. "If someone else had the right patterns..." He sucked in his cheeks and grimaced.

"Malcolm?" Felix said. Somehow he managed to sit forward in his chair and make it look effortless.

Just do it, damn it, Malcolm told himself.

"Where is Blair?" he said.

For the first time Malcolm could remember, his uncle looked off-balance. He shifted in his chair. "I'm sorry, who?"

"The one yesterday, in the school. Who made the force fields to stop the klek. Where is she?"

"You saw that?" Felix said and then quirked his head. "How do you know her name, Malcolm?"

"How do *you*—" Malcolm began, but he was stopped by a lurching sensation in the pit of his stomach, like he had just slammed into a brick wall. *I shouldn't be surprised*, Drew's voice said in his head. "Oh god. Oh crap. He was right about us. Did you kill her?"

"Who have you been speaking to, Malcolm?" Felix asked.

His grandfather growled deep in his throat, then stood, hands planted on his desk. "That's enough," he said, looming over Malcolm. He somehow looked even taller than usual. "You shouldn't have gone down there, and none of this is your business. We have been in control of this situation for decades. You are a child, and you don't get to demand answers to your idiotic questions. You don't understand anything."

He really *was* taller, Malcolm realized. And there were gouges in the desk where his hands rested.

Malcolm had never seen his grandfather use his power before—not in person. He could absorb material around him, use it to make him bigger, stronger. When he'd watched it on old footage, seen his giant grandfather go toe to toe with even the biggest klek, he had cheered. But up close, it was terrifying. He wondered if his grandfather was doing it intentionally to intimidate Malcolm, or if he'd lost control of his power in his anger. Malcolm wasn't sure which possibility was worse.

He rose to his feet.

"Sit down," his grandfather spat at him.

"No," he said, meeting his grandfather's eyes squarely for the first time since they had entered the room.

"Father, please, I'm handling—" Felix began, rising from his chair.

"No, you're not. You can't control him, can't do what's needed. Never could. It's time he learned his place. Malcolm, sit down." Malcolm's grandfather walked around the desk toward him. With each step, a part of the hardwood floor came with him and his grandfather grew a little bit more.

"No," Malcolm said again, embarrassed to hear the quaver in his voice. He stepped sideways, toward the windows.

"Malcolm, please, just listen," Felix pleaded.

"Sit down NOW!" his grandfather roared, huge hands reaching for Malcolm.

"No," Malcolm said weakly one more time. And then he brought his armor up and kicked out behind him. The window shattered into tiny pieces that pattered on the ground twenty-three stories below. Malcolm looked at their faces—his grandfather's, lined now with wood grain and curled in a rictus of rage, and his uncle's, startled, confused, sad. He turned away from them both and jumped out into the open air.

TWELVE

He went south, jumping as far and fast as he could, eyes constantly turning back over his shoulder. After a few jumps he saw a faint blue figure take off from the roof of the Tower, curving down through the green glow of projected castle ramparts on top of the Inandaya Bank building.

For a moment Malcolm stopped. He wanted to go home. When something went wrong, Felix and Aleid were the ones who helped him most. He wanted their comfort. But they were the ones he was running from now. He felt completely, utterly alone.

He leapt down into an alleyway and dropped his armor, then kept moving at a steady run. He heard the boom of his aunt passing overhead but forced himself not to look up. If she spotted him, he had no chance of escaping anyway. But she kept flying, and he kept running.

He ran, not keeping track of how far or how long. He just kept moving, focusing on his next footstep, the din of the city surrounding him, washing away his thoughts. The crowds on the sidewalks began to thin. The flight paths of pods fell away behind him, and he stopped seeing drones hovering over people's shoulders. The din faded until he could hear his own footfalls, *shush, shush*, as they carried him down street after endless street.

He finally stopped. There was a burning sensation in his chest. He bent over and tried to breathe deeper into his lungs, but his muscles were too tight. He didn't recognize where he was—somewhere residential, with bungalows on either side of the street, a park with a playground and stunted trees just behind him. He couldn't see anyone around.

He sat down on the curb, still panting, and pulled out his drone. "Hover on," he wheezed. "Open messages. Respond to—" The drone cut him off with a short buzz. Malcolm looked at it and saw a red light blinking on its side. "What does that red light mean?" he asked. A screen popped open with two words on it: *No connection*.

He looked around, wondering if he had somehow gone out of range of the drone network. But that didn't make sense because the drones used the same connection as the ambient power grid. They worked everywhere, unless...

They cut me off. Of course. He wondered for a moment if they could cut his powers off too, since those were apparently powered by the same nanotech. But when he tried, his armor came up just fine.

He grabbed the drone and tapped it against his forehead. *Texting Drew wouldn't help anyway. He's never going to talk to me again. What am I going to do?*

His sylf vibrated happily against his head, and he pulled it back to look at it. The red light was still blinking, but there was also a green notice light rotating around it. *It buzzed when I was talking to my grandfather and Felix.*

"Open message," he said, letting the drone go. It retreated a couple of feet and projected a display. It was an email from Gatekeeper. Or Darla, he remembered his uncle calling her. **Here's the list, including 153. You should've stayed to talk.** Attached at the end was a file. Malcolm tapped on it tentatively, not sure if his drone would have downloaded it or if it would still be somewhere on the network. But the file popped open at his touch.

It was a spreadsheet, with names, addresses and "solutions" listed in bullet points. The file that Ibrahim's information had come from. There was Ibrahim's name, two-thirds of the way down. And Blair Thomas, right at the end, number 153 on the list. Maybe he could still save her. He scanned right, searching for something he could use. His heart fell. *Family transfer to Seattle*, it said. "How did they move her so fast?" he muttered to himself.

In the last column there were two words: *Major alteration*. He frowned. Ibrahim's file had said *moderate alteration*. And the rest of the entries listed alterations too. In some cases *minor*. In some cases *no alteration necessary*. He scrolled to the top of the spreadsheet. The column was labeled *Memory*.

My family really is messing with people's memories. How? Are they using the nanotech?

He closed the file and clutched his drone close to his chest. A moment later he pushed it away and fumbled with it until he found the off switch. *What if they're tracking me with it? Can they do that? They can probably do that.* He stuffed it as deep into his pocket as it would go. He sat still, trying to catch his breath. Even though he'd stopped running, he still felt like he was at a full sprint.

What the hell am I going to do?

He passed a little diner, and through one of the windows he saw a screen displaying the news. He stopped when he saw his own face. It was a picture from his debut—him stiff-collared and looking dazed. He couldn't hear the audio, but the caption at the bottom of the screen said, *Malcolm Gravenhurst Missing.* He read the crawl underneath. *Youngest Gravenhurst leaves home in confused and agitated state. Family concerned for his mental health. Potentially dangerous.*

And there was his uncle's face on the screen, concerned, loving, beseeching. A number to call with information about Malcolm flashed in the caption. The man who he'd thought loved him most in the world, lying about him on television. Malcolm felt the hot prickle of tears behind his eyes, and he didn't fight them.

I can't stay here. Someone will recognize me. He sniffled, wiped at his wet cheeks and walked on, head down. He wondered if he could get all the way to Seattle, try to find Blair. But no, outside Porthaven he had no powers. And he had no cash either, he suddenly realized. If he tried to access his accounts through his sylf, his family would definitely know. He'd never really thought about money—not until it wasn't there.

So if I can't go get Blair, I need to tell someone who can. His shoulders sagged. Drew had said Kazue would kill him if he showed up. He didn't know what her powers were, and he had a feeling he didn't want to find out. But he needed to tell them. And not just about Blair, he realized. All his family's secrets were sitting there in his head, pressing, screaming to get out. He needed to tell someone.

He started running for the rail yard.

He moved cautiously between the trains, waiting to be attacked. Once, his footsteps startled a squirrel, which climbed to the top of a railcar and chittered angrily at him. Malcolm nearly jumped out of his skin. But otherwise the rail yard was empty. When he reached the red boxcar, he saw that a light was on inside.

Please be Drew, he thought as he knocked lightly on the door. *Please be Drew.*

The door of the car squealed open and Malcolm took several steps back. Kazue looked out at him and then jumped down onto the ground. Without a word she started walking toward him.

"Look, I'm really, really sorry. I screwed up." She was getting closer now, and Malcolm retreated. "But I have this—"

She raised her fist, and something flashed between her fingers. He just had time to raise his armor before her punch landed, and then he was sailing backward through the air. He hit a cargo container and went straight through the metal, ending up sprawled in the dusty interior. The armor across his chest was shattered, and his ribs felt tight, like his lungs didn't have enough room to breathe. He'd never been hit so hard in his life—not in training, not even by the klek.

"Ow!" Kazue said outside the container. "Goddamn it, that hurts!" He could see her through the hole he'd made in the container, rubbing her fist and walking toward him. As he stood up she grabbed one of the nearby lengths of rail-road track, bending the metal like it was made of rubber, and snapped off a piece of the rail. As her arms flexed, light flashed across her skin. She hefted the rail. "Here. This will be better. Now come out here so I can hit you again."

Malcolm stayed put. "I know you're mad, and I totally—"

"Mad? Your goddamn family kidnapped my girl-friend!" She raised the rail and came toward him.

"I know where they took her!" he said desperately as she jumped into the container with him. He backed away, then tripped and fell. She hefted the metal rail over her head. He squeezed his eyes shut and tried to transfer all the armor he had left to his head.

The blow didn't land. He waited. Nothing.

He cracked his eyes open, but the armor around his head was so thick now that he could barely see through it. He dropped it slowly, letting it fold away until he could clearly see.

She still had the rail raised, but she was holding it more loosely now. She met his eyes. He dropped the rest of his armor. It probably wouldn't do him any good anyway.

"Where?" she said.

"Seattle. Her and her mom. And…the file I have says they did something to her memory too. Like Ibrahim's."

Kazue's hands tightened around the rail for a moment, and he saw that light again, running along the edges of her arms, from her shoulders down to her hands. Her fingers sank into the metal, warping the rail, and then she dropped it. It clanged on the metal floor. She sank down to sit against the wall. She put her hands over her face.

"Where'd you get the info? Gatekeeper again?" she asked through her hands.

"Yeah. She sent me the whole file this time. It's… there were a lot of…" Malcolm was surprised to find his eyes filling with tears, and he swiped at them. "You were right. About my family. About me. I didn't—" He stopped himself. Shook his head. "You were right. That's all."

She slowly dropped her hands and sat forward, legs crossed. "Do you have the file with you? You printed it out or something before you went AWOL?"

"You know about that?"

"It's kind of the only thing the news is talking about right now. Poor Malcolm, traumatized from fighting the klek, lost in the big, bad city. So confused, so lonely." Her tone was dry, mocking.

"Umm, yeah, I have the file. It's on my sylf."

Kazue held out her hand, and Malcolm placed the drone in her palm without turning it on. "So you have, um, superstrength?"

"It's not superstrength," she said, standing and walking out of the container. Malcolm sat there on the floor, not sure what to do, until she leaned back in. "You need to stay with me. Until I get this file onto my computer," she said.

"Oh, yeah. Sure." He stood and followed her out into the open air.

"I still might decide to kill you later," she said, examining his sylf as they walked back to the red boxcar.

Kazue texted Drew. He arrived five minutes later, out of breath. When he came into the car, Malcolm stood up. Then he realized it was weird to do that—like this was a trial, and the judge had just walked in—so he sat down. Drew simply stared at him. He looked…Malcolm couldn't quite read it. Disappointed? Angry? Like he'd smelled something bad?

"Um. Hi," Malcolm said.

"I told you not to come. I told you she'd kill you," Drew said.

"Yeah, you did. I had fair warning."

"You came anyway."

"I didn't—I don't mean to, like, force my way back in here. I can leave if you want. I just wanted to, um, there was a file and I wanted you to have it so you could track down…" Malcolm was having trouble keeping his thoughts together as Drew watched him. He felt guilty, desperate and lost.

"What exactly did you do to get your family chasing after you?" Drew asked.

"It's a long story. Well, not a long story, obviously, because it all happened this morning, but…" He trailed off as he saw the grimace on Drew's face. "Sorry, I'm nervous-talking, which totally isn't helpful right now." He took a breath. "I broke into the secret basement and learned how screwed up my family really is."

Drew sighed, and it looked like he was searching for words. Then Kazue made a coughing sound and Drew turned away. Kazue raised her hand to the display and pushed it across the room to sit in front of Malcolm's face.

"What the hell is this?"

"Um…" Malcolm refocused on the display. "It's the message from Gatekeeper?"

"'You should've stayed to talk'? Did you *meet* Gatekeeper?"

"Oh, uh, yeah. She works in the secret basement. Literally keeps the klek gate. And her name is Darla, apparently."

Kazue scoffed at him and dragged the display back to her desk. She began working through the file. "Are these all people your family disappeared?"

"Yeah, I think so."

Kazue stopped talking, searching through the information, scrolling up and down. Drew watched over her shoulder for a moment, then came and sat on the couch next to Malcolm—but with a significant gap between them, Malcolm noticed.

"Why don't you tell me the rest of that long story. What exactly did you find out?"

Malcolm hesitated, and immediately hated himself for it. What possible reason could he have for keeping his family's secrets?

He pushed that reluctant part of himself aside and opened his mouth. "They never destroyed the gate," he began.

THIRTEEN

Kazue hung up her phone and put her head down on the desk. Drew stood and went to her, putting his hand on her back. Malcolm stayed where he was. They hadn't asked him to leave yet, and he figured he would take as much of their company as he could before they kicked him out of their lives.

"She really is in Seattle," Kazue said. "And she thinks she's been there for three months. She has a favorite bakery."

Drew's hand tensed on her back. Malcolm's stomach curdled.

"Does she remember?" Drew asked.

"She remembers me. She remembers going out with me. She's hazy on you," she said to Drew, "and Malcolm is just, like, a rich guy from the news to her. Doesn't remember her powers at all." She punched the desk, and Malcolm flinched, expecting it to shatter. But it was only an ordinary blow. "How the hell are they doing this?"

Malcolm hesitated, not wanting to call their attention to him, but no one said anything. "The nanotech maybe?"

Kazue wrinkled her lip. "It doesn't sound like they have that kind of control over it."

"Maybe Gatekeeper, with her super brain? Or someone else with powers working for them? I mean, if they've sent 153 people with powers away, how many did they keep around?"

"Damn it, how much does your family suck?" Kazue said.

"I'm s—"

"If you say sorry one more time, I'm going to punch you through a wall again."

Malcolm closed his mouth and tried to sink deeper into the couch.

"What do you want to do, Kaz?" Drew asked softly.

"I don't know. I need to think. You two go away for a while."

Drew nodded and gestured for Malcolm to go outside. As he opened the door and hopped out, Kazue stayed at her desk, hunched over with her elbows on her knees. He wondered if she was crying, but she didn't shake or make any sound.

Drew closed the door behind them and started walking north. Malcolm stood there awkwardly, not sure what he should do. Before he could decide, Drew turned back.

"You coming?" he said.

"Oh, uh, yeah," Malcolm said, hurrying after Drew.

"You got some place to stay?" Drew asked.

"Umm…"

"No, 'course you don't. Probably shouldn't stay at a hotel. You'd be recognized for sure."

"Right, yeah. That and I have no money, so…"

Drew chuckled. "Those are words I never thought I'd hear from you." He bared his teeth, looking like he was mulling over something unpleasant. Without looking at Malcolm, he said, "I guess you better come with me then."

"Seriously?" Malcolm said. "You would—" He struggled against the rush of relief going through him. "No. You shouldn't do that, after I let them take Blair. I should go."

"Man, you have no idea where to go. You *literally* grew up in a tower. You don't know how anything works. Just come with me." As they walked, Drew pulled off his hoodie and handed it over to Malcolm. "Put it on, and keep the hood up."

Malcolm did. It was clearly too big for him, so he rolled the sleeves up as best he could.

"So where can I take you?" Drew asked.

Malcolm listened to the crunch of their footsteps on the ground and tried to summon an answer. "I don't really know. Anywhere my family won't find me, I guess."

Drew nodded.

They came to a sprawling building and skirted around it, jumping a series of tracks. When they came around to the front of the building, Malcolm recognized it as the central train station—which made sense, he supposed, since they were still in the rail yard. They went in, Drew handed Malcolm a ticket, and they both passed through the turnstile. Drew easily navigated a confusing series of overpasses and brought them down beside a waiting grav train, floating silently above its track. He and Malcolm stepped inside. Malcolm sat with his face down and hood pulled low, but no one on the train seemed particularly interested in him.

As the train pulled away, Malcolm realized he had never actually ridden one of the grav trains. It felt something like riding in a pod—the smooth, silent motion—except he could feel momentum more than he could in a pod. He watched the rail yard fall away behind them, the glittering ribbon of the river, the roofs of houses peeking out from behind high fences. The train was faster than a pod, and in what felt like only a few minutes they were across the city.

"Where are we going?" Malcolm whispered.

"To the edge of the city," Drew said.

"Oh. Right." Malcolm retreated further into his hood. *Is he kicking me out of Porthaven?*

"So look," Drew said, leaning in close. His ear was right next to Malcolm's, less than an inch away. "I'm still pissed off."

"Right. Sure."

"But I honestly didn't expect you to do what you did. When you said you would help Blair, I thought you would, like, ask your uncle nicely or something. I didn't think you would take it this far. This is…something. You actually did something. *Risked* something. Thanks."

"Wish it wasn't too late."

Drew nodded. "Yeah. Would have made things a lot better if you'd got there sooner. Here, this is our stop."

They got out in a residential area Malcolm didn't recognize. They had gone farther east in the city than he had ever been. They left the train station along with a handful of other passengers and kept walking east. They passed silently in front of imposing brick houses. The road they were walking along was wide and busy—regular cars, no pods. Malcolm could see glimmers of green space a few blocks away, and the houses were getting farther and farther apart.

They were heading out of Porthaven. But there were still houses beside them when he felt his powers fail. He stumbled and fell to his knees.

This was the end of the gate's range, Malcolm realized. *I'm too far from my power source. Like I'm just another piece of alien tech.*

Drew noticed Malcolm had stopped, and he turned around. "You okay?"

"My powers don't work anymore. It makes me feel, like, super heavy when that happens."

Drew frowned. "You've done this before? I thought you said you never left the city."

"After you told me about our powers not working, I went to see for myself. And you were right, of course. My armor doesn't work out here, and I feel like I'm made of lead. You don't get all heavy when your powers cut out?"

Drew shook his head. "No. I can't do anything with light anymore, but other than that I just get a little tired, I guess. That's not what it's like for you?"

Malcolm shook his head and pulled himself over to sit on the grass at the edge of the sidewalk. Drew came and sat next to him.

"So," Malcolm said. "You want me to leave the city?"

Drew looked at him, head tilted. "No. Your family seriously messed you up, you know that?"

"Sorry," Malcolm said, working to take deep breaths. "I don't get it though. Why, um, why did you bring me here if you're not telling me to leave?"

"You said you wanted to be somewhere your family can't find you. If you stay in Porthaven they're going to find you eventually—I mean, the cops and media are in their pocket, your aunt can fly at supersonic speed, and they own half the damn city. So if you want to get away from them…" He gestured down the road.

"Oh. But I don't have any money for food or anything."

"You're still a Gravenhurst. You could sell your story or something. People would pay you for that, put you up. Hell, they would probably pay you a lot just to study you, right?"

"Yeah, I guess. You think that's what I should do?"

Drew grunted. "Stop that! I don't think anything. Besides, what I think doesn't matter for this. Why do you keep wanting me to tell you what to do?"

"Because you're, like, the leader of the team."

Drew seemed to sink in on himself. "No. I'm not the leader. Our *team* doesn't have a leader."

"I think you are, actually. It's kind of cool that you don't know it. But it's obvious that everyone listens to you, looks to you to know what to do."

"I don't want that. I want everyone to have a say."

"I'm not saying they don't. You listen to everyone— you're really good at that. No one's getting bossed around. But *I* can see how Kazue and Blair rely on you, even if you don't want to see that."

Drew breathed deep. "That freaks me out. Ibrahim said something like that to me once too. That if we were going to be a team, I should be the leader. And then, when they came for him, I wasn't even there."

Malcolm felt a pang of guilt at the mention of Ibrahim and watched the same feeling play out on Drew's face.

"The fact that you don't want to be a leader, that it scares you," Malcolm said, "I think that's why you're good at it. I know I'm not part of the team or anything, especially not now. But I'd rather follow you than anyone in my family. I'm not asking you to keep me safe. That's up to me. Just tell me what you think I should do."

Drew sighed. "Even if you're right, it's not gonna work like that. You can't just stop following Gravenhurst orders and come follow mine, because I didn't ask for that. I'm not gonna tell you what to do." He turned to face Malcolm. "What do *you* want to do?"

Every thought seemed to flee Malcolm's head. He wasn't sure anyone had ever asked him that question. Not like this. Not for something that mattered.

"I...I don't know, I guess. This is so..." He pulled in a breath through tight lips. "The things I want are kind of stupid sometimes. Can I say it, even if it's stupid?"

Drew shrugged.

"All I ever wanted was to be a superhero. I thought I was going to be one, but..." He flicked a quick look at Drew, but he was just watching him, listening. "You're not going to tell me there's no such thing as superheroes?"

Drew's brow crinkled in such a perfect look of incredulity that Malcolm almost laughed. "You kidding me? As soon as I found out I had powers, I started fighting street crime. You think I just randomly decided to do that?"

"You—really?"

"Hell yes. If I didn't have to keep everything out of the news, I'd have a costume, a code name, the whole nine.

It's not easy to think of a light-themed name that hasn't been used in comics somewhere though. Best I could come up with was Diffraction, and that's kinda dumb, and it's not even really what I do." He shrugged again.

Malcolm felt like his face was hurting, and he realized he was grinning. "I actually tried for years to get my family to do patrols. And when I became a Guardian, I thought if I could show them it would work, that we could make the city safer in other ways. But…"

"That wasn't really what they were about."

"No. Not really."

They sat in silence for a moment, the hum of cars on the road keeping them company. "So," Drew finally said. "What do you want to do? Say this was a comic. We're in a comic right now. What would you do?"

Malcolm's head didn't feel so empty this time. "I don't think I could walk away. How anticlimactic would that be? Unless I was a bit character and not really a superhero. I don't want to be a bit character. I mean, if there's a problem, I should try to fix it, right? Even if the problem is my family." He looked farther down the road, toward the hints of green beyond the city. Then back toward the jagged downtown skyline, the glimmering of projected light around the improbable silhouettes of Porthaven's skyscrapers. "Especially if the problem is my family."

He raised one heavy arm. He tried to bring up his armor, and between the pale hairs on his skin something glassy glimmered for a moment as his power tried unsuccessfully to rouse itself. He let the arm fall.

"I've gotta stay, don't I? No, sorry, I turned that into a question again. I can't leave. Not until all this is... fixed? Broken? I'm not sure which applies here. But I'm staying."

Drew put his hands on his knees and stood up. "I am seriously glad to hear you say that, Malcolm. Because I don't think Kaz and I can take the Gravenhursts down by ourselves. Even if you're a bit of a screwup, we could use your help." He put out his hand to Malcolm.

"You're gonna go after my family?"

" 'Course we will. This is our city, and your family is going to destroy it. They think they have the gate under control, but they obviously don't. Come on. You can stay at my place tonight, and tomorrow we can figure out what to do."

Malcolm sat there, smiling at Drew, then trying not to smile because he was pretty sure he looked like a fool. Then wondering why he was worried, because he was fairly certain he *was* a fool, so why not look like one? Then realizing Drew had been holding out his hand for a really long time, and it was starting to get awkward.

Malcolm took Drew's hand. Drew pulled and Malcolm pushed, and he managed to get to his feet.

"Man, you weren't kidding," Drew said. "You feel like you weigh a ton."

"I know."

"What's that about? Do your powers make you lighter for some reason? Why would they do that?"

"I honestly have no idea," Malcolm said.

"Weird."

Malcolm could only nod. He still felt like he barely understood anything, even himself. But at least now he had a goal. Take back the city from his family.

Drew walked at his side, keeping his steps slow so Malcolm could keep up as they made their way back into Porthaven.

FOURTEEN

It turned out that Drew's place wasn't far away—his father was a lawyer, his mother was a doctor, and they had a sprawling house in the east end that reminded Malcolm of the homes of stockholders he'd had to visit with his family.

"I thought you said you couldn't afford a sylf," Malcolm said.

"*I* can't. My parents aren't into sharing."

Drew checked the wide garage to see if anyone was home. When he found it empty, he let Malcolm into the house. They walked through a pristine entryway and a blindingly white kitchen then down into a basement with dark carpet and old wood paneling. Drew set him up in a room he said no one ever went into, with a narrow futon and a sleeping bag that smelled vaguely of sap.

"Just to make sure this is clear, you're not here. My parents would not be cool with this, and my dad would call your family in a second."

"Yeah, I got it," Malcolm said. "I can be quiet. Despite all evidence."

Drew smirked, then closed the door and went upstairs. Malcolm camped out for the night. When Drew's parents came home later, Malcolm listened to the hum of their conversation through the ceiling. Despite being secretly stowed away in the basement of a house he had never seen before, he felt strangely comfortable.

Malcolm pulled out his sylf and switched it on, purely from force of habit. When it chirruped and blinked a red light at him, he turned it off again and waited to see if anyone had heard the noise. But the susurrus of conversation continued. He thought he heard someone laugh. He tossed his sylf between his hands, itching to turn it on and check his messages.

He tried to think ahead, to the plan they would have to concoct. One thing he could offer was knowledge of the Tower—its layout, its security. But as he tried to catalog useful details, his thoughts were drawn again and again to his family. He wasn't scared of the security guards, but his grandfather terrified him. He'd always been frightening, but now Malcolm didn't know what he could be capable of. And his aunt and uncle...he felt a betrayal so deep it ached in his bones. They had loved him, cared for him. He had loved them back. Still loved them, blindly, unreasonably. When his parents had died, Felix and Aleid had—

The sylf dropped from his hands as a new train of thought seized him. Grainy images of a giant klek flashed through his mind, along with the face of his nanny, the feel of the gritty carpet on the floor of the nursery. The anxious face of his grandmother. His mother and father, who existed for him only in photographs. The memories flowed, faster and faster, like an avalanche.

They died for this, Malcolm thought. *For* this. *Not for me. Not for Porthaven. For the lie.* Had it been that important to them? More important than their own lives? More important than Malcolm's life? *I don't have parents because...because...*

He gripped the sides of his sleeping bag, fingers twisting into the slippery material. And then, when the tears came strong enough that he couldn't keep quiet, he buried his face in the musty futon so no one would hear him.

When they went back to the boxcar the next morning, Kazue glared at Malcolm.

"Where, um, where are things at with Blair?" he hazarded.

"She's on a bus," Kazue said. "I called her again last night. Should be here in a couple days. Just thinks she's visiting me. Under the impression that we broke up because she moved. Maybe once she's here we can undo whatever your family did to her." She pointed at Malcolm. "You're lucky she remembered me."

"That's...that's really good. I mean, that they didn't make her forget you."

"Maybe," Kazue said. She dropped her threatening finger. "Why does your face look like that?"

Malcolm frowned. He had hoped the puffiness would go down as they traveled, but apparently it hadn't.

"I cried last night. Like, a lot."

Kazue snorted.

"We should talk plans," Drew said, and they all settled into their seats. "What are we doing?"

"I mean, the obvious thing to do would be to go punch down the door of the Tower," Malcolm said. "But I'm not sure that will get us anywhere."

"Sounds satisfying though," Kazue said.

"I'm talking more big picture. What's our goal?" Drew watched them both with his intense eyes.

"To shut down my family?" Malcolm suggested.

"Shut down the *gate*," Kazue said. "That's the real threat. That's where your family's power comes from."

"Plus it's getting worse," Drew said. "More klek attacks, and it sounds like even the Gravenhursts have no idea why. They don't have as much control as they think they do."

"What?" Kazue said with mock surprise. "Rich white people thinking they can control everything while the world falls apart around them? How did that happen?"

Drew didn't laugh, just nodded sadly.

"You in for that, Malcolm?" he said. "Make the gate our target?"

"Yeah," Malcolm said. "For sure. But how do we break the gate? My uncle said it was pretty much indestructible."

"Yeah, but that was over fifty years ago." Kazue nodded and spun to face her computer. "I figure if anyone knows the gate's weakness, it would be Gatekeeper. I've been looking again at all the info she dropped, seeing if it looks different now that we have more context." She shook her head. "Still can't believe I didn't put that one together. Gatekeeper. Gate. Anyway, I came up blank. There's nothing there that might help us take down the gate."

"So what do we do?" Drew asked.

"Ask Gatekeeper directly?" Malcolm said.

"Yeah. That's what I thought too," Kazue said.

"But would she help us?" Drew asked. "She works for your family."

"If she's handing out information behind their backs, she's probably not completely on their side," Malcolm said. "I mean, she sent me a full list of everyone they've exiled, even after knowing I gave Ibrahim's info to you."

"She'll help us. Trust me," Kazue said. "In her forum posts you can tell she's mad. 'Course, if we take her off the gate-keeping, it sounds like we might be neck-deep in klek for a while."

"So once we get her, the gate will be running like it was when it first fell?" Drew said. "Hundreds of klek every day?"

"We don't really know," Kazue said. "It's underground now. But keeping it running without running rampant sounds like a complicated job, and I doubt the Gravenhursts are up to it."

"That's probably true," Malcolm said. "But I think we need her if we want to stop it."

"Yeah," Kazue said.

"So how do we get her? I mean, my family isn't going to let her go, and we can't just punch our way through them." Malcolm looked at Kazue. "Well, I can't anyway."

Drew and Kazue were looking at each other oddly, and then they both turned to Malcolm at the same time.

"…What? Why are you looking at me like that?"

"You said you wanted to help, right?" Drew said. "Maybe we can't fight our way through your family. But we might be able to move them out of the way."

"They actually don't leave the Tower a lot. We could wait for the next klek attack, but who knows how long that—"

"No," Drew said. "I was thinking more along the lines of bait."

Malcolm looked from Drew to Kazue, and realization dawned. "Oh, you want me to—oh." He clenched his hands together. "I'm not sure that's such a good idea. I would have to, like, talk to them face-to-face. I was hoping more to, like, sneak our way in. Maybe if you put us all in shadow—"

"The Tower is lit 24-7. You don't think they'll notice a big blob of shadow walking through the front door?"

"You said you wanted to help," Kazue said.

"I do. But I don't want to actually fight my family if I don't have to."

"Maybe you won't. Maybe you can just talk to them long enough to keep them away from the Tower."

"Have you met my family?" Malcolm said. "I'm pretty sure if I don't give in and go home with them right away, someone is going to punch me or energy-blast me or something, and then I'll have to fight, and it's going to be a thing." He pulled his hands apart—the clenching was starting to hurt. "If I do this, there's no going back."

"So?" Drew said. "Do you want to go back?"

Malcolm looked at them. He searched his mind for an alternative. He found nothing.

He put his head down in his hands. "Damn it. My family sucks."

"Um, yeah," Kazue said. "Welcome to reality."

FIFTEEN

It took about ten minutes for the first camera drones to show up, and another five for the police. Malcolm stood watching them from his perch on top of a parking garage. "I don't want to be here, I don't want to be here," he murmured under his breath. It made him feel better.

They had picked this spot because it was easily visible from the square across the street—plenty of room for gawkers and news crews—but a long way from the Tower. The drones had kept their distance at first, but now camera drones and small, silvery sylfs buzzed around him like a cloud of flies.

He scanned the sky. He had thought he'd seen his aunt a few minutes earlier, but she hadn't approached yet.

A long, sleek police pod rounded the corner of a high-rise and flew in close. The way it flew silently through the sky suddenly struck Malcolm as eerie, menacing. "Malcolm Gravenhurst," the speaker on its roof blared. Malcolm waved. "Come down to ground level."

Still being polite, Malcolm thought. *I wonder how long that will last.* "No, thank you!" he shouted back, hands cupped around his mouth.

"We are going to send someone out," the pod speaker said. Malcolm shrugged.

The pod drifted downward, and one of its sides slid open. But then it immediately closed, and the pod moved off again without another word.

A moment later a familiar black pod flew up over the neighboring building and came down on top of the parking garage. The doors opened and three people got out—Felix, Aleid and Eric.

"I don't want to be here," Malcolm whispered.

The three of them walked forward, and the drones backed off a few yards. Felix and Eric watched him closely, like he was a bomb that might go off. Aleid stayed slightly behind the others, her eyes hooded and inscrutable.

"Malcolm," Felix said. "It's good to see you."

"Hi," Malcolm said.

"We're glad you're safe," Felix went on. "We've been worried."

"Yeah. Me too."

"Have you decided to come home?"

"Umm...I don't know," Malcolm said.

"Dude, don't be dense," Eric said. "Come back to the Tower."

Eric's voice sounded friendly, but there was something in his eyes—something akin to the flashes of enjoyment Malcolm had seen when they sparred.

"This is not the place to discuss family matters," Felix said. "Please, Malcolm. Come home, and we can talk there."

Malcolm took a long, slow breath and then shook his head. "I don't think I can. This is—we aren't what I thought we were. I'm sorry. I really actually am, and I wish none of this was happening, but..."

Aleid closed her eyes, and Eric huffed. Felix watched Malcolm silently. After a moment he looked out at the crowds below—the police cars, news vans, people crowded behind them—and then considered the swarm of drones in the sky above the square.

Felix squinted. "Why are we here, Malcolm?"

"I just wanted to talk to you, I guess."

"You could have come to the Tower if you wanted to talk."

"I wasn't sure you'd let me leave again."

Something was happening to Eric. He looked angrier now, and not just at Malcolm. He kept glaring at the back of Felix's head.

"But why here? You chose a very visible place to wait for us—apparently to tell us you aren't coming home."

Malcolm swallowed. "I don't know. I wanted, um, to see you."

Eric huffed again. "Dad. Just do it."

Felix held up his hand to Eric without looking at him. "I'm hoping that won't be necessary. Malcolm, you aren't planning anything public here, are you?"

Eric clenched his hands into fists.

"What's going on?" Malcolm said.

"I asked you a question," Felix replied. "Are we here so you can air our family grievances publicly?"

"Family grievances?" Malcolm said. "Can you really call them that when they affect every person in—"

"Choose your words carefully," Felix said, gesturing to the camera drones.

"Come on, Dad!" Eric said. "What are you waiting for?"

"It is a lot to process. I understand that," Felix said to Malcolm, ignoring Eric. "It's overwhelming. Confusing. But we are your family. We want you to come home."

For a moment Malcolm was actually tempted. Even with Eric twitching in anger beside him, Felix was such a steady, reassuring, warm presence that Malcolm wanted to run forward into his arms. But he took a shaky breath and stepped backward.

"No. Home isn't what you told me it was. It's—"

"Screw this," Eric said, and he sprinted straight at Malcolm.

Malcolm brought his armor up and prepared to jump away, but Eric skipped forward and swept his foot across Malcolm's legs at just the right place. Malcolm fell to the concrete.

"Hey!" Malcolm said as he struggled to get up. "Eric, what—"

He was interrupted by Eric's heel coming down on his face. He felt it even through the armor, the blow unnaturally hard as Eric shifted his weight and momentum perfectly to strengthen the kick. Eric had never hit Malcolm that hard before. The armor held, but for a moment Malcolm thought it wouldn't. "Eric, stop!"

"I shouldn't have to do this!" Eric shouted. "Why is *he* special?"

"What are you talking about?"

Eric wrapped his hands around Malcolm's wrist and pulled him up. For a moment Malcolm thought Eric was helping him back to his feet, but Eric kept pulling. He flipped Malcolm over his shoulder, sending him skidding across the pavement and against the railing at the edge of the garage.

"Stop it!" Malcolm said.

"Wish I could, dude," Eric said. "But neither you or my dad is going to do what needs to be done, so it's up to me."

Eric planted his feet and pivoted, landing three swift punches on Malcolm's head. His armor vibrated, and Malcolm's ears rang. A crack opened.

"Hey!" he said. "I don't want to fight you!" He scrambled to his feet.

"Dad, do it already!" Eric shouted over his shoulder.

Felix stood there, frozen, eyes wide. Eric cursed and pushed Malcolm over the railing.

Malcolm fell, headfirst, five stories to the ground. He heard a horrible crunch as the crack in his armor turned into a fissure. Brighter daylight poured into his eyes as the gray armor over his face collapsed.

He shook his head and stood, looking at the cracked pavement around him. Eric was coming down the side of the garage, jumping from level to level. He came to a perfect landing and assumed a fighting stance. Then he paused.

"Just give up, Mal. You know you can't beat me."

"You don't understand. They're not what you…the gate is still here."

"I know about that," Eric said.

"You do?"

Eric nodded. "I do now. It doesn't matter. You have to come home, and I honestly don't care if you're conscious or not."

"Why are you so angry at me?"

"You know how old I was when my dad first used his power on me?" Eric said. "Six. I wanted a toy, and I wouldn't shut up. He made me forget the toy existed until Melissa told me about it years later." As he spoke, he moved cautiously toward Malcolm.

"Power? What are you talking about?"

"When I was sixteen and wrecked a car, he made me forget how to drive. He didn't let me learn again for five years. But you?"

He used his toe to flip one of the broken chunks of pavement at Malcolm's still-unarmored head. Malcolm blocked it with his hands, but in that moment Eric leapt forward and landed a stinging strike to his right temple. Malcolm swung, but Eric was already spinning away.

"I don't understand," Malcolm said.

"I know!" Eric roared. "Why do you think I'm so pissed off? If he'll do it to me, why doesn't he do it to you? What makes you so special?"

He leveled another kick at Malcolm. Malcolm ducked and immediately saw that it had been a feint. Eric's fist came straight at his face. He turned his head and took the blow on his cheek, reeling away.

Eric paused, hands on his knees, taking deep breaths. Some of his anger seemed to drain away.

"Come on, dude. We've had this fight a million times in training," Eric said. "You know you can't hit me. Just give up and come home."

Malcolm gritted his teeth and focused. The armor around his head reformed, and a gap opened on his back. Eric shook his head and sprang at him.

Malcolm kicked out, but Eric ducked under his foot and tripped him. He landed hard on his unarmored back. He didn't stay down but stood and jumped away, opening some space between them. Eric sprinted forward.

He's right, Malcolm thought. *I've never been able to beat him.*

Eric was on him again, and when Malcolm tried a punch, Eric grabbed his arm and pulled himself past, then turned to land a blow on Malcolm's unprotected spine. Malcolm groaned as he leapt away again. He needed space and time to think. *I'm stronger than him, but how does that help if I can't touch him?*

Eric caught up to him almost before he could turn around and landed a dizzying sequence of blows to Malcolm's chest, arms, legs, keeping him off-balance and preventing him from using his strength. He hooked a heel behind Malcolm's knee and knocked him to the ground again, then hammered on his chest, pounding his vulnerable back into the pavement. Malcolm shifted his armor again, exposing his arms to close the gap. Eric leapt lightly away. He looked grim—an expression Malcolm had only seen on his cousin's face in his movies until now.

He'll keep hitting me where I'm vulnerable. I can't stop him. He watched his cousin, bracing himself for another attack, and an idea struck him. *Maybe I shouldn't try to stop him. Maybe...*

He stood and got into a proper fighting stance, then shifted the gap in his armor to his chest, guarding it well with both hands.

Eric watched this, bouncing on his toes. "You know what?" he said. "Never mind what I said before. Don't give up. I want to do this." He came at Malcolm again.

He struck hard and fast. Malcolm did his best to keep him at bay, using every scrap of training to deflect his cousin's blows. But bit by bit Eric forced his guard away, opening up his vulnerable chest. He managed to knock Malcolm back on his heels and sent him stumbling, and then he struck at the open patch over Malcolm's heart.

Malcolm shifted his armor.

He hit the ground with Eric on top of him, their eyes locked. Then Eric looked down, and so did Malcolm. There was Eric's fist, pressed painfully against Malcolm's sternum. The armor was wrapped around it up to his wrist.

Eric pulled hard, but his hand was trapped inside the armor. "That's…that's pretty clever," Eric said. "Points for that."

"Thanks," Malcolm said.

"Go ahead," Eric said. "Hit me. I can't dodge, and you've been waiting years for this."

Malcolm frowned at his cousin. "What? Why would I have been waiting years to hit you?"

"Oh," Eric said. He looked genuinely surprised. "I just thought because I always win…I thought we had, like, a rivalry thing."

"No. I thought we were just, you know, friends. Family."

"Huh," Eric said.

Malcolm hugged Eric to his chest with one arm and stood. He grabbed a nearby parking meter, bent it and wrapped it around Eric's leg. Once he was satisfied it would hold him, he dropped his armor and stepped back. Eric pulled against the meter a couple of times, then gave up.

"You could have at least pinned me in a sitting position or something. This is going to get really uncomfortable." He looked up, and Malcolm followed his gaze.

Felix was at the edge of the parking garage, looking down at them. And Aleid was there too, hovering in the air above him. Neither of them made moves toward Malcolm. He raised his armor—still with a gap on his back—and leapt to the top of the parking garage.

"He's okay," Malcolm said.

"I know," Felix replied. "I know you wouldn't hurt him. Aleid?"

Malcolm braced himself, but his aunt shook her head.

Felix sighed. "Malcolm, please come home with us. I'm begging you. I don't want to do this."

"Do what?" Malcolm said. "I don't know what you're talking about, I don't know what Eric was talking about. Can someone just say something that makes sense? All of this, everything since my birthday, makes no..." Malcolm trailed off. His uncle was breathing raggedly, and there were tears running down his cheeks. "Uncle Felix?"

"I have no choice," Felix said, more to himself than to Malcolm. He pulled his sylf out of his pocket, did something on it that Malcolm couldn't follow and put it away again. But as soon as he was done, all the camera drones that had been buzzing around them suddenly turned away, flying down toward the crowd of reporters. Aleid watched them go, her expression mournful.

"Did you do that?" Malcolm said. "What's going on?"

Felix just shook his head and fixed Malcolm with a piercing stare. "Let the words I speak stir your memory," he said softly, sadly. Malcolm suddenly felt like he was falling forward, directly into his uncle. The world around them blurred, but his uncle's face became crystal clear as he opened his mouth and spoke again. "Blair. The girl with powers. Remember her."

Lights burst across Malcolm's vision, bright flares that blinded him and sent him stumbling to his knees. The flares turned into sharper images—images of things Malcolm had seen, but moving too fast for him to follow. A flash of Blair's face. The edge of the city. An infestation of klek coursing through a school hallway.

There was an itch at the back of Malcolm's head. As he reached up to scratch it, he realized his armor was gone. When had he dropped his armor? The itch swept forward, encompassing his entire head, and it began to prickle painfully. He felt his mouth open in a scream, but he couldn't hear his own voice. And all the while, the images sped past, even when he closed his eyes. A shy face, offering him a smile. Fingers intertwined, black skin against light skin. The broken couch in the boxcar, plans spinning out as he talked through the Gatekeeper problem with—

Suddenly it stopped. Malcolm was lying on the roof. *When did I lie down?* He tried to stand up, but it was like the connection between his brain and body was twisted. He tried to move his arm and his stomach clenched. He tried to roll over and his neck arched. He stopped moving, panic coursing through him.

"Did you do it?" Aleid asked from somewhere much closer. "Did you erase that girl and whatever she told him? Will he come with us now?"

"No," Felix replied. "Erasing takes time, and I don't think we have time. I saw something."

"Saw? What do you mean you 'saw something'? You told me that's not how this works."

Malcolm tried once more to move. This time all he got were twitches from his muscles.

"It's not, generally," Felix said. "Trails of memory aren't something I see. They're more like a scent I can follow. I can't read minds. But it can be different with family."

"Different how?"

"Aleid, there's something you need to—"

"No. No, Felix, you tell me what this means. Because you've explained how your powers work, and I thought I understood, and you've used them on family before, on your own children, and now you've used them on *Malcolm*, and you're telling me they don't work the way you said. Tell me what you just did to him!"

Whatever was happening to Malcolm's body, his ears still worked. He could hear Felix's soft steps, Aleid's heavy tread as she moved closer to Malcolm. He lay still, trying to wrap his head around what he was hearing.

"Sometimes I get partial impressions. See hints of the memories when I use my power on family."

"And what else?"

"Aleid, this—"

"You're not telling me everything, Felix. I know you. What. Else?"

"The erasure. It isn't as…clean. Normally minds fill in the gaps by themselves, based on context and a few suggestions from us. With family, I don't know if it's that the context doesn't shift as much because we don't move them away, but the blanks remain blank."

"Did this happen with Eric? Melissa?"

"…Yes."

"God. No wonder they hate you. No wonder your wife left and tried to—"

"Leave Marta out of this, Aleid. That isn't what's important now."

"Not important? Felix, you just ripped a hole in Malcolm's mind, and you—"

"No, I didn't! I didn't erase anything, because Blair wasn't the only one I saw in there. There were others, and they were saying something about the Tower. Aleid, I think he lured us away. I think something is happening at home, and I need you to go. Now."

There was silence. *Oh crap. He knows about Drew and Kazue.* Malcolm opened his eyes and saw a blur of blue sky and smudged white clouds. He tried again to move, and this time his body partially responded. He rolled over sluggishly, face scraping against the concrete before he could get his hands under him. He could see Felix and Aleid, tall, angular blurs against the sky.

"Wait," Malcolm said. "Don't." The words came out garbled and indecipherable. The blur that was Aleid came closer, crouching over him.

"Fine," she said. "I'll go. But I'm not leaving him here with you."

Malcolm felt a firm arm wrap around his ribs, and then he lost his breath as his aunt took off carrying him. They soared through the air, Malcolm limp in her arms. If his muscles had been working, he was pretty sure he would have thrown up.

"Don't. Don't hurt them," Malcolm said. He wasn't sure Aleid heard, but a moment later she cursed under her breath and swerved to the right. They landed, and she set him down. He felt grass under him. Somewhere not far away there was water flowing and a dog barking.

"What have you done, Malcolm? Everything was simple. Or no, not simple. Never that. But it was settled. And now… what did you do?"

"Don't want to hurt anyone," he said.

"That's not how things work out."

As his vision cleared, he could see her gritting her teeth.

"I have to go stop whatever foolishness this is." She moved as if to pick him up, then stopped. She cursed again, louder this time, and suddenly she was taking off into the air without him. He heard the boom as she reached super-sonic speed.

Clumsily, Malcolm managed to roll onto his hands and knees. He was in the parkland that ran along the Lockheed River. Just in front of him was a copse of trees with a path cutting through. Around and behind him was green grass, dotted with picnic tables. He wasn't sure why she had left him here, but he knew he didn't want to be here if she came back.

He considered giving chase. If she was going after Drew and Kazue, he wanted to be there. But he felt so weak, and his armor wouldn't even respond. He had no chance of reaching the Tower in time. "Please be okay," he whispered into the air. Then he stood and hobbled toward the rail yard, head still spinning.

Drew and Kazue were already at the boxcar when he arrived. Drew's shirt was sweat-drenched and scuffed like he'd taken a fall, but he looked otherwise unhurt. Kazue sat at the computer, looking like nothing had happened except that her fingers speeding over the keyboard had bloody knuckles. Malcolm pulled himself up into the car. Everything hurt, but the relief of seeing them safe gave him energy.

Drew turned toward him and shook his head. "We couldn't get Gatekeeper out. Your aunt came back."

"I know," Malcolm said. "She left. My uncle..." And then the world seemed to tilt around him, and his legs weren't listening. He tipped sideways, and his head banged against the metal wall.

Drew was there in a second, pulling him over to the couch. "Are you okay? Are you hurt?"

"It was my uncle," Malcolm said. "He did something to my head. He's...he's the one who changes people's memories." Malcolm heaved himself along the couch until his head rested on the arm. A spring was poking into his neck, but he felt too tired and dizzy to move again. "He figured out you guys were going after Gatekeeper. That's why my aunt showed up."

"So he read your mind?" Drew asked.

"I guess."

"Does he know where we are?"

"I don't know," Malcolm said. "I didn't even know he had powers until today. I don't know how it works. But he said it can be different when he does it to family."

Drew looked around nervously.

Kazue shrugged. "If he knows everything Malcolm knows—not to mention everything Blair knows—we can't really escape them for long. They'll know this place. They'll know where your family is, Drew. We'll just have to wait and see." Kazue returned to typing. "I actually wondered if it might be Felix. Seemed weird, one guy without powers in the whole family."

Malcolm forced himself to sit up. "Can you tell me what happened to you guys?"

"We got in," Drew said. "I melted a tunnel through a back wall, and Kazue dug us into the basement. No security, no one hurt. But we barely started explaining the situation to Gatekeeper when your aunt got there and chased us out."

"Didn't even get her autograph," Kazue said.

"Had to do some damage on the way out," Drew said. "Kaz punched the front doors down and then ran us both out of there at high speed. Got a little more public than I would have liked."

"You punched the…holy crap, Kazue, those doors are sturdy. *I* can't even get through those things. What kind of superstrength do you have if you can—"

"Not superstrength," Kazue said.

Drew shook his head and sighed. "She says she has, like, batteries that store up 'potential kinetic energy.' She can be weird about it."

"I'm not weird about it. I'm precise," Kazue said.

"So what do we do? Wait to see if my family is going to find us?" Malcolm asked.

Drew wiped his sweat-slicked hands on his pants and shook his head. "Not just wait. Come up with another plan."

SIXTEEN

No one came.

Malcolm couldn't sleep much that first night, between the nervousness and the pounding headache that showed up once his head stopped spinning, so he sat awake, waiting for the sound of fists pounding on the boxcar. But no one came that night. Or the next day. Whatever Felix had done to Malcolm, he at least didn't seem to know where Drew and Kazue were.

Drew had gone to school and home. Back to regular life. Which left Malcolm and Kazue at the boxcar to watch the Gravenhursts spin the story in real time.

People had witnessed Kazue's high-speed run away from the Tower. No one had gotten an image of her face, but plenty of drones had captured video of her hightailing it between cars—someone who was clearly not a Gravenhurst, using powers.

Except that version of the story only lasted about an hour. Malcolm's family soon claimed credit, saying the woman was using a new mobility aid they had invented. And they backed it up with real tech—or at least footage that made it look real.

Slim leg braces that used hover engines to let people without use of their legs walk again. At superhuman speeds. They'd even found someone who looked vaguely like Kazue from behind, and paraded her out as they announced the new product line. It would be available to the public in two weeks. And the media switched tack immediately. Instead of endless questions, the Gravenhursts had yet another exciting product launch on their hands.

Malcolm was still the big story though. Too many people had witnessed his fight with Eric for it to be hushed up. Felix was still pleading for news that might bring Malcolm home, but there was a new level of urgency in his warnings now, a new sense that Malcolm was something dangerous.

More than one network was bandying around the word *supervillian*.

And in the midst of all this, Malcolm and Kazue were trying to think of a way to get to Gatekeeper. Without the element of surprise on their side. By midafternoon the best plan Malcolm had come up with was to curl into a ball and cry.

"Hey," Kazue said from her perch at the computer. "I got—oh, hold on."

Malcolm looked over at her screen and then jumped to his feet. "Is that a live feed?" he asked. On one half of her display there was a video of large klek crashing through the corner of a building. "Is there another klek attack?"

"Yeah. That's what I was going to say. But something else popped up too. Something new from Gatekeeper."

Malcolm was bouncing on the balls of his feet. His fingers itched. Kazue noticed and rolled her eyes. "The klek aren't your business right now. Focus."

"I know. But—"

"Your family handled them without you for a long time, right? The news we need to pay attention to is here." She pointed to the other side of the screen, where there was no video of huge robots, no rubble flying through the air.

"What, um, what is it?" Malcolm said, trying to keep his eyes where she directed them.

"Gatekeeper just dropped a message on one of the forums. This make any sense to you?"

Malcolm moved closer. It said, **Hey, friends of Ibrahim. Ping.**

"Is that the whole thing?"

"Yeah. No attachments."

It was a post at the end of a long thread discussing one of Gatekeeper's other revelations, about the emissions the klek gave off.

"What does that mean?"

"I'd say nothing, except this is Gatekeeper. It's got to mean something."

"Maybe her account was hacked?" Malcolm suggested. This was answered with such a glare from Kazue that Malcolm backed up several steps.

"Friends of Ibrahim. That's gotta mean us," Kazue said.

"Right, that's who I said I gave the info to. So what does 'ping' mean? Is she just, like, saying hi in a weird way?"

"You don't even know what ping is, do you?"

"Um…no." His eyes flicked over to the video feed. One of the klek was climbing onto the top of a long building. *Is that the Calvard Center mall?*

Kazue snapped her fingers in front of his face to regain his attention. "Ping's a network test. Signal bounce-back between computers. Tells you the status of the other computer, or the connection speed, or..." She trailed off, staring at her display in a way that made Malcolm think she wasn't really seeing it. "Oh. Oh hell."

She started typing frantically, and her computer spat out new projected displays with new files open. "You said your family controlled when and how often the klek came out. I thought you said they controlled that."

"That's what they said. That they could limit it. Only not really, I guess, because they don't know why they're coming so fast now." He squinted at the new display on Kazue's right. "What's that graph?"

"Klek attack frequency."

"Yeah, I looked at that the other day. It's been getting faster for a long time, with—"

"Two blips. One after the giant klek."

"That's when they stopped feeding the gate for a while. After my parents and grandma died."

"Second blip is this month, when the frequency jumped way up."

"But what does that have to do with—"

"Ping. Bounce-back."

Malcolm struggled to make the connection. When he did, it felt like a pit had yawned open under his feet. "You think the klek attacks are like bounce-back? Like, a signal?"

"The gate gets a signal, spits out a few klek to send a return signal. Makes sense with the data."

"A signal to what?"

"Your family was right. The klek attacks aren't an invasion," Kazue said, and for once she turned away from her computer and looked straight at him. "I'm guessing they're just the beacon for the real thing."

Malcolm shook his head. "No. No way. Not after this long. It's been decades. Wouldn't we know that by now? Wouldn't it already have—"

"Space is big, Malcolm. Decades is small change."

"Oh man. Oh man oh man oh man." He blinked fast. "Okay, so if that's true, then the more frequent attacks mean the bounce-back is happening faster now. And today's attack is…" He counted in his head. "Four days since the last. Before that it was six days. And four before that."

"Zeroing in. If I'm right."

"Might you be wrong?"

Kazue grimaced and didn't answer. "I'm gonna text Drew."

"We still need Gatekeeper."

"No kidding."

Malcolm stared at the screen, his eyes inexorably drawn back to the pandemonium on the news feed. The klek were still at it. One of them seemed to be burrowing straight into a building—which Malcolm could now see for certain was Calvard Center, one of the busiest malls in the city. People were running and screaming on the street. Malcolm stared hard at the screen.

"Hey, how long since the klek attack started?"

Kazue looked up from her phone. "Umm…eight minutes."

"Why isn't that building evacuated? Where is my family?"

Kazue looked more closely at the screen. "They're not there?" They watched mutely for a moment. But there were no signs of the Gravenhursts on the scene. As they watched, a stray klek leg caught the camera drone, and the news switched to a different one that was farther away. From this new angle, they could see three more large klek.

"Where the hell are they?" Malcolm muttered.

"Crap," Kazue said, turning her eyes to Malcolm. Another minute ticked by, Malcolm watching the screen, Kazue watching him.

"Um," Malcolm said, "I know you don't know my family. But you don't think they would, like…not fight the klek or something. You know. To make me come where they could find me?"

"Because they know you couldn't just leave the klek to rip the city apart?"

"Yeah. But they couldn't either! I mean, we…they…"

"I'm pretty sure they could do that," Kazue said. "They're doing that."

"Crap. Crap crap crap."

"So what are you waiting for?"

"But I shouldn't go, right? It's a trap."

"Yeah. A really good one, baited with innocent people who didn't agree to this. Your eye is twitching."

Malcolm moaned. "Damn it. I have to go."

"I know you do," Kazue said. "That's one of the few things I think is cool about you. All the crap about being *guardians* that your family has been selling us for decades, you actually believe it. But you better do everything you damn well can to escape after you're done. If they get you and brain-scan you again, they're gonna know about this place. And I really don't want to move."

"Okay," Malcolm said. "We can talk more about ping and stuff when I get back."

"Good," she said.

As he approached, Malcolm listened for the sonic boom of his aunt's flight, but all he could hear was crashing and screaming. He leapt on top of the building across the street from the mall and paused to survey the scene.

Half of the mall had collapsed, and two klek were storming through it, clicking in strange patterns to themselves. The streets were deserted now. The screams were coming from inside the mall. He picked out two other klek climbing neighboring buildings. One huge klek was tearing at the remaining half of the mall.

"Let's try to make this quick," Malcolm said to himself. He gauged the distance, gathered himself and jumped into the air.

He hit the top of his arc and started down toward the klek. It shifted at the last moment, digging itself deeper into the mall, and Malcolm landed on one of its legs instead of the main body. He managed to bring his feet down on the highest joint, though, and the leg snapped off. It flailed on the ground for a moment before falling still.

The klek reared back out of the building, clicking furiously. It slammed one of its remaining legs down on Malcolm, but Malcolm dug his feet into the ground and brought his hands up to meet it. The barb crumpled against his palms. When the klek tried to pull away again, Malcolm held on and let it pull him into the air. He began climbing the leg, punching handholds into its metal shell. The klek shook its leg, but Malcolm kept his grip and climbed higher. It tried hitting him with another of its legs but did more damage to itself than to him. Within moments he had reached the robot's main body, and with a grunt he flung himself against it, bringing both fists down. Its shell crumpled with his first blow and ruptured completely with his second, baring what looked to him like a storm of moving parts and fizzing wires, the pieces so convoluted and so fast that his eyes couldn't follow them. He struck at them indiscriminately, digging his way into the center of the machine blow by blow, until he felt the klek cant sideways. When it crashed to the ground, he was thrown out of the machinery. The giant klek beside him lay still, its broken body sparking.

A rush went through him at the sight. He felt powerful. No, he decided. It wasn't that. He had felt powerful before. This was something new. He felt capable. Competent. *Bring on the next*, he thought.

He turned just in time to catch two razor-sharp barbs in the chest instead of the back. He crashed down onto the ground and felt his armor crack across his ribs.

The other klek—the one that had been on the mall roof—had come down on top of him. Two of its legs pinned him, two others were braced on either side of him, and the fifth was still dug into the roof of the mall. It looked like a deformed metal hand gripping the ruined building.

It pressed down on him, slowly widening the crack it had formed in his armor. Malcolm pushed up, but from this position it was hard to get the leverage he needed to move the legs off him.

Then the legs moved on their own. Malcolm watched, bewildered, as the klek swung into the sky, pivoting on one of the legs that had been on the ground. At the end of that leg stood Kazue, glowing around the edges.

She had her arms wrapped around the klek's leg, and she slammed the entire thing down onto the rubble. It cracked against the ground. Its joints immediately doubled back on themselves and tried to lift the klek again, but from somewhere behind it a blinding-white torrent of energy lanced into the robot's body. When Malcolm could blink the stars out of his eyes, he saw that the klek had been disintegrated, the rubble all around it charred.

"What the…"

Kazue turned and nodded to him. At the same time, Drew clambered up the side of a large slab of concrete. The shadows on his body were wavering strangely.

Malcolm scrambled to his feet "You're here!" he said. "Drew, was that you with the—" Malcolm held out his hands like he was firing one of Melissa's energy blasts. Drew nodded. "Holy crap! I didn't know you could do that!"

"Never have," Drew said, flexing his fingers and grinning. "Usually I'm fighting people I don't actually want to hurt. That felt pretty cool."

"But, um…" Malcolm looked up and saw at least a dozen camera drones hovering over the area.

"Drew's idea," Kazue said.

"If the Gravenhursts aren't going to handle it, someone else has to," Drew said. "Besides, maybe it's time to change the game."

A scream behind Malcolm caught his attention, and he turned back to the wreckage of the mall. The collapse had cut the building in half, and he could see into several floors, like a cross section. There was movement on more than one floor, and as Malcolm watched, one of the supporting pillars creaked and bent. A portion of the roof crumbled and slid down.

"We've gotta get those people out before the other half collapses," Malcolm said.

"You're probably the best for that, with your armor," Drew said. "If your armor is still working after that hit."

Malcolm checked himself. "Yeah, I think it's okay. Ish."

"Good," Drew said. "You go save those people while Kaz and I hunt down the other klek." He and Kazue immediately started running toward the street. Malcolm wanted to stay and watch them, but there wasn't time.

He leapt to the third floor of the mall, where he heard the most noise. A group of people clustered near the back wall, pulling desperately at the rubble clogging the stairwell. Malcolm counted around a dozen of them.

"Hey, come this way," he said. "I'll get you out."

A middle-aged man in shorts turned to him with panic in his eyes. "But those things—"

"The ones right outside are gone."

"Don't listen to him," a boy who looked like he was about ten said from the middle of the crowd. "He went crazy, remember?"

Malcolm grunted. "Look, first, that's ableist—don't call people crazy. Second, you're in a collapsing building and I'm offering to get you out. Do you really want to argue?"

The middle-aged man and a woman came quickly. Malcolm ran with them to the broken side of the building, hoisted them both onto his shoulders and jumped down to the ground. He set them on the rubble and then leapt back up. There was a crowd waiting for him, all but the boy, and Malcolm carried them down two at a time. Others were gathering on the lower floors now, clamoring for his help as the building groaned and shifted. Malcolm moved them all out, watching the cracked pillar nervously as he worked.

When he was done, Malcolm stepped back and scanned the floors for more movement. He didn't see anyone. *Just that stubborn kid left*, he thought.

Suddenly the bent pillar snapped, and the entire right side of the building tilted, concrete cracking and raining down around Malcolm. He leapt for the third floor.

The space was choked with dust and rubble, and he could barely see, but he picked his way in deeper, to where he thought the stairwell would be. "Hey!" he called out. "Hey, kid, are you still in here?"

"Help!" came the frantic response.

Malcolm hurried forward as the ceiling cracked and groaned above him. Finally he found the boy, pressed against the wall next to where the stairwell had been. The opening was now fully covered in rubble, and so was one of the boy's legs.

"I'm sorry, I'm sorry, please please please…" The boy was speaking so fast Malcolm could barely understand him, and there were tears streaming down his face.

"Hey, hey, it's fine. We're going to be okay," Malcolm said. He stepped forward and pulled at the rubble on the boy's leg, but it was pinned in place by two stories' worth of collapsed building. Malcolm set his feet and pulled as hard as he could, but it only moved a fraction of an inch. He looked at the rubble and back to the boy. "Okay, hold still, all right?" The boy kept muttering, but he nodded his head. Malcolm tried to gauge the length of the boy's leg. He brought his foot down on the concrete as hard as he could, past where he thought the boy's foot would be.

The slab cracked, and the boy cried out. As the slab crumbled, the rubble on top of it began to shift. Malcolm turned and wrapped his arm around the boy, pulling him up and away, trying to get to the open air. But the entire ceiling was cracking above them now, the open space in front of them closing, and Malcolm knew they wouldn't get out.

He put the sobbing boy down and got onto his hands and knees above him. "Tuck your legs in and hold still!" he shouted as the building collapsed around them.

The weight hit Malcolm's back, trying to crush him, pushing him down on the boy. His arms trembled and his armor groaned, but it held, he held, concrete falling all around him, piling on top of him until he screamed from the strain, his cries mingling with the boy's.

And then suddenly it was over. The roar of the falling building gave way to silence. Malcolm stopped screaming. He couldn't move. His arms and legs burned with the effort of holding this small space in the wreckage. He could feel a web of fine cracks in the armor across his back.

Everything was quiet. He pried his eyes open to look down at the boy, then tried to open them again when it didn't work. It took him several blinks to realize his eyes were fine—he couldn't see because it was pitch-black.

"You okay?" Malcolm asked.

"We're buried," the boy said, strangely calm.

"Yeah."

"Can you get us out?"

"I don't think I should move," Malcolm said. "It might make more fall on us. But I have friends here, and one of them's stronger than me, so I think we should just stay here and see if they can get us out."

"Okay."

Malcolm drew a ragged breath and exhaled through pursed lips. He could hear the boy breathing—quick, open-mouthed breaths.

"What's your name?" Malcolm asked.

"Umm…Mal."

"Oh, hey. Short for Malcolm?"

"Yeah. My, um, parents named me after you."

"Oh. That's—really? Why would they do that? You're what, ten?"

"Eleven."

"So when you were born, I would have been four or something. They didn't know what my powers were yet, or what kind of person I was. All they would have seen were photographs, right?"

"Yeah, but it happens with all the Gravenhursts. There are, like, sixteen Malcolms in my grade at school. You didn't know that?"

Malcolm started to squirm, but the concrete on his back groaned, so he stopped. "That kind of sucks."

"Oh?"

"I mean, for you it sucks. 'Cause then, like, every time I screw up you have to be, like, 'Oh, there's that guy I'm named after being a dick.' It's not even about you, but your parents made it—"

"Should we, like, stop talking? So that we don't run out of air?"

"Oh," Malcolm said. "I don't know. Is that a thing I should be worried about? I've never been trapped under rubble before." He shut his mouth.

They waited in the dark and the silence. After what might have been several minutes, the boy muttered, "This rescue sucks."

Malcolm tried to think of something clever to say, but it took him too long and then the moment was gone, and anything he said would have just made the silence even more awkward.

There was a thump above them, and Malcolm felt the rubble on his back vibrate.

"Oh, thank god," he said. "I think they're coming to get us."

There was another thump, louder this time, and another. With each one the weight on Malcolm eased. Finally, with a boom that hurt Malcolm's eardrums, the final piece of rubble lifted off his back.

Malcolm stood and pulled the younger Malcolm to his feet. "Thank you, Kazue. I don't think I could have—" He turned around just as his aunt Aleid landed hard on the rubble beside him. "Oh," he said. "Hi, Aunt Aleid."

She grabbed Malcolm by the shoulders and burst up into the air.

"Whoa!" Malcolm shouted. His aunt twisted as they flew, making Malcolm's stomach lurch. He couldn't tell which way was down anymore. "Aleid! Aleid!"

Suddenly the ground was coming at him, and he hit it at full speed. The web of cracks in his armor split and crumbled, baring his torso, and then they were flying up into the air again.

He scrabbled at the hands under his arms while trying to get his armor to spread over his vulnerable areas. His aunt didn't have his enhanced strength, but she was stronger than any normal person he knew, and with his armor thinned it was hard to dig his fingers under hers. "Stop!" he said. "Let me go!" With one final push he got her fingers loose, and then he was falling through the air. But a moment later his aunt was back, grabbing him under his armpits and bearing him down toward the ground.

Her jaw was set, every muscle in her neck clenched. Her eyes were focused not on him but on a point past him on the ground.

"Surrender, Malcolm. Before I have to hurt you."

"Just stop, Aunt Aleid!"

He struck at her, but the blows didn't even make her flinch. They both knew he couldn't hurt her. She drove him into the ground at an angle, and then they were scraping along the pavement, weaving between cars. The road wore at his armor like sandpaper, scraping it steadily away. He transferred every bit of armor he had left to his back, leaving his front completely open.

"Stop!" he shouted into his aunt's face. "Stop, please! You don't want to do this!"

"You're right, I don't," she said. "So surrender!" Her eyes finally met his. "Please, Malcolm!"

"I can't! The klek, they're—something worse is coming! The gate isn't under our control!" The last of his armor wore away, and suddenly his back was burning.

His aunt lifted him off the street and into the air. Without the armor on his face, he could feel the force of the wind against his skin, so strong it chafed his cheeks. "What is that supposed to mean? What could you know about that?" she asked.

"The people I've been with, they think…" It was hard to catch his breath in the rushing air. "…the attacks are coming faster because the signal's bouncing back faster…"

They stopped suddenly. He looked down. They were far above the city, almost at cloud level. And he had no armor left. He gripped his aunt's wrists so hard his knuckles went white.

"These people. They think it's like radar?"

"They called it ping," Malcolm said. "Gatekeeper called it that. We have to…"

His aunt watched him. "Have to what?"

"I don't know. But we have to stop. Our family is making it worse."

Her jaw clenched even harder.

"I mean, you left those klek alone to lure me out, right?" He knew from the way she cringed that he was right. "How could you do that? How could a Guardian do that? How is any of this under control?"

And then they were flying again, spiraling toward the high towers of downtown.

"Where are we going?"

"Home," she said. "We can figure this all out at home."

Malcolm didn't struggle to get free. He took stock of himself. Judging by the wind on his skin, his jacket had been scraped through in places, and his entire back stung. But on his left calf he felt something hard and smooth—a small patch of armor that had survived his aunt's attack. He tried shifting it upward onto his hand, and it responded.

He looked down. They were lower now, below the rooftops and slowing down. His aunt's face was set in a grim, inscrutable expression, the one he had seen in her countless battles against the klek. She brought them down until they were just a few feet above the road, yellow lines flashing past.

Malcolm closed his eyes and tensed. He knew this would hurt.

He shifted the armor to his ribs, under her right hand, and then dropped it again instantly. Her grip was suddenly gone and she reached for him, but he fell, banging against the pavement. He rolled to a stop.

"Ow," he said. He couldn't feel his right arm. As he stumbled to his feet, he found one of his legs didn't want to hold him. He limped over to the sidewalk before looking for his aunt.

She had managed to stop herself. She was hanging in the air a few blocks away, looking back at him. Her eyes met his and he stayed frozen, waiting for her to give chase. There was no way he could outrun her. But she just hung there, staring at him, before slowly turning away and flying toward the Tower, leaving him bruised and bleeding on the sidewalk.

He watched her until she was out of sight, uncertain what had just happened. *That's the second time she's let me get away. Why?* Finally, when he could no longer see the vibrant blue of her flight suit, he stumbled southward, the stares of the crowds following him. *Maybe she doesn't like any of this either. The way she argued with Felix on the parking garage... and she didn't look happy about letting the klek attack go so long.*

He looked around, searching for Drew and Kazue or the klek, but Aleid had flown him far from the battle, and he couldn't hear any crashes or screams to guide him back.

Not that I could help in the shape I'm in. I hope Drew and Kazue are okay. He limped slowly south, ducking down the first secluded alley he could find.

SEVENTEEN

Malcolm was the first one to reach the boxcar for once, and he found the sliding door padlocked. His first instinct was panic—perhaps the klek had hurt his friends, or his family had taken them captive, or worse. He wanted to go out and search for them, but he could barely move. His back hurt so much it made him dizzy. One of his knees had swollen to twice its usual size. And the sensation had started to return to his right arm, but now it prickled maddeningly. He sat down in the shadow of the boxcar and tried to massage the blood back down into his fingers.

When Drew and Kazue came up beside him, he could have wept.

"You're okay," he said, and Drew nodded.

"Kaz ran out of juice, so we had to bus it," Drew said. He took a duffel bag off his shoulder and dropped it on the ground. "You don't look good."

"I had a fight with my aunt and then jumped out of her hands when she was flying," Malcolm said. "Oh, and the mall fell on me."

"Oh," Drew said. Kazue unlocked the door beside them, and it clattered open. "I think we have some bandages inside. And—Kaz, any ice?"

"Nope."

"Okay. I'll go see Mrs. Jindal later."

"Thanks," Malcolm said. He managed to pry himself off the ground and get inside.

"No bleeding on the couch," Kazue said. She sat slumped just inside the door. It looked like she had tried to make it over to the computer but collapsed partway there.

"Are you okay?" he asked.

She nodded. "Gets like this when I drain my batteries. Hard to move. Think you can shut up for an hour so I can sleep?"

"Yeah. Sure."

She nodded, then curled up where she was on the floor and didn't move again. He opened his mouth to comment on the lack of a bed in Kazue's home, but Drew put his finger to his lips. Malcolm nodded.

Drew knelt on the couch and reached behind it. He retrieved a roll of bandages and a battered plastic box, and gestured for Malcolm to come closer. Malcolm sat gingerly on the edge of the couch, trying to keep his blood off it—though as he looked down, he realized there were several stains on it already that looked like they might be blood. Drew slapped a bandage on Malcolm's forehead in a place he hadn't even realized he was bleeding and then twirled his finger in the air. Malcolm frowned at him.

Turn around, Drew mouthed.

Malcolm stood and turned, and heard an intake of breath from Drew. Malcolm took off the tattered hoodie and, with some hesitation, his T-shirt as well.

"There's some gravel in here. I'm gonna try to take it out," Drew whispered at his shoulder. Malcolm nodded and gritted his teeth as he felt Drew's fingers on his tender back, brushing and plucking at the scraped skin. It stung, but not as badly as he expected. He realized he'd never had someone he knew do this kind of thing for him. He'd been injured plenty of times during training—once even been burned by Melissa's energy blasts, when she'd started a sparring match before he was ready. He still had a scar across his thigh from that. But it had always been the nurse on staff who'd tended to him. Having someone he knew, someone he trusted, do this felt different. More awkward, but less painful.

Drew wiped something wet across Malcolm's back, and then he started applying the bandages. Malcolm raised his arms so Drew could wrap them all the way around his body. He felt very aware of Drew's arms encircling him with each pass of the bandage. When Drew fastened the end, Malcolm turned around.

"Thanks," he whispered.

"Your aunt did that to you?" Drew asked softly.

"She wasn't trying to kill me. I don't think."

Drew blew out his cheeks. "Well, it's ugly but not too deep. Should be fine. Anything on your leg that needs binding?"

Malcolm shook his head. "Just banged up," he whispered, his eyes flicking to Kazue to make sure he hadn't woken her.

"Okay. I'll go get some ice for that."

"Thank you," Malcolm said.

Drew went out of the boxcar and closed the door as softly as he could. Kazue didn't stir.

Malcolm looked around. He grabbed his T-shirt and pulled it on, despite the gaping hole in it. And then he lay down on his stomach, the torn and bloody hoodie rolled up under his head. The floor smelled awful—like rust and old urine—but his back felt better in this position, so he didn't move. He lay with his eyes open, watching the door.

He woke with a start, feeling something was wrong with his leg. The hoodie under his head was damp where he had drooled, and for some reason his leg felt wet too. He rubbed at his face and tried to sit up, but his back flared with pain. It felt like the skin there had shrunk, and now it was several sizes too small. Slowly and carefully he rolled onto his side.

There was a half-melted bag of ice propped against his knee, which explained the wetness. His knee was numb, but the swelling had gone down. As he shifted position the bag fell, water sloshing out and dribbling through the door. Malcolm picked up the bag and propped it against the wall, then looked around.

There was no light coming in through the gaps around the door. Kazue was in exactly the same place she had been, and Drew lay on the couch above him, sleeping. His long legs hung over the far end of the couch, pointing toward the computer desk.

Malcolm eased himself into a seated position, grabbed the hoodie and used it to mop at his wet pant leg. As his knee thawed, he could feel some pain, but much less than before. The knee was stiff, though, and he didn't relish the thought of using it. He reached behind him and felt the bandages. They were crusted with dried blood.

He went to lie down and realized his pillow was now sopping wet. He lay his head on the floor and absently reached into his pocket for his sylf. Then he remembered it didn't work anymore. Without its network connection, and with all the important files transferred off it, it was just a silver ball. It would have been nice to check the news, see what people were saying about Drew and Kazue. See how his family had tried to spin this new story against them.

After trying to get back to sleep for a while, he pulled himself up to sitting, eased the door open and slipped outside. His knee was stiff and didn't want to bend much, so he hobbled just a few feet away and sat himself down. He breathed in the greasy rail yard air. Above him, the few stars that could penetrate the city lights glimmered. He gazed up at them. They'd looked a lot clearer from the top of Gravenhurst Tower. He missed his bed. And clean clothes. He was pretty sure the boxcar stink had seeped into his skin as he slept.

Now that he was looking, he could see that the eastern sky was lighter than the west. It must be near morning.

He started stretching out his arms. His right arm hurt, but it seemed to be working fine again. He went through his pretraining stretches three times and then tried to bring up his armor.

It came slowly, but it had grown back somewhat during his rest. He could muster enough to cover his arms and torso.

He tried shifting it down over his bruised leg and stood up tentatively. His leg held him with only mild discomfort. He walked the length of the disused train, feeling his muscles loosen as he moved.

"Oh my gosh," a voice said behind him. He spun and saw Blair standing at the door of Kazue's boxcar, hand extended and frozen midair. Her eyes didn't meet his, because they were fixed on the armor covering his leg. "You're the new one. Malcolm, right? Gravenhurst?"

"Umm..." Malcolm dropped his armor, stumbling when his bruised leg took his full weight again. He looked at Blair's round face and wide, open eyes. "You don't remember me?"

"Of course I remember you. You're famous." Her face fell, and her eyes flicked to the boxcar at her side. "What are you doing here though? Was there—did the klek—"

"Oh! No, no, everything's okay. Kazue's okay, since that's who you're probably worried about."

Her hand pressed against the boxcar door, like she was holding it closed. Her eyes narrowed. "How do you know Kaz?"

Malcolm blew out slowly. "You don't remember meeting me? At all?"

"No. Because we've never met. I think I would remember."

"Oh crap, I'm really not the person who should do this with you. Or...or maybe I am, because my family are the ones who..." Malcolm raked his hands through his hair, then gestured to the ground. "Is it okay if I sit down? My leg kind of hurts." Blair nodded slowly. "Thanks," Malcolm said, easing himself onto the ground. "Your bus just got in?"

Blair looked even more suspicious, but nodded. "I'm in town to see my girlfriend."

"I know," Malcolm said. Blair's eyes were fixed on him as if he were an aggressive dog that was getting a little too close. Malcolm's eyes kept trying to slip away from Blair's, down to the ground, but he forced them to stay up. "We've actually met before. Just, like, a few days ago. And you don't remember because…because my family did something to you."

"I was in Seattle a few days ago," she said, frown deepening.

"You actually weren't. My uncle—Felix Gravenhurst?— he messed with your memories. Made you move out of town. He did it because—this is going to sound really bizarre, and I know that—but he did it because you have powers. Like the Gravenhursts do. They made you forget that too."

The look of concern on her face was only growing now. But Malcolm didn't want to stop yet.

"I could have warned you, but I didn't. I could have stopped them from sending you away. Making you forget. I'd say sorry—I actually am saying it, I'm saying sorry right now, because I'm sorry—but I know apologies don't really cover something like this."

Blair burst out laughing. Malcolm smiled nervously back at her. "I don't get it," she said. "I don't get what's happening right now."

"Um, Kazue's inside, and Drew. Maybe you should talk to them. Someone you know." Blair didn't move. "Oh! And as for your powers, you make, like, walls. Glowy blue energy force-field things. But you should really talk to your friends about this stuff. I'm gonna…go for a walk, I guess. Give you a chance to talk. I'm sorry."

He brought his armor up on his leg again and started walking away, then paused. He didn't look back at her. It felt too hard.

"One more thing. I liked you. You were nice to me when you didn't have to be. I wish I had done better for you."

"Are you okay?" Blair called after him. "You look awful. Are you hurt?"

"Yeah," he said, then kept walking away. He heard the door squeak open behind him and Kazue shouted joyfully. He ducked between two railcars, hopped the coupling and sat down. He dropped his armor. He didn't want to overuse it because it didn't regrow while he was using it, and he had a feeling he'd need it soon.

The eastern sky was showing signs of blue now. It looked like a cloudless day. The sun wasn't up yet, but it must be close now.

When he returned they were all outside the boxcar. Blair looked stunned, her eyes unfocused. Kazue glared at Malcolm as he approached, but Drew just looked sad.

"Did she—did you remember?"

Blair shook her head slowly. "No, but..." She put her fingers together and then drew them apart, creating a blue square of light in the air. It flickered out almost immediately. "I don't remember, but I believe now. Don't really have a choice, do I? Not if I can do this." She made another force field. This one stuck around, and Blair stared at it. "I should call my mom. Tell her I got here."

"I don't think you should," Drew said. "The Gravenhursts probably already know you're gone. We don't want to give them any more information than we need to."

Blair looked sad and lost, but she nodded. "That makes sense, I guess." She leaned in to Kazue, and Kazue wrapped her arms around Blair.

"I want to know how we undo this," Kazue said, eyes on Malcolm. "How the hell do we get her real memories back?"

"I don't know," Malcolm said. "I really, really wish I did."

"We still need Gatekeeper," Drew said. "And she might be our best bet for this too. She's worked with Malcolm's uncle for a long time. Maybe she knows how to fix what he did somehow."

"Back to planning how to get Gatekeeper out of the Tower?" Malcolm said.

Drew's lips pursed. "Yeah. But there's a complication. Come check this out."

Malcolm followed Drew into the boxcar while Kazue and Blair stayed outside. The computer's projected display had a news site open. And there, in a large photograph at the top of the page, was a picture of Drew and Kazue. Drew had light swirling around his hands.

"It looks like they couldn't cover this one up," Drew said. "Too many people saw us use our powers. It's everywhere."

"How much do they know?"

"They got my name pretty quick. Haven't figured out Kazue yet—she's been off the grid for a long time. But people sure know her face now."

Malcolm stared hard at the picture. "So they know my family has been lying to them?"

Drew shook his head. "Not that easy. The Gravenhursts are playing it that they're as surprised as everyone else. And they're billing us as the reason you went off the rails, saying we've turned you traitor. Everyone's looking for us—the media, the police, the Gravenhursts."

"What? You saved all those people. My family didn't even show up."

"According to most accounts, the Gravenhursts took out those klek and fended us off at the same time." Drew shrugged. "The point is, I doubt we can get close to the Tower now."

Malcolm stared at Drew. "So what do we do?"

Drew shrugged. "Honestly, man, I have no idea. Lie low for now, I think. See if we can help Blair."

"And what about you? Your family?"

Drew puffed out his cheeks. "As far as I can tell, they're fine. Media's got them under siege, which might actually protect them from something worse."

Malcolm winced, knowing that "something worse" was *his* family.

"I can't go home for sure, which hurts. Wish I could explain all this to them."

Malcolm nodded. "Yeah. I'm sorry."

Drew looked at him, but his eyes still seemed far away. "I know you are. You're not your family."

"Okay," Malcolm said half-heartedly. "Hey, do you have an extra shirt?"

"Oh, right." Drew went to the duffel bag he had brought the night before and threw a faded black shirt to Malcolm.

Malcolm pulled off his tattered one and replaced it. "Thanks," he said. He slid the door open to go back outside, but froze with one foot out the door. Kazue and Blair were just outside, pressed against each other, kissing.

"Umm…"

"Maybe we should give them the place for a bit," Drew said at his shoulder.

"Yeah. Right." Malcolm stepped outside softly, armoring his leg so he could walk without limping. Drew came behind him, tapping Kazue on the shoulder and gesturing to the open door before walking after Malcolm. Malcolm turned away but heard the girls' footsteps moving toward the boxcar as Drew came up beside him.

"I'm gonna go check in on a few people around the neighborhood. With all this, I haven't been keeping up my patrols. Want to come?"

For a moment Malcolm's heart sped. He remembered the bright, uncomplicated feeling he'd had after they'd stopped the robbery for Mrs. Jindal, and he craved it. He closed his eyes and breathed deep. "No. Thanks though. I have something else I was going to do."

"Okay. Maybe give Kaz and Blair a few hours to talk and…everything. And stay out of sight?"

"Sure."

"Good. See you back here."

Drew headed off to the west, while Malcolm hurried south. Within minutes he had no idea where he was. He knew where he wanted to go—where he needed to go. He was just having trouble getting himself to go there. His plan felt simultaneously like something he should have done long ago and the most foolish thing he could possibly do.

It took him an hour of aimless walking to talk himself into it.

EIGHTEEN

He saw the red of Orin's jacket and almost turned back. Orin had been the Tower's doorman for longer than Malcolm had been alive. He was a fixture in Malcolm's memories, there at the cusp of the world outside, always ready to see him off and to welcome him home. He didn't want to get Orin mixed up in whatever happened next.

But he couldn't turn back now. He'd been spotted several blocks out, and a crowd had gathered in his footsteps—not surprising, since he had to keep his injured leg armored the entire time. The crowd was keeping its distance, but he could already hear sirens. If his family didn't know he was coming, they would soon. It was now or never.

The front doors were pristine, as if Kazue had never been there—which made sense, since the Tower staff would have set the mites to work fixing things almost instantly. He stepped up to the doors and Orin held them wide, his easy smile spreading across his face until he recognized Malcolm, and the smile dropped.

"Hey, Orin," Malcolm said.

"Malc—um, Mr. Gravenhurst. No one told me you—"

"No, no one knew. But I'm coming home. Can you let me in?"

Orin stepped back to let Malcolm through. "I must say, you are a welcome sight. We have all been worried."

"I know," Malcolm said. "I, um, things got a bit out of control."

"Is that what you call it?" Orin said, but he reached out and squeezed Malcolm's arm affectionately. Malcolm let himself smile—a genuine one. He'd always liked Orin. "I'm sure you will get more than one earful, but I for one am happy to have you home."

"Thanks." Malcolm felt a moment of comfort—which ended abruptly as he saw Orin's other hand signaling to the guards at the security desk. There were several of them, more than usually manned the desk, and they were all coming toward him now, eyes fixed on him through their glowing green visors. Malcolm's reflection warped and twisted across the surfaces of their silver armor.

"It's okay," he said to them, raising his hands. "I'm not here to fight. I just…I just want to see my uncle. I want to come home," he said. He knew he sounded desperate. He hoped they would interpret that in his favor.

"Malcolm, don't be afraid. We've been instructed—the guards—it's a precaution, you understand." Orin looked genuinely afflicted, and Malcolm felt another kick of guilt.

"You don't have to come with me. I remember the way." He attempted a smile and felt it fail.

Two of the guards were wearing stun gloves, and Malcolm saw them spark in a way that showed they were primed.

But they seemed reluctant to lay hands on him. They fanned out, blocking him from the exit.

"Seriously, Orin," he said. "I just want to go upstairs."

"If you don't want to go with the guards, then let me call your uncle here," Orin said. "I'm sure he'll want to see you right away."

"No, honestly, that's okay. I know I screwed up, but…" As he spoke, Malcolm began walking backward, toward the elevators. The guards started closing in on him. Apparently his grace period was over. "Ah crap," he said, then armored up as best he could and turned.

He ran for the elevators. The guards broke into action immediately—they were well-trained, but Malcolm was quicker on his feet. He lowered his shoulder and slammed through the elevator doors without stopping, bending the metal and spilling through into the darkness of the elevator shaft. He fell the few stories to the basement, just managing to position his armor to cushion the fall.

As he got back to his feet, he heard shouting above him, and the machinery of the elevator whirred to life almost immediately. He sighed. He hadn't really counted on his ruse lasting long, but this was a bit ridiculous.

He gathered his thoughts and reached up to pull open the elevator doors. He hauled himself into the basement and was momentarily blinded by a flash from one of the lights around the gate.

"Hey, Gatekeeper? Sorry, um, Darla?"

"Prefer Gatekeeper, actually," her gruff voice said from the far side of the room.

Malcolm walked around the gate and its lights and saw Gatekeeper sitting on her swivel chair, typing furiously. She looked exactly as she had the last time he'd seen her, save that her hair looked even more unkempt.

"Okay. Gatekeeper. Can we talk?" He looked back at the elevator. "Fast?"

Gatekeeper's eyes shifted between the gate and the array of computer monitors and then she turned to him. "As long as it's fast."

"It'll have to be, or security is going to chase me down here to lock me up."

"Oh," she said and turned briefly to her computers and made a few more furious keystrokes. "There. That should buy us some time. I'm guessing it'll take them about five minutes to figure out I messed with the fingerprint scanner."

"Thanks," Malcolm said.

Gatekeeper shrugged. "So. What's this about?"

"Well, um, I came to get you out of here."

She blinked several times before she said anything. "Why?"

"Because we're trying to figure out how to stop my family, and we need your help."

Gatekeeper watched him, eyes flat and unemotional. "Is that why those other two came down here?"

"Yeah, that was Drew and Kazue. Ibrahim's friends. I mean, we don't want to force you. We just thought...I mean, Kazue was sure you'd want to help. That you didn't like—"

"How the Gravenhursts run things? I don't. They don't know what they're messing with, but they keep messing with it anyway. So you, what, want me to turn the gate to your side or something? Turn off their powers?"

"No. We want to destroy the gate, turn off all the powers. Because of the ping—the, um, signals to something out there." Malcolm waved upward.

For a second Malcolm saw a twinkle in Gatekeeper's eyes. "Figured out my message, did you?"

"Kazue did."

"Good on her. But to destroy it…that would be tough. Probably too late, but maybe we could…" Gatekeeper trailed off and turned back to her computers.

Malcolm could hear sounds coming from the elevator shaft now. Thumping. Raised voices. He inched farther into the basement.

"So, Gatekeeper, do you think—"

"Yeah, I'll come. But I'm going to need a couple of minutes to rig this to run itself. The gate's always thinking, trying to figure out the pattern of light so it can exploit it. An automated program won't be as good as having me here, but we might get a couple of days before it starts building an army."

Malcolm heard a clunk from the elevator shaft. A moment later something dropped to the bottom. Malcolm watched in horror as his grandfather stood up inside the shaft. He was easily eight feet tall, and his skin was mottled and shiny— exactly like the marble floor of the lobby, Malcolm realized. His grandfather stepped out of the shaft and into the room, and as he did another figure slipped down off his back—Felix.

"Oh. I guess they didn't need the fingerprint scanners," Gatekeeper said, still typing.

Malcolm's grandfather surveyed the room and spotted Malcolm and Gatekeeper on the other side of the gate.

"Malcolm," he said.

"Hello, Grandfather."

"Darla, did he disturb you?"

"Shut up. Working," she said.

He nodded and turned his eyes to Malcolm. As he walked toward him, the concrete on the floor seemed to crumble and flow up his pant legs. His marbled skin turned gray and pitted, and he hunched his shoulders to keep his head from scraping the high ceiling. His expensive suit was absorbed into his stony skin, leaving him looking like a huge statue. Felix stayed by the elevator. Malcolm kept a nervous eye on him, but he was hard to see between all the flashing lights.

Malcolm found himself backing away from his grandfather. Gatekeeper didn't move an inch.

"You turn your back on us?" his grandfather said, his heavy strides bringing him closer and closer to Malcolm. He passed Gatekeeper without even glancing at her. "You want to undo everything we've accomplished? Everything we've built for you? Our decades of work, our sacrifices?"

"It's not under control, Grandfather. The gate is—"

"You think this is out of control?" He actually laughed, a rough, scraping sound from the pit of his stony belly. Malcolm wasn't sure he had ever heard his grandfather laugh. "This is nothing compared to the first klek attack. Your grandmother and I almost died a dozen times a day. We saved the city. We brought the gate to heel. But you wouldn't understand what we did, what we had to do."

"Grandfather, please listen. The klek are—"

"I expected better from you, Malcolm. I hoped for better. But I can't keep placing my faith where it isn't warranted."

He suddenly jumped forward. Malcolm barely leapt clear in time as his grandfather slammed his fist down where Malcolm had been. The blow cracked the floor.

"Stop!" Malcolm said. "Please!"

His grandfather let out a guttural growl and came at Malcolm again, growing as he absorbed mass from the floor. He expanded until he had to get down on all fours, craggy shoulders brushing the ceiling. The contours of his face had turned jagged. One huge arm swept forward, and Malcolm ducked.

"I don't want to fight you," Malcolm said. "I never wanted to—"

His grandfather lashed out again. Malcolm dodged the hand and simultaneously brought his limited armor up over his arms. He grabbed his grandfather's wrist and yanked him forward onto the floor. Malcolm dropped his armor to his legs and sprang over his grandfather's back, landing on the other side.

"Felix, what are you waiting for?" his grandfather shouted as he struggled to turn around in the tight space. "End this!"

Malcolm turned with dread toward his uncle, but Felix still stood frozen by the elevator. And now that Malcolm could see him without the flashing lights between them, he noticed that his uncle looked different. There were bags under his eyes, a haunted look on his face.

Behind him, the elevator car slid to the bottom of the shaft and stopped. Its arrival seemed odd to Malcolm, but he didn't have time to think about it. His attention was fixed on Felix, waiting to see what he would do. The golden light from the elevator car, reflected off its mirrored walls, illuminated Felix from behind, making his shadowed face even darker.

"Father, I...please," Felix muttered.

Malcolm's grandfather grunted. "Fine. I'll take care of it," he said. He came at Malcolm again.

Malcolm was caught flat-footed, and he barely got his arms up to deflect his grandfather's blow. He was knocked into the wall, shattering computers and monitors, and a sharp pain shot through his back. He was pretty sure he was bleeding again.

With a growl Malcolm's grandfather crawled forward and wrapped a stony hand around Malcolm, pulling him away from the wall and pinning him to the floor. "Careful of the computers!" he shouted at Malcolm. "If Darla can't—" He suddenly paused, eyes flicking around the room. "Felix, where's Darla?"

Felix looked around the room, as did Malcolm. She wasn't there. And the elevator car was gone now.

His grandfather's eyes flared, and he pressed down on Malcolm with a hand that had grown almost as big as Malcolm himself. "Do you know what you've done?" he shouted at him.

Malcolm felt the vestiges of his armor groan under the pressure. "Please, Grandfather," Malcolm said. "Just stop."

His grandfather only pressed down harder. Malcolm got a grip on his finger. He stole a little bit of armor from his legs and torso, groaning as he felt the pressure there increase. But the armor reformed over his hand and forearm, and he pulled.

For a moment he thought his strength wouldn't be enough. Then he heard a *crack*, and his grandfather's finger snapped off at the base, raining concrete powder over Malcolm. The hand pulled back, and Malcolm scrambled away.

"Oh crap, I'm sorry! I didn't mean to—"

His grandfather put his hand down over the broken finger, and it flowed back into his skin, the digit immediately regrowing. "I thought you didn't want to fight me," he said and then lunged forward.

Malcolm turned and ran the other way, putting the gate between him and his grandfather. Without realizing it, he had come within a few feet of Felix. His uncle was breathing hard, eyes fixed on Malcolm.

Oh crap. I didn't think this through, did I? Maybe Felix didn't find out where Drew and Kazue were before, but now, if he uses his power on me again, he could see where the boxcar is.

"Uncle Felix. Please don't."

Felix didn't respond. But his grandfather took advantage of Malcolm's hesitation. He lashed out and caught Malcolm from behind, sending him sliding across the concrete floor. Malcolm got up fast and leapt forward over the next blow, landing on his grandfather's shoulder. He pulled back his fist, transferred more armor up to his arms, then froze as his grandfather turned his face to him. His grandfather's eyes were huge now, and the gray of concrete, and yet they looked exactly the same. The same eyes that had looked down on him his entire childhood. The same look of weary disappointment. Malcolm let his fist drop.

His grandfather chuckled. "Is that all you can do?" He raised his hand and swatted Malcolm off his shoulder. Malcolm fell to the floor. His head was spinning. His back didn't want him to get up. He got up anyway.

What am I doing here? I don't want to fight my family—not like this, toe to toe. But I told Drew I was in this. That I wanted to fix what my family broke.

His grandfather swung, and Malcolm dodged. He was against the wall now, pressed between two desks.

So how far am I willing to go? How much will I let this cost me?

Malcolm found his feet, shifted his stance. Almost all his armor was on his arms and shoulders now—just a thin gray shimmer over his injured leg to keep it working.

"Enough play," his grandfather said and swatted at Malcolm with a massive, open hand.

Malcolm stepped to the side and punched his grandfather's arm, digging in his feet and twisting his core to drive the blow home. There was a *crack*, and his grandfather's arm fractured at the wrist. As his grandfather's eyes widened in surprise, Malcolm stepped forward and brought his other fist down on his grandfather's shoulder. There was another *crack*, and this time his grandfather yelped.

"I don't *want* to fight you. But that doesn't mean I won't," Malcolm said. He cocked his fist, aiming for the huge stony slab of his grandfather's cheek.

Every nerve in his head suddenly lit up. Somewhere behind him he heard a voice—his uncle's voice. "Let the words I speak stir your memory. Blair. Drew."

His head was itching, then prickling painfully. Malcolm felt himself topple, felt his armor folding away, and through eyes that were swiftly losing focus he saw his uncle moving toward him.

"Nnn..."

The rush of images started as it had on the roof of the parking garage, but this time longer, clearer. The alley where he'd first met Drew. Mrs. Jindal. Tears mixing with gravel, streaking his fingers with mud. The feel of a pillow pressed against his face to mute the crying. Blair, confused and scared the night she returned.

Things slowed, that single memory playing out in full. And then more came. Melted ice against his leg. Kazue hefting a length of railroad track. His memories, circling and circling Kazue's home in the rail yard, the one place they had all been safe.

The images suddenly stopped. Malcolm opened his eyes, but everything swam around him. Once again it felt like his brain and his body couldn't communicate. But this time Malcolm didn't stop trying. He lay on the floor, twitching and twisting, trying to get his muscles back under his control. The mental impulses wandered through his body, finding their way slowly.

He could see two blurry figures above him. Felix and his grandfather. His ordinary grandfather, flesh and blood. Malcolm tried to blink, tried again when it didn't work, and finally his eyelids listened. His vision began to clear.

"Were you able to see anything?" his grandfather asked, adjusting his cuffs. His suit looked like it was caked with concrete powder.

"I believe so," Felix said. "It's not easy. I've never used my power this way intentionally before. But I saw shapes. Shipping containers. A red one, again and again, with white graffiti." He pursed his lips. "A railcar, perhaps?"

His grandfather nodded, pulled a drone out of his pocket and released it into the air. "Security, we have a location," he said to it, and it chimed at him.

Felix's eyes had fallen again to Malcolm. Malcolm flinched away, but his uncle just looked down sadly at him. "I didn't want to," he said. "Why did you bring it to this?"

Malcolm's head was beginning to ache again, but panic sent his heart racing and urged him on. He focused on his legs and found the right mental connections. And then, praying it would work, he called on his armor. Gray facets unfolded, ghosting out through his pants before solidifying around his legs. And before his uncle could do anything more, Malcolm brought his legs under him and pushed off sideways, toward the elevator.

He skidded into the empty shaft. He felt clumsy, dizzy. But he could hear feet pounding toward him—he had only moments. He got his legs under him, looked up and saw a spray of light above him where the lobby doors were broken. He leapt.

He got his arms up over the edge of the floor. They didn't want to hold him, but he kicked a foothold into the concrete wall of the elevator shaft and pushed himself out into the lobby.

It was still buzzing with security—people who weren't part of the conspiracy, Malcolm was pretty sure. People just trying to earn a paycheck. But he didn't have time to be careful. His uncle and grandfather knew where Drew and the others were. Malcolm sprinted for the doors, knocking the guards in their silver armor out of his way. As he raced outside, he just had time to see Orin against the wall, his weathered face lined with fear, grief, confusion. And then Malcolm was out on the street, his heart pounding frantically against the inside of his ribs.

NINETEEN

There were sirens ahead of him. He leapt onto the nearest rooftop and saw a fleet of police pods racing south, scudding over the buildings. The Gravenhursts and emergency services had the only pods with clearance to fly that high.

He came down on the lead pod with a hard kick, forcing it onto a rooftop. Two shocked police officers stared at him through the tinted windows. Malcolm tried to ignore them as he kicked his leg deep into the front end of the pod, killing its hover engine.

"Freeze!" he heard an officer shout behind him—and it occurred to him that with only half of his armor available, they could easily shoot him dead. But he kept scanning the sky for the other pods, hoping the cop would hesitate. Only one of the other pods had stayed behind and was circling overhead. Three more were several blocks away, still hurrying to the rail yard. Malcolm leapt after them.

He managed to land on another pod, but he couldn't keep his feet on its slippery surface. He slid down over the side. At the last moment he transferred his armor and lashed out, punching his fist through the door. He was dangling in the air, suspended by one arm.

He pulled himself up and wedged his other hand into the hole made by his fist, then pried. The metal of the pod squealed, and the entire door came loose in one of his hands. Malcolm threw it to the ground.

Four police officers in full riot gear—faceless helmets, powered armor with the Gravenhurst logo on both shoulders—turned their heads toward him. They all had guns drawn. An alarm was going off inside the pod now, mingling with the whine of the siren. "Warning," said the gentle computer voice. "Pod integrity compromised. Emergency landing procedures initiated."

"What the hell are you doing?" one of the officers shouted at Malcolm. "Get off the pod!"

"Sounds good to me," Malcolm said. He glanced down, then released his hold, putting the armor back around his legs to land safely on a roof a few yards down. The pod spun and bobbed through the air, making its way between buildings toward street level. Malcolm looked around and was pleased to see that all the police pods were now focused on him, keeping their distance but circling above him. Then he realized he could hear more sirens. He looked into the distance. There were more pods now, coming from other parts of the city, converging on the rail yard. He couldn't stop them all.

I have to get my friends out.

He leapt farther and faster than he ever had before. The police pods chased after him, but he left them behind.

He passed the rest of the fleet, racing ahead until their sirens were only a faint murmur in the air. He didn't slow. When he reached Kazue's boxcar, he left a crater in the ground with his landing.

He pulled the door open. Drew was already standing there, hands glimmering with light.

"Malcolm?" he said. "I thought that was a bomb going off. You can't—"

"Police. Coming. They know where you are," Malcolm said, panting. "We have to run."

Surprise lit up Drew's face, but only for a second, and then he was moving. He grabbed his bag and another from behind the couch. Kazue came out, clutching her computer in one arm and Blair in the other. As they emerged Malcolm saw them register the sirens—louder now, so many that it seemed like all of Porthaven was wailing.

"Where do we go?" Kazue said.

"The place I met you," Drew said, and Kazue nodded. Without a word Blair hopped up on Kazue's back—an awkward configuration, given Blair's larger body and Kazue's smaller one. But Kazue took off running without pause, legs flashing with each step. Drew listened to the sirens for a second. "Can you carry me?" he asked Malcolm.

Malcolm nodded and bent one knee, presenting his back. Drew strapped the bags over Malcolm's shoulders, then climbed on himself. This was awkward too, Drew being so much taller than him, but Drew wrapped his legs around Malcolm's waist, above the armor, to keep them off the ground. It hurt when Drew pressed himself against Malcolm's bandages.

"Go west," Drew said, and Malcolm jumped.

Drew started swearing as soon as they left the ground, but by the time they hit the zenith of the jump his curses had transformed into a wordless moan. Behind them Malcolm saw a line of police pods descending into the rail yard. Malcolm made sure to land on the ground, not a rooftop, and kept his next jumps low, trying to stay out of sight of any pods that might still be in the air. Drew held on tight.

"Where should I be going next?" Malcolm asked after they had made a few more jumps and the sound of sirens was fading.

"Um...can we just...can you stop for a second?"

Malcolm slowed gradually, over several jumps, to keep from jarring Drew too much. Once they were stopped, Drew unwrapped himself from Malcolm, walked on unsteady legs to a nearby brick building and threw up on the ground.

"Okay. That was...you do that all the time?" Drew said, wiping his mouth with the back of his hand.

"You get used to it."

Drew shook his head. "I don't think I do, no. We can walk from here."

They started walking. They were in what looked like an industrial district. Malcolm had never been here before—had no idea this part of the city even existed. The advent of tech like the repair mites had changed how manufacturing was done in Porthaven. Now you could easily reproduce almost anything with the right licenses from the Gravenhurst Company, of course. Malcolm knew the history, but he'd never understood it until now. Here were the actual physical marks of the change, all around him—

countless buildings empty, lifeless. Before the Gravenhursts, and after. Porthaven had once been a city like any other on the planet. His family had changed it into something else. Something better, Malcolm had once thought, but now he knew that wasn't true.

Malcolm followed Drew mutely. Drew's steps grew steadier as he walked, and he stood straighter.

"Okay. Can you tell me what just happened?" he asked.

Malcolm nodded. "I, um, went to get Gatekeeper, but I ended up fighting my grandfather and my uncle Felix. Felix got into my head and found out where you were."

Drew kept walking without looking back. The muscles in his neck were tensed, Malcolm noticed.

"He make you forget anything?"

"No." Malcolm waited for more questions, but Drew just kept walking. "I tried to stop the police pods that were coming, but there were too many. It was actually kind of cool. I jumped on this one and took the door off, and the cops inside, like...um, can you forget I started telling this story? A story that starts with 'It was kind of cool' and ends with Kazue being chased out of her home probably isn't actually cool." Another silence, footsteps echoing off the walls of empty factories. "I'm sorry," Malcolm said.

"Yeah. You always are." Drew sighed. "So what happened to Gatekeeper? You didn't get her?"

"She left on her own. I don't know where she is now."

"She left without you?"

"Um, yeah."

"So you banged your way in there to get her, and she just walked out on her own?" Drew actually laughed.

"Yeah. I guess that's about right."

"Oh man, Kaz is going to love that." Drew's laughter died away. The smile didn't linger on his lips.

Malcolm was tempted to laugh himself—simply to break the silence—but he couldn't. His throat felt knotted. The way Drew had said it. *You banged your way in there.*

"I screwed up again, didn't I?" Malcolm said. Drew didn't answer, just raised an eyebrow in Malcolm's direction. "I'm sorry about Kazue's place. I should have...I don't know. I knew what Felix could do. I should have thought."

"So why'd you do it?" Drew still wasn't looking at him.

"I don't know. I felt, like, this panic. My family has screwed up so much, and I just hate thinking about that, and I wanted to do something, you know? Stop it. Change it. Do something right for once. You guys were all talking about getting Gatekeeper out, but it wasn't your family that was keeping her tied to the gate in the first place. I kept thinking you shouldn't have to do it. It's not fair that you have to do it."

"And it didn't occur to you that your uncle might get in your head?"

"I guess I didn't want to think too hard about it. I just wanted to do something before I, like, spontaneously combusted. I know that doesn't make any sense."

"Nah. It makes sense. For you it makes sense. I mean, you're a Gravenhurst."

Malcolm nodded, then frowned. "I don't...what does that mean?"

Drew sighed—a huge, weary sigh that made Malcolm fall back a few steps.

"It means you got raised in all of that. Even if you don't buy into everything your family does, you got raised rich, white and superpowered. It occurs to you that you want to fix a problem, but it doesn't occur to you that you might not be the one who should. It occurs to you that you'd like to protect your friends, but it doesn't occur to you to ask if they want your protection. You didn't have to think about stuff like that before, so you don't. You're a Gravenhurst."

As he talked, Drew didn't look at Malcolm, yet each word went right through him. He could feel them in his chest, like shrapnel.

"I don't—I didn't mean to—" He took a long breath, in and out. "Am I off the team?" he whispered.

Drew spun around and finally looked right into Malcolm's eyes. His usually calm face was clenched in anger. "No, don't do that, Malcolm. Don't make this an 'am I in or am I out' thing, because that's not fair. That puts it all on me. It's never that simple." He rubbed the sides of his head. "This is why I never wanted to be the leader."

"You—" Malcolm began, but Drew wasn't done.

"You know what this is like for me? I gotta keep doing the math every damn day you're with us. You're a good guy, but you got blind spots a mile wide, and I gotta calculate the risk to me and the people I care about. I like you. I want you around, and it should be that simple. But you're gonna screw up, and it's gonna hurt me, or Kaz, or Blair. I have to keep figuring out if you're worth that. Since I met you, Blair has had her memory wiped and now Kaz has no place to sleep. You gave us the info on Ibrahim and you tracked down Blair, and I know that cost you, but the math just gets harder and harder. And I'm tired of doing that, figuring out the odds. Forget whether it's fair that I have to fix what your family broke. I shouldn't have to be running the damn numbers every second I'm with you. *That's* what's not fair."

Malcolm nodded slowly. Silence stretched between them. All around them the world seemed dead and still.

"So…if it's that hard," Malcolm began. "And, I mean, yeah, I can see that. That I've done a lot more harm than good for you guys. I just, um…" Malcolm blew out a long breath and tried to stop his head from spinning. "You said you want me around?"

Drew looked at Malcolm from under a knitted brow. "Yeah, man. 'Course I do, or you wouldn't be around."

"Okay. Um, why?"

A small smile curled Drew's lips. "Really? You wanna ask that *now*?"

"Yeah, you're right. You're telling me off, and it's not the time." Malcolm blew his cheeks out. "But actually yeah. I'm asking. I get why you're mad at me, but I don't get why you like having me around, and I feel like that's something I could really use right now."

Drew was still smiling, which Malcolm took as a good sign. Finally he shrugged. "Because you get that all of this is cool. That first night you jumped on me and then you geeked out about my powers…Blair's too chill to geek out like that. Kaz doesn't really get excited about things either— too much has happened to her, I think. She's all scar tissue. I like having someone else around who sees it for what it is. Complicated and dangerous as hell. But still amazing."

"I thought that was annoying. Because, like, underneath I'm still kind of geeking out about your powers. When you laser-blasted that klek? Holy crap, dude."

"Ibby got it too. When we found out about each other's powers and started practicing…even if our powers come from the gate and we have to shut the whole thing down, it still means that all of this is possible, you know? That this kind of thing is possible. That the universe isn't…"

"Boring," Malcolm suggested.

"Yeah," Drew said. "Exactly." He sighed. "So what do we do now? Where are the odds at, Malcolm? We're running out of places to hide. Are you gonna screw it up again?"

Malcolm took a deep breath. The thought of it terrified him, made him want to run as far from Drew and the others as he could. But…

"I can't promise I won't screw up. But if I do, you'll know about it beforehand," Malcolm said. "No more making decisions for everyone."

"Part of the team?" Drew said.

"If that's okay with everyone else."

Drew let out a long breath, then nodded. "I'm good with that. So who gets to tell Kaz it was your fault?"

"Um. Me. But, I mean, if you could be there to encourage her not to kill me, I'd like that a lot."

They walked on, not saying anything more, until Drew pointed them toward a large gray building—another empty factory, anonymous in the crowd. There were large *For Lease* signs out front, half covered in graffiti. The back of the factory abutted the edge of the river, and part of the building had slumped down toward the water. A tall chain-link fence surrounded it, collapsed in places. Drew pushed the gate in the fence open, and Malcolm noticed that the lock looked melted.

They closed the gate behind them and walked around the side of the building. Drew went to a window empty of glass and climbed through.

Malcolm followed him in. "What is this place?"

"I used to come here to practice my powers with Ibrahim. This is where Kaz found us. And then she found Blair and brought her here too. This was where we all trained. Haven't been back in a while."

"How long ago did you meet Kazue?"

"Five years now? Three for Blair."

"Did Kazue live on her own already?"

Drew nodded. "She doesn't talk about her past, so don't even try."

Malcolm did the math. He guessed Kazue was sixteen or seventeen, so she would have been only eleven or twelve when Drew met her. Living on her own. Malcolm would have been ten, training in his family's state-of-the-art gym, Eric and Aleid testing his limits, Felix watching from the sidelines with that subtle smile of his.

They walked through a small office, across moldering cardboard and into a cavernous room beyond. "Kaz?" Drew called.

"We're here," Kazue answered.

It took Malcolm a moment to pick her and Blair out in the shadowed room, standing in front of a broad concrete column a few yards away.

"You weren't followed?"

Drew shook his head.

"Okay. What the hell did Malcolm do this time?"

Drew turned to Malcolm. Malcolm nodded and told them everything.

Kazue's reaction wasn't what he had expected. He was braced, ready to dodge. But she just said, "Huh," then turned and walked away, into one of the smaller rooms off the main area. Malcolm looked at Blair, but she seemed as puzzled as he was.

"Kaz?" Drew said. "What are you doing?"

"Checking my equipment," she called back. "Should get online in case Gatekeeper tries to make contact." They heard clattering. Drew raised his eyebrows at Malcolm.

"I thought you would want to kill me," Malcolm said when Kazue re-emerged.

"I do, but that's not new, right? This is kind of your MO."

Malcolm flinched. He wished she had thrown a punch instead.

"So what do we—" Malcolm began, and that was as far as he got before he crumpled to the floor.

It took a long, dizzying moment for his brain to catch up with his body. One moment he was standing, and the next he was flat on his back, feeling like he was buried under a ton of sand.

"What happened?" he asked. "Did I faint? Was there an earthquake?" He tried to stand, but the weight was too much. He tried pulling up his armor to give himself some strength. But it didn't respond. Something was wrong with it.

Drew suddenly appeared above him. "You okay?" he asked, his eyes darting back and forth between Malcolm and the far wall.

"Something's wrong with my power," Malcolm said. "How far away from downtown are we here?"

"Not far enough for that," Drew said. "Can you stand? Something's happening outside."

"What do you…" He trailed off as he became aware of a sound. It was unlike anything he had ever heard. A whining noise, high-pitched, that seemed to set his bones vibrating at the same frequency. He'd mistaken it for a ringing in his ears. "What is that?"

"I don't know. Come on."

With Drew's help he got himself up, and they limped to the window they had come through. Malcolm noticed now that, though his knee still hurt a lot, it could hold a little weight. He practically had to pitch himself out the window headfirst to get through, but he managed. Kazue and Blair were already on the street. At least, he thought it was them— the streetlights were all out, and he could barely see.

"Do you know what it is?" Drew called.

"No, but power's out everywhere," Kazue called back.

As they emerged onto the street, Malcolm saw she wasn't exaggerating. He couldn't see any lights anywhere. It was like Porthaven had vanished. No lit windows. No headlights. No dreamlike projected skyline. There were only huddled dark shapes stretching as far as he could see, ill lit by a crescent moon.

"I think the entire ambient grid is down," Kazue said. "What the hell did you do this time, Malcolm?"

"I didn't do this one," he said. "At least, I don't think I did." Another thought occurred to him. "Hey, my power is screwed up. Is anyone else's?"

Drew held out his hand and concentrated, then shook his head. "Nothing."

Kazue flexed her fingers and stamped her foot a few times, the frown on her face deepening. "So what could knock out the city's power and ours too?"

Something in Malcolm's pocket buzzed, and he nearly toppled again, this time in surprise. With clumsy fingers he pried his sylf out. It had been in his pocket, powered off, for so long that he had forgotten it was there. As soon as it was clear of his pocket, it rose into the air, chiming and vibrating.

"I thought the grid was out," Blair said.

Kazue checked her own phone. "It is."

"It wasn't even turned on," Malcolm said.

The sylf spit out a wide green display, lighting up the cracked street around them.

Meet me in Camden tomorrow morning. Look for the light. Gatekeeper.

"Gatekeeper?" Kazue said. "How did she turn on your—"

But the sylf cut her off with another message. **Don't get yourselves killed before you see me.**

As soon as this second message was complete, the display flickered out, and the sylf fell to the ground, dead.

Before they could do anything—fatal or otherwise—a *crack* reverberated across the sky, and suddenly there was light. The droning sound he'd noticed before rose until Malcolm's bones hurt from the vibration. They all spun around and saw a strange glow in the sky above downtown— like an aurora borealis, but spherical and expanding. As they watched, the lights flared and then vanished, leaving something behind.

It was huge and silvery, pyramid-like but rounded at the top. Dim violet lights ran along channels in the thing's surface in strange patterns and rhythms.

It began to descend, and long appendages unfolded from its bottom. They flexed and moved, spreading out as the thing neared the ground. Five vast, multi-jointed legs.

It came down directly over Gravenhurst Tower. The bottom of the pyramid landed on the top floor and kept moving down. With a *crunch* that rang across the dark city, the top of the Tower crumbled. The thing continued to descend until its legs touched the ground. It stopped moving. Everything was horribly still.

Then the screaming started. Distant, but in the quiet the sound carried.

"Uh…" Malcolm said, "is, is that…"

"Ping," Kazue said.

TWENTY

They started toward the screaming—all of them, without even talking about it—but Malcolm ran out of steam after about a block. He bent down to lean on his good knee and just kept bending until he was in a crumpled heap on the ground.

"We can't do this," Blair said as she came back to help him off his face. "Kaz? We can't help right now."

"Can't you see that?" Kazue said, gesturing toward downtown. "That's—it's—it's an actual alien invasion, Blair!"

"I know. But we don't have our powers. Malcolm can hardly walk."

"So leave him!" Kazue said. "His family brought this damn *thing* down on us, and people out there are…we have to go!" She started walking again.

"Kaz, wait!" Blair left Malcolm's side and ran after Kazue.

"Hold on," Malcolm said to their backs. "I think I can…" He got to his feet and started limping after her. His heavy footsteps rang out in the silent city. "I'm coming." And then Drew's hand touched his arm, stopping him.

"Don't get yourselves killed," Drew said. "Right? Kaz! Gatekeeper said not to get ourselves killed!"

A block away, Kazue slowed to a stop. Blair caught up with her, and after exchanging a few words they both turned around.

"She must have known this was gonna happen," Drew went on. "And she's right—if we try to go help right now, we probably won't survive. A single klek could take us all out, no problem. We're in no position to help."

Kazue kept turning to stare at the huge thing hunkered over downtown Porthaven.

I wonder if my family is still alive, Malcolm thought. *If any of them were at the top of the Tower...*

"We don't even know what it is," Kazue said. "We don't know what's happening."

"Gatekeeper might," Drew said. "And she's gonna be waiting for us. Camden's not exactly close, and we won't be moving fast." He glanced at Malcolm as he said this.

"We just ignore it?" Kazue said.

"No. We do what we can. Which, right now, is walk to Camden."

Malcolm cleared his throat. "When you say it's not exactly close, are we talking about, like—"

"Five miles, I'd say," Drew said. "It's north a bit. Up the hill."

"A hill?" Malcolm groaned. Drew stepped closer, like he was going to help Malcolm, but Malcolm waved him off. "No, I got it. I just...I don't think I'm going to like hills."

They all stared at one another for a moment, the only sounds Malcolm's breathing and the distant screams. Blair nodded, then Malcolm and finally Kazue.

"Okay. Let's get going," Drew said, starting to walk. They moved slowly, keeping pace with Malcolm.

Malcolm hadn't known a night could feel so long. Every few blocks he had to stop to catch his breath, sit down and let his legs recover. The sounds of distress continued from downtown—crashes, shouts, strange trilling clicks that didn't sound like klek but didn't sound like anything human either. They crawled through the city, time dragging past them on even heavier feet than Malcolm's.

As they left the industrial district, the effects of the blackout became more apparent. There were cars stalled on the street and others crashed into lampposts or fences or walls. When the ambient grid went down, every piece of machinery in the city had shut off. Malcolm wondered what had happened to anyone who'd been in a pod. At least all the cars appeared to be empty.

Whenever they stopped, Malcolm looked around, studying the windows of shops, apartments. Sometimes he caught a flash of movement, the wan purple light from downtown reflecting off something that might have been a face. But as soon as he looked, whatever it was withdrew into shadow.

Malcolm's lungs burned. His legs had moved beyond burning, and now they just felt numb. Sometimes when he tried to move them, they simply ignored him.

"Ready to go again?" Drew asked. He was sitting on the curb while Malcolm lay where he had stopped, right in the middle of the street. The hill that Drew had warned him about loomed ahead.

"What time do you think it is?" Malcolm said.

"I don't know. Maybe…" He looked at the sky. "Nah, I have no idea. Not morning yet."

"And are we close?"

"Just up that hill, man."

Malcolm felt like groaning, but even groaning took effort. "Okay. Let's—"

"Hey! I see a light!" Kazue called to them from up the hill. She and Blair had taken to scouting ahead whenever Malcolm stopped.

Drew stood and walked toward them. "Sunrise?"

"No, like, a light in a window!"

Drew jogged up the rest of the hill, took a look around and then came running back down. "Come on, Malcolm. It must be her."

"How does she have light without the grid?" Malcolm asked.

"Same way she turned on your drone without the grid?" Drew said as he tugged at Malcolm's arm. "You can ask her when we get there." Once Malcolm was on his feet, Drew tucked himself under Malcolm's arm and they started struggling up the hill together. The slope was gradual, but to Malcolm it felt like climbing a sheer cliff face.

They had to stop after a few yards, both Malcolm and Drew kneeling to rest, panting and dripping with sweat. Feet came pounding toward them, and Malcolm managed to turn his head just enough to see Kazue and Blair approaching.

"Damn it, Malcolm," Kazue said, grabbing his other arm and clenching her teeth as she helped him stand. Blair stepped in behind him and put her hands on his back, like she was going to push him up the hill.

"Okay, stop," Malcolm said. "I mean, thank you, but stop. You don't have to carry me. You go ahead and meet Gatekeeper. I'll catch up."

Drew started to shake his head, but Malcolm pulled his arm off Drew's shoulders. "Seriously," he said. "I've slowed you down enough." He climbed a few more yards, using both arms and legs.

"I'm good with that," Kazue said, and she started up the hill again.

"You sure?" Drew said. "It's a big hill."

"I know. But it sucks being the guy you have to drag along. It's, like, too literal. Like I'm a crappy metaphor. Just go. I'll get there."

Drew and Blair set off more slowly. At the top of the hill, Malcolm saw Drew turn and look back at him. Malcolm had only moved a few more feet, but he waved Drew on.

They disappeared over the curve of the hill, and Malcolm set himself moving again. A few steps, stop to rest. A few steps, stop to rest. As he climbed, the sky turned from star-spotted black to washed-out navy.

"Sun's coming up now," Malcolm said to himself. "I don't even know what day it is anymore." By the time he reached the top of the hill, most of the stars had vanished from the sky.

And now he could see what the others had seen. In an apartment building up ahead there was a light on in a third-story window—the only light in the city, aside from the sickly violet glow from the strange ship.

"Third story," Malcolm muttered. "I hate you, Gatekeeper." But he set off walking, faster now that the hill was behind him, and trudged through the open door of the building.

When he reached the third floor, he was greeted by the last thing he expected: Kazue's smiling face.

"Um, did I miss something? Or were you just enjoying watching me drag myself up these stairs?" he panted at her.

"Both," she said. "Hurry—you're gonna like this."

"Hurrying isn't really a thing I can do right now," Malcolm said. "I think my legs fell off." He lifted himself up another step, crawling closer to the landing where Kazue waited. Drew and Blair had joined her now too. They were all smiling.

"Have you guys...seen anyone else?" Malcolm asked between grunts of effort. "Place looks...empty."

"People are evacuating, Gatekeeper says," Drew answered. "Now come on, Malcolm. Get in gear."

"This is the highest gear I have," Malcolm wheezed as he finally got his hands onto the top step. He stopped to lay his head down on the landing.

From where he lay he saw an open door, and beyond it the warm amber light of lightbulbs. And not just that, but also the glow of screens—honest-to-goodness old-fashioned computer screens. Several, it looked like, spread out on a small table, with Gatekeeper's head bobbing back and forth between them all.

"What is this place?"

"An empty apartment Gatekeeper took over after she left the Tower, she says," Drew told him. "She scavenged most of this equipment after the evacuations started."

"Oh. Okay," Malcolm said, taking deep breaths. "I just need another minute, and then I can—"

"That's it," Kazue said. "I know I'm supposed to save my juice, but this is boring." She leaned down, grabbed Malcolm under the arms and heaved him up over her shoulder as if he were light as paper. Flashes of light ran along her skin.

"Huh? What?" Malcolm spluttered as Kazue hauled him into the apartment. "You—you got your powers back?"

"Kaz, we said we would let it be a surprise," Drew protested as he entered the apartment behind them.

"Surprises are boring. Let's get this done." She walked swiftly through the apartment, which consisted of a narrow hallway, a living space now crowded with electronics, and a kitchen about the size of Malcolm's old closet in the Tower. She went to one of two doors off the living area and entered a bathroom, where she dumped him into the bathtub.

Malcolm wondered for a moment if they wanted him to shower—he was drenched in sweat and probably didn't smell too good. But the upper half of the shower was crammed with metal frames and wires, tiny LEDs blinking down at him in a rainbow of colors. "What are we doing?"

Gatekeeper bustled into the room, and Kazue stepped out. The older woman's hands flickered over the electronics, fiddling with controls he couldn't see.

"When the aliens arrived, they sent out a signal to shut down human use of the nanites," she said. The way she spoke low and didn't look at him made Malcolm feel like she was talking to herself rather than him. "Lucky for us, I've been studying these things for decades, and I know—hold on." She pressed a series of buttons, and the tub Malcolm was lying in came alive with electricity. He flinched, but when it touched his skin it didn't hurt—it just made his hair stand on end.

The lightshow stopped, and Gatekeeper frowned down at him. "Hmm. Should have worked. I was going to say I know how to fake the signal, get your nanites up and running again. Worked on me, worked on your friends. But something's off." She reached down and grabbed his chin, staring hard into his eyes. "How much do you weigh?"

"With or without powers?" Malcolm asked.

Gatekeeper puffed out her cheeks, hurried from the room and came back a moment later with what looked like a jeweler's magnifying lens. "Open your mouth," she said. He did, and she peered inside with the lens. Malcolm could see some kind of digital display light up across the glass. "Huh," she said. "You've got a hell of a lot of nanites in there." She pulled away and returned to the controls of the machine above Malcolm, twisting dials and flipping switches. "This might feel weird."

This time when the electricity hit him, it really did hurt. It felt like every cell in his body was jumping around, pulling him apart. And then it stopped. He sat up woozily. It suddenly occurred to him that he *could* sit up—like normal, like he didn't weigh a thousand pounds. He raised his arms, testing, and then got to his feet.

"Put up your armor," Gatekeeper said.

Malcolm obeyed and felt a thrill of joy when he saw the gray facets of his armor unfolding from his skin, covering him. And the armor came up fully—complete coverage, even though he hadn't rested to let it recharge. Gatekeeper bent close to his chest, staring at his armor with the lens.

"Fascinating," Gatekeeper said.

"What is?" Malcolm asked.

"Your armor. It's actually a lattice of nanites. I thought it would be an energy field like Blair uses, but it's constructed of the nanites themselves. No wonder it took so much juice to get your powers running again."

"That's why I felt so heavy?" Malcolm asked.

Gatekeeper nodded. "You actually are that heavy—you and your nanites together. They're constantly using hover tech to accommodate the extra weight. Hmm. Now that we've hijacked them, I wonder if…"

She was still staring at him, her face uncomfortably close.

"What is it?" Malcolm asked.

"Nothing for now," Gatekeeper said, "Bears some thinking about. Now get out of my bathroom. I need to pee."

She bounced in place while Malcolm let his armor drop, stepped out of the tub and left the bathroom quickly. Once Gatekeeper closed the door behind him, he took a moment to relish the feeling of free movement—and then almost fell over as he put weight on his sore knee. But he steadied himself and smiled. He felt human again—which was odd, he supposed, to feel more human when his alien powers had been restored to him. He walked out into the living room, where the others were waiting. Drew was at the window, looking out. Kazue and Blair were on the couch, curled up against each other, hands entangled.

Malcolm paused, staring at their hands. For a moment it felt jarring, in the middle of all of this, to see their fingers entwined—simply because it was so normal. Normal didn't seem right after what he had learned about his family. After the aliens' landing. It was like the entire world had shifted sideways under him, like normal didn't even exist anymore.

And yet this one thing hadn't changed, even after Blair had lost part of her memory. Blair and Kazue were still most comfortable when they were touching. He smiled at them, grateful in a way he couldn't explain. He got a scowl from Kazue in return.

"Hey, did you ask about the memories? Blair's—"

"She doesn't know how to fix it," Kazue said, her scowl deepening.

"I'm all right," Blair said, pulling herself closer to Kazue. "I have you to remind me of what I forgot."

Kazue rested her head on Blair's shoulder but kept on glaring at Malcolm. Malcolm bore it—he felt like he deserved every dirty look Kazue could throw at him.

"Okay," Gatekeeper said, emerging from the bathroom and sitting down in front of her screens. "You wanted my help. What are we doing now?"

They all looked at each other blankly. "Um, I guess…" Drew started. "I mean, we thought you might have ideas. You told us not to get killed before we saw you."

"Yeah, because I needed you to tell me what I'm supposed to be working on. Don't you have a plan?"

Drew puffed out his cheeks and reluctantly shook his head. "We did, sort of. But not for this. Not for aliens landing and shutting everything down."

"Okay, then come up with one," Gatekeeper said. "Fast."

"Any suggestions?" Malcolm asked her.

"Nuh-uh. No, that's not what you said. When you came to the basement, you said you needed my *help*, not my *suggestions*. If you told me you needed me to come up with a plan, I would have told you to go somewhere else. I'm not…I don't do plans. I'm good at figuring out how things work. I just want to figure things out for you."

She wasn't looking at them and was still typing away on the keyboards. All Malcolm could see on the screens were fields of numbers, moving too fast for him to follow. But even with her back to him, he could see she was shaken. She was breathing hard, and her fingers were stabbing the keys like she was trying to drive them through the table.

"Okay, yeah, we can come up with a plan," Malcolm said placatingly. "We do the plan, and you help us figure out how to make it happen."

Gatekeeper nodded once, sharply.

"We can do that, right?" Malcolm said to the others. They looked at him uncertainly. "We were planning to destroy the gate. Would that do anything, or is that pointless now?"

"Who knows? But now that we have our powers back, maybe we should get out there," Kazue said. "See if we can save some people."

Malcolm nodded, but Drew shook his head again. "No, I don't think that's the best play. We really do need a plan, otherwise we're just rushing in. And"—he glanced at Malcolm—"we've seen what happens when we don't think things through."

Malcolm nodded, swallowing the lump that had suddenly formed in his throat.

"Okay, let's take a minute to figure out what we know, because now we don't just need to understand how to destroy the gate, we—man, I can't believe I have to say this—we have to stop an alien invasion. So let's compare notes, see what we know and what we don't. Does that sound good?"

Everyone nodded, even Gatekeeper. Her breathing had slowed, and she even looked over her shoulder at Drew.

"Good. I think we've got proof now that Gatekeeper and Kaz were right about the ping thing. What do we know about the aliens?" Drew said.

"Um, nothing really," Blair replied. "We haven't even seen one yet, assuming that's what's in the ship. Maybe it's just more robots."

"No," Gatekeeper said. "It's not more robots—unless the aliens *are* robots. But this is the real thing for sure, because they stopped the maintenance routine when they took full control of the nanites."

"The what routine?" Malcolm asked.

Gatekeeper looked around at all of them, blinking fast. She seemed to have trouble making eye contact with people. "I, you know, like to figure out how things work. And this tech—the gate, the nanites—is part of an advanced system way beyond human thinking. But we think they somehow *accidentally* gave humans powers? That doesn't really make sense, 'cause it would be wasteful. Sloppy. And this stuff isn't sloppy. It's pretty much perfect. Nothing wasted, everything built to purpose. So a long time ago I came up with a theory about that. Do...do you want to hear it?"

"Yeah, of course," Drew said.

"Okay. Good. The other Gravenhursts never wanted to know. They just wanted me to work. Okay, so if the gate is like a probe, looking for planets that suit the aliens' needs and sending back a signal, then what the gate needs is time."

"Why?" Malcolm said.

"Space is big, remember?" Kazue said. "Takes time for the aliens to actually reach us."

Gatekeeper nodded. "We don't know what the aliens want, but they had to plan for local wildlife. They needed to know the probe would stick around even on inhabited planets, and who the hell would keep around an alien probe that keeps spitting out robots? It needed incentives. Reasons people would want to keep it running. So powers first, and then even the klek became an incentive, because they were free alien tech that could be repurposed. Once the Gravenhursts thought they could keep the gate under control, they were doing exactly what the aliens needed. Maintaining the gate."

"That's what you meant by 'maintenance routine'?" Malcolm asked.

Gatekeeper nodded.

"That actually fits. My family called the gate, um, an opportunity. Not an invasion," Malcolm said. "That was what Felix said."

"Yes. Never could convince them it might be both," Gatekeeper said.

"Okay. So what does that tell us about the aliens?" Drew asked. "They're smart, obviously. And they make efficient systems. Think about that. Let's assume everything they sent to Earth has a purpose. If that's true, what else can we infer about their plan?"

They all sat in silence for a moment. Gatekeeper turned back to her computers and looked instantly more comfortable. Malcolm watched her fingers speed over the keyboard, wishing his own brain could move that fast, wishing he could see the big picture. *But maybe it's not about the big picture. Maybe it's the small stuff.*

"The nanites," he said tentatively. "There must be something more to them. Because if the system is perfect, why would they make all those nanites and then just shut them down?" He looked up. "Even before the aliens arrived, most of the nanites weren't really doing anything. They're in every person, but they only give powers to a small fraction of them. They build the klek, but not all the time. Why would they multiply and spread so much if those were their only jobs? Even with us using them for the ambient grid, most of them are just sitting around. There are too many of them for a perfect system."

Kazue sat straight up. "Terraforming?" she said. "Or something like it? Maybe now they'll start working on changing the atmosphere, making it habitable for the aliens."

"Okay. That would make sense. Does that fit, Gatekeeper?" Drew said.

Gatekeeper stopped typing and looked down at the floor, her eyes flickering back and forth like she was reading something there. "They haven't shown that capability before, but maybe. There are enough of them." She clicked her tongue a few times and then shook her head. "Not enough data to tell." She started typing again.

Drew sighed. "She's right. I think Malcolm's onto something with the nanites, but if we're going to figure this out, I think we need more information. Which means we need to go scouting, see if we can lay eyes on these things."

"Maybe while we do that, we can see if anyone needs our help," Blair suggested, squeezing Kazue's hand. Everyone nodded.

"That sounds like a plan," Drew said. "We go, help where we can, see what we can see and then bring notes back here to put a few more pieces together, come up with a way to stop this whole thing."

"Um, this sounds good, and I really do want to get out there and help people, but we've been up all night," Blair said. "I don't think any of us are in shape to make useful observations, let alone fight aliens we don't know anything about."

Kazue grimaced.

"I'm sorry, Kaz. I know you want to get going."

Drew rubbed his face. "Blair's right, but we shouldn't rest too long. A couple hours, just to recharge? Then we go."

They all stood up. Kazue and Blair took the bedroom, and Drew went to the couch and lay down. Within seconds he was snoring lightly. That left an oversized chair for Malcolm or Gatekeeper. But Gatekeeper was still at her computers.

"Do you want the chair to sleep on?" Malcolm said. "I'm fine on the floor."

"I don't sleep," she said. "Not since the nanites. Besides, I want to see if I can get some access to the city's network, so I can observe directly when you all head out there."

"Oh. Okay then." He went to the chair and curled up, listening to the clack of keys. He was exhausted, but his brain was still spinning. "Hey, can I ask you something?"

"Go for it," Gatekeeper said, still typing.

"Why did you help them all those years? My family? I mean, I'm not trying to accuse you of anything, because I did it too. I just…you're smarter than me. I figure you must have a good reason, and maybe it will help me figure out how guilty I should feel right now. Because I don't really know."

Gatekeeper stopped typing, but she didn't say anything. Not for a long time. Then she slowly turned her head toward Malcolm. No eye contact, but her attention was clearly directed at him.

"I think about that a lot," she said. "It's hard for me to explain though. It's not like I planned it. Like I said, I'm not good at plans. My brain works so fast in some ways, but in other ways it just…doesn't. So…"

She took a deep breath and fell silent for another long stretch. Malcolm waited.

"I guess…I mean, at first I only wanted to figure it out," Gatekeeper said. "It was all so big, so new, and I always felt like I was getting closer to understanding it. And the Gravenhursts let me work on it all the time, so I didn't have to worry about anything else like food and stuff. I hated worrying about stuff like that, so it was nice. And then…" She shrugged. "I just kept working. Kept figuring it out."

"But they made you a secret. Down in that basement all that time, and no one even knew—"

"Don't care about that. I don't need anyone to know. But eventually I did figure out that your family wasn't…right. Wasn't doing it the right way. Took a while, because that's not the kind of thing that usually sticks in my brain. But I did know what they—what *we* were doing was wrong. I didn't know what to do about it though. I guess I felt like it was too late. I tried getting information out, but it never seemed to go anywhere. Not until you started poking around."

Her eyes flicked up for a moment and met Malcolm's, and he took a breath. Gatekeeper's voice was always so flat and unemotional that he had almost started to think of her as an extension of her computers—brilliant and cold. But her eyes held such raw, unmasked emotion that it staggered him for a moment—fear, confusion, guilt. Malcolm's family had misused her for the past few decades, and she had felt every moment of it.

She turned away but didn't start typing. "I'll be honest with you. I don't know if we can do anything at this point. Creatures who can build all of this…I don't know if we even have a chance. But thanks for, you know, getting me away from the gate. Asking me to do something different."

"Yeah. I mean, thank you. If we're going to do this, we need your help. And…and I'm sorry for what my family did. To you."

"Okay. Helping your friends sounds good to me."

"Me too." Malcolm lay back in the chair and closed his eyes as the sound of her fingers on the keyboard started up again. He felt exhausted. As he curled deeper into the thread-bare upholstery, the sound of Gatekeeper's typing seemed to swirl around his head, drowning out his thoughts, and he sank into sleep within moments.

TWENTY-ONE

It felt like Malcolm had just closed his eyes when Drew tapped him on the chest. "Time," he said. Malcolm nodded, uncurling himself from the chair. He went to the bathroom, passing Kazue, who was standing in the doorway of the bedroom. Kazue nodded to him, and Malcolm, surprised by the friendly gesture, just blinked at her. In the bathroom he ran some water and rubbed it into his face like he'd seen people do in movies. It actually kind of worked—he almost felt awake when he came back out to the living room.

Gatekeeper handed them all coffee, which only Drew and Kazue drank. After that they left the apartment without too much discussion. Out on the street Blair climbed onto Kazue's back, and Drew climbed onto Malcolm's.

"Can you, like, run? Instead of jumping?" he asked.

"I guess," Malcolm said. "It's not as fast."

"But it doesn't end with me throwing up all over you," Drew said. "Just try to keep pace with Kaz, okay? We stick together on this one."

Kazue set off, and Malcolm followed. Kazue flew through the streets, each stride taking her half a block.

Malcolm started to fall behind—he wasn't used to moving like this, fast and low. He watched her legs, the way she planted her feet—knees always bent, he noticed, toes never reaching forward but instead carefully pushing at the ground behind her with quick thrusts. Almost like her body was a skateboard that she was propelling forward. He mimicked her, and his running became more fluid.

As they drew closer to downtown, the effects of the attack became more apparent. There was rubble in the streets from the buildings that had broken when the grid went down— no more hover tech meant that impossible architecture suddenly had to wrestle with gravity again, and more than one skyscraper had broken under the strain. They passed a condo tower with a pod embedded in it halfway up—one of the long limousine-style pods, its sleek back end jutting out several yards.

The klek ship loomed over them, its violet light dimmer in the sunshine. This close, they could see that the ship was never quite still. Its five legs shifted and flexed subtly, like a living thing.

Everywhere they went, Malcolm searched the windows for people. He saw no one. He hoped that meant they had all evacuated. He feared it meant something worse.

I was a Guardian. I was supposed to be a Guardian. I was supposed to stop things like this. He wasn't sure if the feeling lodged in his chest was sadness or anger.

Still dozens of blocks away from the Tower, Kazue slowed to a stop. As Malcolm stopped beside her and the echoes of his footsteps faded, he understood why. He could hear a rhythmic thumping somewhere up ahead. Without saying anything, they all moved off the street and huddled against the closest building, creeping along the wall. The light from the ship throbbed subtly. A loud crash echoed through the streets nearby, making them jump. Blair stretched her hands out and constructed a shield in front of them.

"You're getting good at that again," Malcolm whispered.

"Even if I can't remember, I think my body does," she whispered back. "As long as I don't overthink it, it works."

She carried the shield with them as they walked on.

At the corner of the building they all peered into the next street. Half a block away there was a cloud of dust in the air, and through it they saw a gaping hole where the front door of a high-rise would have been. In the shadow of the hole something moved.

At first Malcolm thought it was a klek. It moved the same way, on multi-jointed legs that bent in all directions. But these legs were thicker, almost as broad as tree trunks. And there were four of them, not five. As it came through the dust, Malcolm could see other differences. Where the klek were clearly artificial, this creature looked partly organic. Pinkish flesh showed between metallic plates—plates that were embedded into the creature, not worn. Like the klek, its body was bulbous, with no discernible head. There was a bundle of machinery on top of it, which Malcolm thought might be an array of sensors. When the creature changed direction, it did so without turning, as if it had no front or back. And it was big. Half again as tall as Drew. Malcolm swallowed.

"Like the robots weren't creepy enough," Kazue said.

Drew had his lips pursed, watching the creature. One of its legs bent upward, curling to reach the broad top of its body. It lifted up the bundle of machinery and then, with two of its legs, deftly manipulated it, reconfiguring until it looked like a long tuning fork with a tangle of suspended wires at the top that reminded Malcolm of the gate. It planted this in the ground with one hard thrust.

"Okay," Drew said. "It doesn't look like it's noticed us. We'll stay here and w—"

Drew was cut off by a prolonged scream from somewhere inside the building. At the sound, the alien hunched itself up and then scuttled through the hole into the dark interior.

"Crap. Change of plan," Drew said. "I'm going in. Malcolm, with your armor you stand the best chance of not getting hurt here, so you take on the alien and keep its attention away from me. Kaz, Blair—who the hell knows what's going to happen, so you stay ready. If it looks like Malcolm can handle the alien, hang back and watch, get that data we need. If not, do what you can."

Everyone nodded. Drew walked forward, raising his hands, and the daylight flowed away from him, leaving him as a patch of shadows on the bright street. He disappeared into the darkness of the building as Malcolm hurried after him.

After passing through a small, dark-carpeted lobby, Malcolm entered the core of the building—an atrium that stretched all the way up to a broad skylight at the top. The interior walls were all glass, revealing hallway after hallway stacked on top of each other. *From the upper floors, the view into the central atrium must be dizzying,* Malcolm thought. Down at the bottom there was a broad-branched tree, and a pond half-filled with rubble. Broken glass crunched under Malcolm's feet.

He found the alien not by sight but by sound. It was several stories up, climbing the sheer glass sides of the atrium. Each step it took made a strange sucking sound. Whoever was in the building was still screaming, somewhere higher up. Malcolm couldn't tell where Drew was anymore—there were too many shadows in here.

"Here goes," he said, leaping for the alien.

He flew straight toward the creature's body, his aim true. But midway through his jump the creature paused its climb and suddenly leapt toward him, all four legs bending backward to reach for him. Malcolm raised his fists, but it swatted him out of the air like a fly. He crashed through the branches of the tree, snapping several, and came to rest on the ground.

He stood. There was the alien, just a few yards away, perched on the rubble in the pond. Malcolm sprang at it, aiming this time for one of its legs. But the alien spun and hit him, deflecting him away through the glass one story up.

He righted himself. So far he hadn't done any damage to the alien, but it hadn't affected his armor much either. He could keep going like this for a long time. But he was supposed to be learning about the aliens, seeing how they worked. And he wanted to know if they had weaknesses.

"Let's try something else," he said under his breath. He jumped down to the ground floor, advancing on the alien at a walk, one arm forward, the other up to guard his face, like in one of his sparring matches with Eric. The alien waited for him, swaying slightly.

He ran the last few steps and kicked with his right leg. The alien blocked this with one of its own legs and met his follow-up punch with another block. Malcolm moved faster, putting his full strength and speed into each strike. He spun, fists and feet lashing out, moving in and out to attack from different angles, at joints, body, metal, flesh. His blows descended on the creature in a storm, flying faster than Malcolm's own eyes could track them.

Not a single hit landed.

The creature loomed over him, casually blocking his every strike with its four broad limbs, moving faster than something so big should be able to. Malcolm felt like he was six again, just starting his training with his tall, super-powered cousin, no strength to help him, no armor to protect him. He could almost see Eric's smirk emblazoned across the silvery metal and sunburn-pink flesh of the alien's body.

Malcolm stepped back to reassess, and that was when the alien finally struck. It tipped up on its forward legs, then flipped right over and came down on him with its other two. Malcolm didn't have time to dodge. He was pinned to the floor.

The alien's feet were smooth metal caps, but as he watched, their surfaces fractured and claws unfolded from inside, clamping onto his armor. They looked like the barbs on the robotic klek feet, but while the robots had one claw per foot, Malcolm counted eleven on each foot of this creature. And once they were dug in around his armor, they began to vibrate. He felt his body thrumming, making him immediately feel dizzy and nauseous. The claws began to sink slowly through the surface of his armor.

He breathed in to scream and then the alien was suddenly swept aside by a bright blue wall of light.

As the light knocked the alien clear, sending it back against the glass walls of the atrium, Blair ran up. Her hand was extended, pushing at the force field she had just used to save Malcolm.

"Are you okay?" she asked, extending her other hand to help him up.

"Um, yeah." He checked his armor. He could see the holes where the claws had sunk in, but it was mostly intact. "Yeah. I think so. Thank you."

The alien was pinned against the glass by Blair's force field but, as they watched, it shattered the glass behind it and slipped into the hallway beyond.

Blair let her field dissolve, and at the same time Malcolm saw Kazue sprint into the building, running toward the alien at full speed.

"Be careful!" Malcolm shouted. "It's really—"

She kept running. The alien lashed out at her with two legs, claws fanning out. With a roll, Kazue went under its blow and came up, punching the alien's body right in its center with a flash of light. Malcolm heard metal crumple.

"—fast," he said.

The alien leapt clear, then balanced on one leg and swiped at her with three others. Kazue was forced to jump back, but she moved in again, grabbing one of its legs and twisting it. The alien struck out at her at the same time, and Malcolm gasped, but a blue force field appeared and stopped the blow from landing. Blair walked slowly forward, hands raised to shape the air as more force fields appeared next to the combatants.

Malcolm watched. The alien wasn't making it easy, but Kazue and Blair were winning the fight. *I couldn't even land a blow, and I spent my entire life training to fight the klek*, he thought. Kazue's fighting style was obviously untrained but effective. She was fast, strong and fearless. But the alien also looked slower, less poised, against her. *What's going on? Should I go help? Could I help?* Kazue and Blair looked like they had it handled. *It can't actually be faster when it's fighting me, can it? Am I just jealous that they can beat something I can't?*

A sound drew his attention away. He heard a shout and clattering from a floor midway up the atrium. Malcolm backed up to see better and saw debris flung against the glass about a dozen floors above him. A moment later the bulky form of another alien pressed against the glass, cracking it. It wasn't alone.

There were three—no, four—aliens rushing along the hallway. And from the shadows ahead of them, a thin beam of light lanced out, slashing across the lead alien.

Drew. Malcolm watched, tense, as the aliens hurried forward. He couldn't tell where Drew was now. But the aliens seemed to have no such problem. One of them dashed forward and swept the hallway with a leg. Malcolm saw Drew's tall form fly backward, the shadows around him shredding away.

Oh no.

Drew hit the wall and slid down. He wasn't getting up and the aliens were surging toward him. Malcolm flexed his legs and jumped.

The leap seemed to take forever, everything moving in slow motion. He flew through the air, up one floor after another. The aliens ran, clambering over each other in their hurry to reach Drew. Drew shook his head, like he was trying to clear his vision.

I'm not going to reach them, Malcolm thought, watching the aliens close in. *Come on*, he urged himself. *Up. Up. Faster.*

He moved faster.

Midair, with nothing beneath him, his momentum shifted, and he soared the last few yards to the floor where Drew lay against the interior wall. Malcolm struck the atrium glass, broke through and hurtled straight into the side of one of the aliens.

This alien didn't block his attack. Malcolm's momentum carried them both into the wall, one of the alien's legs punching through in a rain of plaster.

The rest of the aliens recoiled, surprised. But their hesitation didn't last long. As one, all three of them came at Malcolm.

Malcolm didn't stay to fight. He jumped away, swept Drew up under his arm and leapt back out through the glass. Drew, still groggy, mumbled something that sounded a lot like "Aw crap."

As they arced smoothly downward, Malcolm looked up. The aliens were coming after them, jumping down into the middle of the atrium. He wished he could fall faster— and again his momentum shifted, taking him swiftly toward the floor. He regretted it a moment later, fearing for Drew. Malcolm wrapped his arms tightly around him, but their landing was surprisingly soft. He touched down right beside the hole the aliens had punched into the building.

"Blair! Kazue!" he shouted. They turned just as the other aliens landed behind him. Blair raised a force field over herself and shouted for Kazue. Kazue, meanwhile, grabbed the leg of the alien she had been fighting and swung it.

It flew through the air and collided with the other aliens, knocking them sideways. She ran, picking up Blair as she went. They were all pelting away from the building seconds later, moving so fast that Malcolm wasn't even sure if the aliens had followed them out of the high-rise.

"Malcolm?" Drew said. He was blinking hard, his eyes starting to focus. "Are we—"

"We're out," Malcolm said. "What happened to you?"

"I found the person who was screaming. Got them going down the stairwell and then drew the aliens away so they could escape. But the aliens knew where I was, even when I made it pitch-black. I couldn't get away."

"What?" Malcolm asked.

"The shadows didn't slow them down. Not for a second." He rubbed his head and shifted uncomfortably in Malcolm's arms. "Thanks for coming to get me."

"Yeah," Malcolm said. "I'm not sure how I did it exactly." He gritted his teeth. "I think we all better talk to Gatekeeper."

TWENTY-TWO

"Oh no. No no no no…"

At first Malcolm had no idea why Kazue had started muttering to herself. All he knew was that she picked up speed. He tried to keep pace but gradually fell behind.

And then he saw the smoke.

Out here the devastation of the alien attack wasn't so apparent. The buildings were empty but intact—this area had none of downtown's creative architecture, so the buildings had survived the failure of the grid. But up ahead, at the top of the Camden hill, a plume of smoke was rising into the air.

He got to Gatekeeper's building a few seconds later. The front of the building was devastated, the brick wall collapsed up to the fourth floor. They could see directly into the apartment where they'd met with Gatekeeper. Kazue was inside, just behind the long couch where Drew had slept.

But that wasn't all. Out on the street was an alien, lying flat on the ground, legs splayed. Blair stood a few yards away from it, a force field up. At first Malcolm thought the alien was dead, but as he drew closer he could see subtle movements.

Joints flexing. Panels in its mechanical plates sliding open and closed. But it didn't seem to register their presence.

"What happened?" Malcolm asked Blair. He set Drew down on his feet.

"Nothing," Blair said. "We found it like this. It's not reacting to us at all. Kaz even kicked it."

"She's not here!" Kazue called from above. "I can't find her!"

Drew took a deep breath. "So, um, the aliens attacked, clearly. Maybe they took her, but…" He clenched his eyes shut. "Sorry. Hard to think this through. I'm still feeling dizzy."

"Kaz?" Malcolm called. "Is there any ice in the fridge up there?" Kazue disappeared into the back of the apartment, reappearing a moment later to throw something down to Malcolm. It was a half-empty bag of frozen chicken nuggets.

"All I could find," Kazue said.

Malcolm held the bag out to Drew. He put it against the left side of his face, where a purple-black bruise had begun to spread.

"If the aliens have her, can we get her back?" Blair asked. "I don't think we can fight—"

She was cut off by a boom from above—a boom Malcolm recognized immediately. He just had time to mutter, "Oh crap," and then his aunt Aleid was there, hanging in the air above their heads.

Blair shifted her shield to cover all three of them. Malcolm braced for combat.

But Aleid held up both hands, fingers spread. "I'm not here to fight you."

Kazue jumped down beside them and walked over almost casually to stand under Blair's shield and glare at Aleid.

"Why, then?" Malcolm asked.

Aleid looked at him but quickly looked away. "Gatekeeper. Gatekeeper asked me to come."

Kazue immediately stepped out from under the shield. "Where is she? Where did you take her?" she shouted.

Aleid backed away as Kazue advanced. "She's safe. I saw the aliens coming this way, and I came to see what they were after. I helped."

"What do you mean, 'helped'?" Malcolm asked.

This time she didn't look at him at all. "Helped her get away. I can take you to her. That's why she wanted me to come here."

"What about that?" Blair said, gesturing to the alien.

"Leave it," Aleid said. "It won't hurt anyone."

"What happened to it?" Blair asked.

"I don't really know," Aleid said. "Gatekeeper did something to it. With, um, a bathtub."

"Is Gatekeeper in the Tower? Or with the rest of the Gravenhursts?" Drew asked.

"No. They don't know I'm here."

The four of them shared looks. Kazue still seemed ready to fight, and Blair looked nervous, but Drew nodded. "Okay," he said. "Take us to her."

A few minutes later they came to a nondescript stretch of trees along the Lockheed River. As Aleid flew in, Malcolm saw Gatekeeper walking erratically between the trees. She looked up as their feet crunched into the underbrush.

"You did it, 'Leid," Gatekeeper said. "Wasn't sure you would."

Malcolm looked around for a moment before realizing Gatekeeper was talking to his aunt. He had never heard anyone call her by a nickname before.

"Neither was I," Aleid said.

"Was the alien still there?"

"Still incapacitated. The rest were long gone."

Gatekeeper nodded and resumed her pacing. "Damn it, I wish I had a computer."

"Why?" Drew said. "How is a computer going to help us right now?"

"Helps me think. Screens help me think, put the thoughts down somewhere I can see them. Otherwise everything just sort of…" She made a strange wiggling movement with her fingers. Finally she looked at Malcolm and the others. "No screens, though, and you've got data. You got data? You fought the aliens?" Everyone nodded. "Good. Okay. Okay. Let's figure things out."

"I shouldn't be here for this," Aleid said. "Stay safe, everyone." She began flying away.

"What?" Malcolm said. "Wait! Aunt Aleid!"

She began to pick up speed and left the cover of the trees. Malcolm armored up and jumped after her, landing on the road that ran parallel to the river just as she began to arc upward into the sky. "Where are you going?" he shouted. She didn't slow. "Aunt Aleid! Can't we at least talk?"

She kept going, and he wasn't even sure she had heard him. But after a moment she slowed and stopped. Malcolm watched her hanging in the open air above him.

"Come down," he said. He had meant to shout the words at her, but they came out soft, pleading.

Slowly Aleid floated back down, and her feet landed on the pavement a few yards away. Her eyes were pointed at the ground.

Malcolm dropped his armor. "Why are you leaving?" he asked her.

"I can't stay here for this part. I don't want to hear what you're planning," she said. "Because any plans you make will go against our family. I don't want to hear it, because if I do, then I will have to make a decision about whether to tell my father."

"This isn't even about our family anymore," Malcolm said. "We want to stop the aliens. Don't you want to..." He trailed off, watching his aunt. She wasn't moving a muscle, save for the flare of her nostrils as she breathed in and out. Short, staccato breaths. "What happened? Something happened, didn't it? What don't I know?"

Aleid appeared to wrestle with herself for a moment, then opened her mouth and let out a long breath. "My father and Felix have...they are communicating with the aliens. Felix found a way to speak to them. They have come to an agreement. It's how I have my powers back."

Malcolm hadn't even thought about that. He couldn't imagine his aunt without powers, so when she had flown in, he hadn't thought it through.

"They...they're working *with* the aliens? Even after..." Malcolm gestured vaguely toward downtown, the gargantuan ship perched over the Tower like a spider on its prey.

"Yes." She spat the word through clenched teeth.

Malcolm stood still, frozen by shock. Or...no, he realized. He wasn't shocked at all. He felt like he should be, had braced himself for the feeling of the ground shifting beneath his feet. But it wasn't there.

"Do you know anything about what's happening outside Porthaven? What is the rest of the world doing?"

"Nothing," Aleid said. "They're used to letting the Gravenhursts handle things like this. And as far as they know, we're handling it. Your grandfather told Eric and Mel to assure everyone that things in Porthaven are under control."

Malcolm didn't feel surprised, but he certainly felt the vertiginous beginnings of panic. "You need to help us, Aunt Aleid. You've got to know that's wrong. Help us stop them before they make it even worse."

"I can't, Malcolm." She hung her head, gray hair falling forward to cover her eyes. "Don't ask me to do that." She stood completely still.

Malcolm walked over beside her. "I'm asking you. I'm asking you to do that. We need to stop them."

As Malcolm drew closer, he realized she wasn't as still as she appeared. Her whole body was trembling. What he had taken for stillness looked more like a struggle now, like every muscle in her body was clenched tight.

"He's my father, Malcolm. I can't turn on him. The most I can do is try not to stand in your way."

Malcolm stood there, trying to find words, any words that might change things. He was angry—the blinding, twisting anger that can only be born from love. There were no words that could change this. Malcolm knew it, but he kept searching anyway.

"How is your back?" Aleid asked softly.

"Only hurts when I think about it. So, you know, thanks for bringing it up."

"I am sorry," she said. "I'm sorry I hurt you."

A wet spot appeared on the pavement between their feet. Malcolm frowned and watched as another two appeared beside the first. His aunt was crying. And now he did have the feeling of the ground shifting beneath his feet. A crack opened in the blinding wall of his anger.

"How is everyone?" Malcolm asked.

"Safe," Aleid said. "Melissa and Eric have left the city. Felix insisted on that much."

"And Felix and Grandfather are still in the Tower?"

She nodded her head.

"Aleid, someone has to stop this. It should be us, the Guardians. Please. Help."

Aleid was silent for long enough that Malcolm began to grow hopeful. He reached out a hand, put it on her arm.

"You always thought better of me than I deserved," she said to him. And then she took off into the air, leaving Malcolm and his extended hand far behind.

Malcolm breathed. Found his lungs didn't quite work. He turned back toward the trees and saw Drew watching him. Malcolm took a step forward, then stopped and sat down on the curb.

A few long moments later, Drew came up beside him and sat. "You okay?"

"Did you hear that?"

"Some," Drew said. "Enough." He grabbed a rock from the road, threw it to the opposite sidewalk. "I always thought she was cool. Even though I didn't like the Gravenhursts. She seemed cool."

"Yeah." Malcolm's head sank down onto his knees. "The weird thing is, I still don't hate them. I just feel, like, sad and angry. I feel like I should hate them by now. It would make things easier."

"Easier, maybe. But then you'd be doing this for the wrong reason. Wouldn't be like you." Drew gathered a handful of rocks, picking each one carefully off the ground. He aimed for a speed-limit sign across the street and began throwing them. "Hearing you talk about them weirds me out sometimes. I mean, they're the Gravenhursts. Everyone in Porthaven—in the world—gets pumped full of the legends. The Superfamily. It's hard for me to think of them as regular dysfunctional people. Makes them seem too much like me."

"Like you? I thought your family was fine."

Drew had found the trajectory now, and each stone he threw pinged off the metal sign.

"You see my parents running in here to save me?" he said. "You ever see them trying to stop me from going out at strange hours? My parents have been ignoring me for years—too busy trying to kill each other. And it's not like mine are the worst. Kaz ran away when she was eight. Won't even talk about why. Blair—well, Blair's mom is cool. Might be why Blair's so nice."

"I…I didn't know about your family."

"'Course you didn't. I didn't tell you. But hey, I guess your family was in the right place, with the right privilege, to turn its dysfunction into an actual global disaster."

Malcolm laughed, even while his heart felt like it had sunk down below his stomach. He watched Drew until he threw his last rock. The bruise on his cheek glistened an oily purple. "How's your face?"

"Good. Except now I smell like chicken nuggets. Come on." He gave Malcolm a hand and pulled him to his feet. "Let's go figure out how to stop your family before they destroy the world, huh?"

TWENTY-THREE

Gatekeeper was pacing between the trees while Kazue and Blair sat shoulder to shoulder, watching her. When Malcolm and Drew stepped in, Gatekeeper hurried up to Malcolm.

"Is it true? You couldn't fight it?"

"Um, uh," Malcolm stammered.

"We filled her in on the fight," Kazue said.

"Oh. Yeah. I couldn't land a hit, and they had to save me."

"Was it faster than you? Stronger?"

"Um, no. I didn't think so. It was more like it was always ready for what I was going to do. Like, maybe it read my mind or something? I don't know. It seemed weird."

"Weird that I'm tougher than you?" Kazue asked.

"No, not that. Honestly, I'm not trying to tear you down. It was just…I've trained, like, a lot for this. I'm good at it. But that alien took me apart."

Gatekeeper was back to pacing now. "I wondered if they could monitor us through the drones. Sometimes those signals the klek sent out seemed to carry data. Looks like I was right."

"You mean the aliens still had control of all the klek tech my family made?" Malcolm asked.

Gatekeeper nodded. "Drones, communications, the whole grid. Makes sense. All those inventions the Gravenhursts released were made out of klek parts. Not even rebuilt much, just dismantled and repackaged."

"So the aliens have been watching us?"

"Definitely you, Malcolm, since you've always been surrounded by their technology. So they already know how you fight. But Kaz and Blair are unknown, because they intentionally kept their powers out of the media."

"And because we're poor," Kazue said. "Could never afford a drone."

Malcolm frowned. "Gatekeeper gets to call you Kaz already?" he asked softly. Kazue smirked.

"But that doesn't explain how they took me down," Drew said. "I mean, I got a couple of hits in with my light beams, but they seemed just as ready for me as for Malcolm. Like they knew exactly where I was even when I was in shadow. They couldn't have studied me, though, because I never had a drone either."

"That…that might be something else," Gatekeeper said. She stepped away from Malcolm and resumed her pacing. As she walked, her fingers twitched like they were moving across an invisible keyboard.

"Maybe they watched you through your parents' drones?" Malcolm asked.

"No chance. I never used my powers in front of them."

"Something about the nanites themselves?" Blair suggested. "I mean, we're all covered in them, right? Could they monitor us through those?"

"Then how did we escape their notice?" Kazue asked, wrapping her arm around Blair's waist. "We've got powers, so we've definitely got nanites too."

"Maybe not exactly monitoring through the nanites, but something else about them," Gatekeeper muttered. A moment later her head snapped up. "Tell me how they moved."

Everyone was silent for a moment. Gatekeeper waved her hands. "Data! Data! Come on!"

"Um, it was disconcerting," Blair said. "They reminded me of crabs—you know the way they scuttle sideways? Except worse?"

Drew nodded. "Yeah. They moved like they had no front. They never turned to face you, just went after you."

"No top or bottom either," Malcolm said. "The one I fought flipped over on me and didn't bother flipping back."

"No directional sensory apparatus," Gatekeeper muttered. And then she was smiling. "Oh, that's…oh, *wow*."

Malcolm looked around to see if anyone else understood, but they all seemed just as lost as him. "Wow what?" Drew asked.

"I think I get it. I think—okay, did you see the alien outside my apartment?" They nodded. "I hit it with the same thing I used on you in the bathtub, except I told its nanites to turn off. I thought it might weaken it, cut it off from its power source long enough for me to get away. But you saw it. It shut down completely." Her hands were beating excitedly against her thighs now, *tap tap tap*. "I think the nanites are their senses. Instead of eyes or ears, they have nanites. The nanites are constantly feeding them information about the world around them. I mean, evolutionarily it makes sense. Why use directional senses when you already know where everything is, in all directions at once, thanks to your omnipresent technology? Whatever natural senses they once had, they left behind."

"So the nanites really are terraforming, only they're not changing the atmosphere," Kazue said. "They're sensory aids."

"Drew, that's how they saw through your shadows," Gatekeeper said. "They don't actually *see* at all."

"Okay," Drew said. "But if that's true, it's deeply bad, isn't it? I mean, not only do these aliens have no blind side, but if we want to make them leave, we probably have to destroy the nanites."

"Better than the gate, though," Malcolm said. "The nanites aren't indestructible, right? Otherwise my armor, which is all nanites, would never crack."

"Better?" Drew shook his head. "Maybe we can destroy some of them. But all of them? Trillions of microscopic robots that are everywhere around us? How are we supposed to do that?"

"With Gatekeeper's bathtub?" Malcolm suggested. "Okay, yeah, I heard how ridiculous it sounds as soon as I said it. But maybe with a bigger bathtu—never mind, I'm just going to shut up."

The others didn't have a better suggestion, though, and silence fell. The only sound was Gatekeeper's tapping.

"There was something else weird," Malcolm said. "I have no idea if this is relevant, but—"

"More data is always good," Gatekeeper said. "Say what you were going to say"

"Okay. Well, when I was trying to get to Drew, I did something I haven't done before. Midjump, I kind of sped up, I guess? Maybe even changed direction a little?"

She squinted at him and nodded slowly. "I wondered about that. Think *up* for me."

"Huh?"

"Try to go up."

"Jump, you mean?"

"No. Try to fly. Like your aunt."

"I ca—"

"Just do it already," Kazue said. "Stop arguing."

"Okay. I'll try."

Malcolm thought *up*. Nothing happened. He closed his eyes and imagined himself lifting off the ground, feeling incredibly foolish.

"With the armor," Gatekeeper said.

He raised his armor and did it again, with no effect.

"I told you, I can't—"

Gatekeeper reached forward, grabbed Malcolm around the waist and tossed him upward. And he sailed off the ground, floating into the air like a balloon. He rose until his head brushed the lowest branches.

At first Malcolm thought Gatekeeper was revealing some unknown element of her own powers. But the second he got distracted and stopped thinking *up*, he started to sink back to the ground.

"What the hell?" Drew said, coming closer. "Malcolm, you—"

"Can't fly, if that's what you're thinking," Gatekeeper said.

And sure enough, Malcolm kept moving downward, even when he tried to will himself higher again. But his descent definitely slowed in response to his thoughts.

"What is this?" Malcolm said as he settled gently onto his feet.

"I actually wondered if this might happen," Gatekeeper said. "When I turned your powers back on, I didn't just set things to how they were. The aliens have turned off human powers, so that door's closed. I had to trick your nanites into thinking you *are* aliens. Looks like that gives you more direct control over the nanites. So those hover engines that keep your armor from weighing you down? Yeah, those listen to you now. Not strong enough to lift you outright, but might give you a bit of control."

"Power upgrade," Drew said.

Malcolm closed his mouth. He had been about to say exactly the same thing.

"The rest of you might find similar effects as you get a grasp on your nanites. They should listen closer now, tap into more energy from the gate for you, things like that."

"More energy?" Kazue said. "Maybe quicker battery recharge for me, that kind of thing? How much power can the nanites draw?"

The others started to experiment lightly with their powers—Drew formed one of his rings of spinning light over his hand, Blair began forming multiple shields, and Kazue bent and flexed like she was warming up for a run. But Gatekeeper was standing completely still, only breathing and blinking. Malcolm couldn't remember ever seeing her hold still before—he hadn't known her long, exactly, but it was jarring not to see her fidgeting and pacing.

"Gatekeeper? Are you oka—"

"Shut up," she said. "Trying to think."

Malcolm shut up, waiting at Gatekeeper's side. Her lips began moving, mouthing words silently. It took a bit of time for Malcolm to work out what she was mouthing: *How much power*. Over and over, the same words.

And then suddenly she clapped her hands together. "The early trials!" she shouted. She grabbed a stick, found a bald patch of dirt on the ground and started scratching lines into it.

"The early trials?" Malcolm asked. "What are those?" The others moved closer to watch Gatekeeper work as well.

"Way back at the beginning, we ran trials on the gate to see how much we could feed it safely. They're fuzzy in my memory, because one of the trials went bad. We *overfed* the gate, accidentally gave it way more energy than natural sunlight would. And it..." She broke off to write some long mathematical equations into the dirt at her feet.

"I didn't know people actually did that," Malcolm said, pointing to the scrawls on the ground.

"Closest thing I have to a screen," Gatekeeper said without looking up. "I have to see this to figure it out. We overfed the gate, and it fed the energy through to the nanites. The nanites don't have batteries themselves—they just use whatever power the gate is feeding to them. When we overfed it, first the nanites went into overdrive and made a bunch of klek, and then the whole system shut down. No one had any powers for a few days, which is why I can't remember too well. Whatever the nanites did to my brain was suddenly gone, and all that information..." She waved her hand in the air beside her head, as if the information had literally dissipated. "When we got it going again, the range was seriously decreased. Couldn't use powers even two blocks away from the gate. Took months before it was back to baseline range."

Everyone watched her work, waiting for her to finish her story. But she didn't say anything more, just kept scribbling in the dirt. They all looked at one another, the silence stretching uncomfortably. Finally Drew opened his mouth.

"So maybe the gate is still the answer?" he said. "If the nanites don't have energy storage and rely on the gate, wouldn't shutting that down also shut down the nanites?"

"Maybe," Kazue said. "But that's like breaking a machine by unplugging it. What's to stop the aliens from just plugging in another gate now that they're here? No, I think we need to break the nanites."

"Couldn't they drop more of those down too?" Drew said.

Kazue wrinkled her nose. "Kind of doubt it, actually. I mean, when the gate landed, there weren't that many nanites with it, and they've been replicating using materials they found here on Earth. It took them fifty years to get up to their current numbers. The gate is just one machine, but the nanites are decades' worth of work. Not so easy to replace, hopefully."

As Kazue talked, Malcolm watched Gatekeeper. Her scrawled equations had now morphed into graphs, bell curves and jagged lines running through the dirt in every direction. Gatekeeper was working so fast now that she was sweating. And smiling. She drew one final upward curve with uncharacteristic gusto and then grinned at them, waiting for a reaction.

"Um," Blair said. "What is it?"

Gatekeeper's grin faltered, and her eyes fell back to the ground. "No upward failsafe."

"Which means…" Drew said.

"The gate. It must not have any internal storage either, because it feeds everything it gets to the nanites. And based on that early trial, it looks like it doesn't have an upward failsafe to keep from feeding too much power to them. It must rely on the klek as a deterrent to make people stop before power levels get too high."

Malcolm saw a spark of realization in Drew's eyes at the same time he felt his own. "So when you overfed it and everything shut down, that was actually the nanites burning out?" Drew said.

Gatekeeper nodded. "That explains the decreased range of our powers. A few nanites must have survived, but nowhere near their original numbers. It took them a while to replenish and spread again."

"So we *can* destroy the nanites," Drew said. "And to do it, we need to feed the gate as much as we can."

"Feed it *light*," Malcolm said and grinned at Drew.

"We feed it enough," Kazue said, "it sends the power through to every single nanite in the city and burns them all out at the same time!"

"Or at least enough of them to make this city a lot less habitable for the aliens," Gatekeeper said.

"But before they burn out," Blair said, "we're going to be feeding a machine that makes angry robots."

"Yeah," Gatekeeper agreed. "Sandra and Hendrik could barely contain all the klek it made. And Sandra could handle pretty much anything."

Malcolm thought about his grandmother. He wished he had known her. Wished he had more than the one fuzzy memory of her in his nursery. *It didn't have to be this way,* Malcolm thought. *If my family had made different choices...*

But we didn't, and now we've turned everything into a mess, and other people have to clean it up for us.

"This is something," Drew said, grimacing. "But I'm not sure it's the right plan. Honestly, even if we could use the gate to burn out the nanites, I don't see how we can make that happen. We would have to fight our way through the aliens to get to the foot of their giant spaceship and then survive an avalanche of klek while I pump light into the gate." Drew shook his head. "I don't see how we can do that. The aliens weren't exactly pushovers, and there are a hell of a lot of them. There are five of us."

As Drew spoke, the growing hope on everyone's faces fell again. But Malcolm's head began to spin, trying to work through an idea that Drew's words had sparked. "No," he said. The others looked at him curiously. Malcolm opened his mouth to explain, but for once he couldn't seem to find any words.

"You don't think we can do it?" Kazue demanded, pushing out her chest like she was getting ready for a challenge.

"No. I meant, 'No, there aren't only five of us.'" Everyone looked bewildered. Malcolm took a deep breath, trying to calm the excitement pounding in his chest so he could think this through and explain it in a way that made sense.

"I was just thinking, um, that it sucks how my family made this mess but other people have to clean it up. But maybe *other people* is exactly what we need. Gatekeeper said before that the aliens have been watching my family. Like, all the time, through the klek tech. They know what to expect from the Gravenhursts. So if we want to beat them, we—*I*—have to do things my family would never do. And for decades my family has been…hoarding these powers. Keeping them for themselves, sending away anyone else who has them. And we have a list of the people they sent away." Malcolm looked around at everyone. Blair was taking a deep breath. Drew was starting to nod. And Kazue was relaxing, even smiling a little. "What if we brought them all back?"

"Gatekeeper, your bathtub thing. You still have that, right?" Drew asked.

"Yep," she said, pointing farther into the trees. "But to clarify, it's not a bathtub thing. I just built it over the bathtub. It's not even attached to a bathtub anymore. Just a shower curtain rod."

"But it could do what you did for us? Turn on powers that have been shut off?"

"In theory."

"I really, really, really like this idea," Kazue said.

"And how do we call everyone? Without the grid we've got no phones, no sylfs," Drew said.

"Think I can manage that," Gatekeeper said. "Might have to keep moving. I'd be surprised if the aliens couldn't track our signal once we start making phone calls to the real world."

"But that sounds solvable," Drew said. "This…this actually sounds like a plan that could work." He smiled, and Malcolm couldn't help but smile back. "I know I shouldn't get my hopes up, but—"

"Hell with that," Kazue said. "Get your hopes up. And then let's go kick some alien butt."

TWENTY-FOUR

They cobbled together the equipment Gatekeeper needed to get a signal out. The first time they made a call it took the aliens almost an hour to find them. After that they had twenty-six minutes, like clockwork. No matter where they were in the city, a squad of aliens and klek descended on them twenty-six minutes after they connected. The days fell into a grueling rhythm: set up, make three or four calls, then move again before they were caught. Malcolm's and Kazue's strength let them move the equipment quickly each time, so they stuck close to Gatekeeper. Drew and Blair took on the other part of their task, meeting new arrivals outside the city, bringing them in to safe locations and running them through Gatekeeper's device to get their powers working again.

For Malcolm, evading the aliens was the easy part. The hard part was convincing people to come. Drew had made the first call—to Ibrahim. But after that Malcolm did the calling. He told the others he should do it because his name would carry weight. People might believe him because he was famous. Even if news reports had turned against him, he was still a Gravenhurst.

But really he did it because he wanted to hear firsthand what his uncle had done. What his family had done. With each phone call the weight of it grew. His uncle had tampered with people's memories, stolen from them—not just powers, either, but friendship, loss, struggle, victory, years of their lives lived in joy and pain. Treated people's minds like they were company assets that could be broken up and sold for parts.

Malcolm told them the unalloyed truth. Sometimes it didn't work. People laughed at him, hung up on him, shouted at him, refused to come. Even Ibrahim refused, which cut Drew's wounds open all over again and came close to making Malcolm finally, genuinely hate his family.

But many people did listen. Many knew, in some way that Felix hadn't been able to edit out, that something had been stolen from them. They heard. They believed. And they came back, one by one.

It was grueling work—constantly running, snatching sleep when they could. But even allowing for exhaustion, Kazue seemed more sedate than usual. Her snide remarks dropped off after only a couple of days. Malcolm thought at first she must be saving up her energy, making sure she had strength when they needed it. But as they spent more time together, away from Drew and Blair, he began to wonder if it was something more.

On their fifth day with Gatekeeper, he finally found the courage to ask. Kazue was sitting against the front window of a clothing store, the willowy, headless mannequins looming over her. Gatekeeper was in the parking lot, setting up the complicated machinery used to make their calls. Malcolm walked over to Kazue.

"Hey, um, are you okay?"

She simply raised an eyebrow at him by way of answer.

"I mean, I know I might not be the one you'd want to talk to. But you seem…I don't know. Distracted?"

Kazue grimaced and didn't say anything. Malcolm waited for a while, then turned around to go back to Gatekeeper.

"I'm trying to figure something out," she said behind him.

He turned around again. "Oh?"

"I'm just not sure why I should want to save this damn city. I mean, I'm not cool with weird crab aliens taking over the whole planet, if that's their endgame. But I'd be fine if they ground Porthaven into dust."

She wasn't looking at him as she spoke, and she spoke softly. Malcolm moved closer to hear, sitting against the window beside her.

"The only good things that ever happened to me here were Blair and Drew. I'm just trying to figure out why I should care." She leaned forward, hunching low. "I know they care about this place. Maybe that's enough. I'm sure as hell not going to let them go face those aliens without me."

She fell silent. They sat together, looking out at the city.

"That makes sense," Malcolm said. "Porthaven isn't what I thought it was when I was a kid, that's for sure. I still feel like I love it, just out of habit. I guess…I guess I feel like I'm fighting for what I thought it was? I want to save Porthaven so maybe it can get closer to that." He scuffed his foot against the pavement. "I know that probably doesn't work for you, though, because you always saw it for what it is."

Gatekeeper straightened up from her work. She held out the clunky headset that would let Malcolm talk to yet another person his family had betrayed. He stood up and walked forward.

"Hey, Malcolm?" Kazue said behind him.

Malcolm paused and looked back.

"I see what you're doing. With the phone calls. Still not cool about what happened to Blair, but...I wanted to say I see that."

"Thanks," Malcolm said. "It's hard, but it really should be hard after everything, you know?" He turned to Gatekeeper and the waiting phone.

"Okay, fine," Kazue said to his back. "You can call me Kaz."

Malcolm turned around. "Oh. Oh, okay. Yeah." He smiled at her. She scowled at him.

They kept going for two more days before they exhausted the list of exiles. Set up, make contact, run. Set up, make contact, run.

By the end of the week there were seventy-six of them.

They gathered everyone in the southern rail yard. The aliens hadn't made it this far out yet—not more than klek scouts, anyway. The yard made sense as a hiding place and as a safe space for experimenting with reawakened powers. All of them were there now, spread out across gravel and tracks—Gatekeeper, Drew, Blair, Kaz, Malcolm and the seventy-six people who had agreed to return to see if they could recover what the Gravenhursts had taken.

Malcolm and the others sat atop a rusted black shipping container. From his perch Malcolm could see Kaz's old home, faded red, *JEST* blazoned across it in bright white. There was still police tape wrapped around it. He could also see the crumpled side of the cargo container Kaz had punched him through. A few more holes had been added to it and the containers around it as people learned to control their powers.

Everyone was waiting, still, listening. The crowd was varied. Some who had returned were even younger than Malcolm—the group had refrained from calling anyone too young, but some parents had brought their children with them, and the team hadn't felt they had the right to turn people away. Some were old enough that Malcolm wondered how they had traveled here at all. Nonelectric wheelchairs had been found for those who needed mobility aids, since they didn't want to tap into the ambient grid if they didn't need to. Faces from palest white to richest brown to deepest ebony watched Malcolm and his friends.

No, Malcolm realized. They were all watching Drew. Malcolm turned his eyes to Drew, as did Kaz and Blair.

Drew turned and smiled at everyone—until he noticed that even Malcolm, Blair and Kaz were looking at him expectantly.

"Oh." He looked out at the crowd, pursed his lips.

"Time for a rousing speech, O leader," Kaz said.

"I didn't even like being the leader of our crew," Drew said in a whisper. "This is…" He shook his head. "Kaz, you're smart and kick all kinds of butt. Want the crown?"

"Hell no," she said.

"Blair?"

"We already talked about this, Drew," Blair said. "You're good at this. You should do it."

"Malcolm? I know you're kind of awkward, but—no, never mind. Can't put another Gravenhurst in charge."

"Yeah, no kidding," Malcolm said.

Drew sighed and hung his head. The crowd was beginning to murmur restlessly.

"I know you don't like it," Malcolm said. "Maybe that's why it should be you. I mean, look at my family. That's what happens when people want that kind of power. And people listen to you. You're good at getting them where they need to be. I know you did for me."

Drew looked up at the sky and grimaced. "Okay, fine," he said. "But I'm not lying to anyone. No false hope. I'm doing this my way."

He stood taller and looked out at the crowd. Even though he hadn't said anything, they seemed to sense his attention and quieted down.

"Um, hey," Drew said. "Thanks. For being here with us. It means we might have a chance. But it's only a chance. So the first, most important thing I can tell you is this: Don't fight too hard." His voice carried across the space, echoing off the railcars. "Don't try to beat the aliens or the klek. This is not a war. Because if we turn it into a war, we will lose. They're more powerful than we are, even with all of us here, because they've got the numbers. What we need—what your job is—is to create chaos. Confuse them. Keep them distracted, keep them spread out."

As he spoke a murmur rose up—people throughout the crowd translating his words for those who didn't speak English.

"While you keep the aliens busy, the four of us are going to try to punch through. Make it to the Tower. And then—

well, if it works you'll know. If it doesn't work—if you're still fighting when the aliens really get themselves organized, just get out. Don't even think about coming after us. Get out of Porthaven.

"You'll work in groups—four or five to a team. Make sure every group has someone with some kind of protective power, someone who can take a hit. Those people run interference, try to keep the aliens and klek off the others. The rest of you, make a show. Do some damage. Stir it up, and when it gets too heavy, get the hell out."

Everyone nodded along. Malcolm looked out on the sea of nervous eyes, the set jaws, the held hands. People started talking among themselves, finding others they could work with. It happened more smoothly than Malcolm expected. Those who could fly found their way to the sides of people who moved more slowly. Gatekeeper walked among them, a paper map in her hand, pointing people to where they might help most. And then they were moving.

A full quarter of the crowd lifted off the ground into flight, some carrying passengers. Energy flashed between fingers—blue, green, gold, electric, flaming, otherworldly. A boy with his father took a deep breath, and suddenly his entire body turned a strange pearlescent hue. The world seemed to shift around him, the air warping and refracting light. His father lifted the boy up as if he weighed nothing and put him on his shoulders, the boy's strange aura now distorting them both. A mild-looking woman suddenly grew to enormous proportions and sprouted four extra arms. She gathered up three other people, deposited them on her now-capacious shoulders and began loping away on her arms and legs, like a bear. The entire crowd was fragmenting and moving off among and over the trains, into the city, to face what awaited them there.

Malcolm watched the prismatic display of powers. And for a moment he felt the old excitement—simple, powerful, hopeful. It didn't replace his fear and guilt, but it sat alongside them, untempered.

"So. Frigging. Cool," he muttered. At his side Drew laughed—a small breath, almost silent—and they shared a smile.

"We should get going too," Drew said.

"Before you do," Gatekeeper said, "there's one more thing."

"Bad news? Or strategy?" Drew said.

"Neither. Bad news maybe. Just need to say goodbye." She looked around at their confused faces. "You know those trials I mentioned. When we ended up burning out the nanites? Well, when my powers went…" She huffed, tapped her hands against her legs. "I figure this is going to be a lot like that, except this time it will be permanent. The nanites changed the way I think, you know? Changed who I am. Once they're gone…" She made a small explosion gesture above her forehead. "I won't really be me anymore. Not Gatekeeper anymore, just Darla. Don't even know how much of this I'll remember. So, yeah. Kind of like goodbye."

Malcolm felt like he had been punched in the gut—and from the looks on the others' faces, he wasn't the only one. Kaz looked like she was on the verge of tears.

"I didn't think," Drew said. "I mean, if we lose our powers that's not so…maybe, um, we should—"

"No," Gatekeeper said, her habitual scowl returning. "This might be a surprise to you, but not to me. I knew this was coming. Still the right plan. And don't worry about me. I set things up. Whoever I am after this, I'm gonna be taken care of." She scanned all of them. "But even if I'm different, if you wouldn't mind coming to see me, telling me who you are, who *I* was…"

"Of course," Malcolm said. "We can help remind you. Get to know you again." He smiled reassuringly, but there was an ache lodged under his ribs that didn't fade. None of this would have been possible without Gatekeeper. And she'd done it all knowing she was erasing herself.

"Excuse me," said a gravelly voice below them. They looked down to see the father with the pearlescent boy on his shoulders. It was hard to look at him for too long, the way light refracted around him.

Drew took a deep breath, gathering himself. Gatekeeper was already climbing down off the container, taking the opportunity to leave without further sentiment. "Um, yeah?" Drew said to the father.

"My boy was just wondering how careful we should be. Because we think once he gets going, it might be hard to control."

Drew jumped down to the ground in front of them. "Well, I mean, watch out for each other. But if you're talking about collateral damage to the city? Buildings and things?" The father nodded. "Yeah, I wouldn't worry too much about that. No one is left in the city except us and the aliens."

Even through the warped air, Malcolm could see the grin that split the boy's face. "Okay. Thanks," the father said and jogged off to join the rest of their team.

Drew stretched his neck from side to side, then looked up at Malcolm and the others. "Plan's still on, even if it stings. Gatekeeper gets to make that choice, not us. So let's go get this done, yeah?"

They all ran together, no one carrying anyone, moving at an easy pace. They needed to let the others get ahead, let the action start, so they would have a better chance of reaching Gravenhurst Tower. They ran side by side down the empty streets of Porthaven.

The first sign that things had begun came from the west. There was a boom, and a mid-rise building shook and then crumbled.

"Um," Malcolm said.

"Wow," Drew said. "You think that was the shiny kid?"

"I like him already," Kaz said.

After the boom the city seemed to come alive around them. Streets that had been silent except for their footfalls a moment before now echoed with clicking, shouting and the crashes of battle. A beam of golden light shot into the air far to the north and then blinked out.

"I guess it's on," Drew said, gesturing everyone to move faster.

They made it into downtown before they saw any aliens. The sounds of combat were loud all around them now, and up ahead they could see klek and aliens thronging the street. Dozens of them, the klek ranging from lapdog-sized to two-story monstrosities. And they weren't being drawn away by the fighting.

Malcolm and the others slowed to a stop. They were within ten blocks of the Tower now, but Malcolm couldn't imagine how they would reach it through all this. He checked his armor nervously. It was good to go.

Kaz and Blair nodded to each other, and Blair hopped up on Kaz's back.

"Stay back a bit," Kaz said over her shoulder to Malcolm and Drew.

"Why?" Drew said. "What are you doing?"

They were too focused to answer. Blair had her hands outstretched over Kaz's shoulders. She pulled them apart to make one of her force fields. Then she shifted her hands and pulled again, and again. The field grew until it filled the street from wall to wall. The aliens and klek had noticed them now, and the klek were surging forward.

"Just keep up," Kaz said. She bent her legs and started running.

Malcolm let Drew hop onto his back and took off after her. It took everything he had to keep up as she ran full tilt down the street, shouting like a thunderstorm, legs flaring with light.

The force field hit the first rank of klek at the speed of a bullet train, and the robots came apart. Silvery limbs and bodies skittered off the shimmering barrier into the streets on either side. Kaz barely slowed. Klek jumped up, trying to escape by climbing the walls, but Blair simply stretched her field higher, catching them all.

Over his shoulder, Malcolm heard Drew laughing. "How long have you two been planning this?" Drew shouted.

"I've wanted to do this since Blair and I first kissed," Kaz said.

Up ahead the klek were beginning to thin. Malcolm could see the Tower on the other side of them—a hole where the front entrance had been, the legs of the alien ship planted on either side of it, humming with violet light. And between their team and the Tower, Malcolm now saw aliens gathering. There were dozens of them. As the force field barreled toward them, the aliens dug their claws straight into the pavement, and each one raised two of its thick legs.

Blair's force field met the rank of aliens and stopped as if it had hit a wall. Kaz gritted her teeth and pushed harder. The aliens slid back a yard, digging furrows in the street with their claws, and then stopped again. Malcolm let Drew down and came forward, pushing against the force field. Once again the aliens gave way, but only so far.

"Blair?" Kaz said through her clenched teeth. "Think it's time?"

Blair nodded. "Malcolm, watch yourself," she said, as she pushed one of her outstretched hands forward and pulled the other back. The stories-tall force field tipped forward and came down on the aliens, crushing them into the pavement. Then the field dissolved, and Blair took a deep, ragged breath as Kaz let her down onto her feet.

The aliens were disoriented, and some had cracks in their metal plates, but they were rising again. Kaz raised her fists in a fighting stance, and Blair, regaining her composure, created two force fields in front of her hands.

"Malcolm, you get Drew in," Kaz said. "We'll handle these things."

Malcolm nodded. As Kaz and Blair ran forward, side by side, he stepped back to where Drew stood.

"Think you can handle one last jump?" Malcolm asked.

Drew grimaced. "Yeah. Dammit." He let Malcolm pick him up.

Malcolm aimed himself above the fray—high above, as Kaz was throwing the aliens into the air two at a time—and leapt. They came down on the other side of the battle, the hole in the face of the Tower yawning in front of them like a mouth. One of the aliens turned toward them, and Drew sent a lance of white light into it before it got close. He got down from Malcolm's arms, took a couple of deep breaths and then nodded to Malcolm. "Let's do—"

Something emerged from the Tower—or rather someone. Malcolm almost didn't recognize his uncle. Felix looked haggard, sunken. He seemed decades older than when Malcolm had last seen him, his dark suit hanging forward from his stooped shoulders. But there was Malcolm's grandfather at Felix's side, tall and stern, the same as ever.

"Malcolm!" he roared. "Enough!"

Oh crap, Malcolm thought. *Of course. Of course they're here. Of course I would have to...why didn't I think...*

Drew laid his hand on Malcolm's elbow, only the subtlest pressure discernible through his armor. "You need to step back for this one?" he asked.

Malcolm's lungs felt shrunken in his chest, inadequate for the size of his body. He stared at his family, letting the confusing blend of anger, guilt and lingering love wash through him, and took a breath. "No," he said to Drew. "Um, no, actually, I think I should do this myself. I mean, don't get me wrong, if I can't do it, then take them apart. But maybe give me a minute? To try?"

Drew looked uncertain, but he nodded. "I'll see if I can help the others."

"Yeah. Yeah. Okay."

Malcolm walked forward. His eyes gravitated to Felix, his thoughts a storm. Every story he'd heard from the exiles reverberated in his mind, the echoes of stolen memories hidden in their interstices. And yet. Here Felix was—shrunken, broken—but still the closest thing to a father Malcolm had ever had. The man who had talked him through nightmares. Who had watched him train and applauded as he came to grips with his growing powers. Who had a smile that he gave only to Malcolm.

There was no smile on his face now. His eyes did not even meet Malcolm's.

"You have caused enough harm," Malcolm's grandfather said, and Malcolm turned his eyes reluctantly from Felix to look at his grandfather. "Stop this. Tell these others to stop, before you undo everything."

Malcolm gritted his teeth. "Really?" he said. "Are we going to do this again?" He took a step forward. "Because we've had this talk, Grandfather. You tell me I'm a child and don't know anything, and I tell you you're doing the wrong thing. I thought maybe we didn't need to do this again."

His grandfather's scowl deepened. "You assume you know everything. But this isn't the threat you think it is. We have been negotiating—"

"With the aliens. I know."

For once his grandfather looked surprised. And it occurred to Malcolm that his aunt wasn't there. Maybe she had decided to leave. It wasn't the most helpful choice she could have made, but it was something.

"Then you should know things are well in hand," his grandfather said. "Our family has been promised safety if—"

"No, we really don't need to do this again." Malcolm started walking forward faster. "So if you're going to sic Uncle Felix on me, just do it already."

His grandfather sighed. "This is disappointing."

"No kidding," Malcolm said.

His grandfather turned and nodded to Felix, who seemed to shrink another few inches.

"Father..."

"Now, Felix. He's giving us no choice."

Felix slowly turned toward Malcolm. His eyes met Malcolm's with such pleading that for a moment Malcolm stopped. His uncle looked withered, but his eyes seemed young—childish, frightened, alone—and Malcolm couldn't turn away.

"Malcolm, I...I didn't want—"

"But you did anyway," Malcolm said.

Felix's eyes flickered down to the ground for just a moment, then came back up and met Malcolm's. "Let...let the words I speak stir your memories," he whispered.

And then the itching began. Malcolm could hardly see the ground beneath him as he fell forward onto his knees, could hardly feel the impact as his present was buried under a flood of memories.

Something was different this time. The flow of memories was more erratic, more random. Before, it had been like being submerged in a river of images and sounds. Now it felt like a whirlpool.

He saw Drew, the first smile he'd ever given Malcolm. He saw his cousin Melissa, looking impatient as they made their way down the red carpet at another one of Eric's premieres. He heard the clink of plates at Sigmund's deli during a busy lunch hour, tasted dough and tomato sauce on his tongue.

He saw a memory he recognized and grasped it, holding it like driftwood in the flood.

He was seven, and his grandfather had scolded him for being disrespectful in front of the mayor—an event Malcolm had pleaded not to attend. Malcolm sat in the grand ballroom, leaning against the windows and staring out at the glimmering green light of the Porthaven skyline. Felix sat beside him and said nothing, but his long-fingered hand rested on Malcolm's back.

For a moment the torrent of memories ebbed, letting Malcolm catch his breath. He focused himself and found another memory, lunging for it through the swirl of noise and light that threatened to drown him.

He was walking into his room. A couple of days earlier he had finally convinced Felix to give graphic novels a try—he'd reluctantly picked *Squirrel Girl*. And that day when Malcolm walked back into his room after lessons, he found Felix sitting on his bed with several volumes spread out around him, laughing quietly to himself. Felix looked up sheepishly, but Malcolm just grinned and picked up one of the volumes for himself.

The flood of memories was definitely slowing now. Malcolm kept going, forging his way through his mind to some of his deepest, warmest memories of his uncle. Moments of pride Felix had shared with him. Moments of loss when Felix had comforted him. The smallest moments— shared looks across the table, the feeling of being curled in his lap as a child, the feel of his fingers as he adjusted Malcolm's tie on the day he became a Guardian. Malcolm gathered them up and held them tight, and slowly his mind cleared. The itch receded to the base of his neck and then vanished, and Malcolm could see the ground beneath his knees. He felt none of the shakiness he'd felt the other times his uncle had used his power on him.

"I can't," Felix was intoning. "Father, I can't, I can't."

And as Malcolm finally stood up—still shaky but strong enough to keep moving—his grandfather growled under his breath.

"Then I will do it, as I always must." And all around him the world began to come apart.

TWENTY-FIVE

The ground beneath his grandfather's feet crumbled and lifted into the air. Concrete fractured into stones, stones fractured into dust and flowed toward him. Broken fragments of the klek, thrown here by Kaz and Blair's attack, joined the flow. The front of the Tower, glass and steel and stone, dissolved, and all were absorbed. And when the cloud of particles cleared, Malcolm saw his grandfather again.

He loomed over the street, a colossus made of concrete and silvery metal, run through with narrow ribbons of glass. The face was a crude caricature of his grandfather's, on an immense scale.

Malcolm stopped walking forward. "Umm…"

"I was trying to build a future for you," his grandfather said, his human voice jarring in that inhuman face. "But you have chosen otherwise." And he slammed a fist the size of a car down on Malcolm.

Malcolm was driven into the ground, and the pavement beneath him cracked. With his grandfather's enormous hand pressing down on him, Malcolm felt for a moment like he was in that collapsing mall again, pinned under rubble.

But his armor held, and as he pushed up, the fist lifted slightly, letting light back in around him. He struggled onto his feet, heaved his grandfather's fist higher, and scrambled out from under it.

He looked up and saw his grandfather advancing on him again, felt the *thud* of his footsteps. Felix was shouting, but Malcolm couldn't hear him through the ringing in his ears. His grandfather didn't slow. He raised a foot and brought it down toward Malcolm. Malcolm leapt away, crashing into a nearby building and barely righting himself before another foot came down where he had fallen. He dodged to the side, pivoted and brought his foot up to kick the side of his grandfather's ankle. The blow opened a crack, pieces of concrete and glass tumbling out. But as soon as they fell, the pieces floated back up again, reabsorbed into his grandfather's body.

"How the hell am I supposed to—"

But he had no time to consider strategy, as another fist came down at him, followed by a swiping backhand. Malcolm dodged them both.

His grandfather hadn't had martial arts training like the rest of the family had, relying instead on his size and endurance for combat. *Maybe I can use that. Use his own weight and momentum against him.* He wasn't sure that concept still applied when your foe was several stories tall.

"Believe it or not, Malcolm, I'm not trying to hurt you," his grandfather said. "Because, as foolish as you may be, you are still family. And family has always been the most important thing to me. If you continue to press this, to threaten my plans, I will use what force is necessary. But you can choose to stop fighting whenever you wish."

Malcolm jumped forward and punched him in the shin. There was a *crack* as a large piece of stone calved off, falling to the ground. The wound didn't close so fast this time.

With a sigh, his grandfather attacked again. Malcolm wove back and forth, avoiding his grandfather's blows. The ground was shattered all around him now, an obstacle course of rubble. He watched for an opening and finally saw it when his grandfather brought both hands down in an open-palmed slap, trying to flatten him. His grandfather would be unbalanced, Malcolm's training told him. He dodged the hands, then leapt forward. He landed on the curve of his grandfather's calf and struck the back of his knee as hard as he could.

His grandfather didn't move an inch.

A spiderweb of cracks spread out from Malcolm's fist, but almost as soon as they opened they began closing again. And before Malcolm could strike a second time, huge fingers wrapped around him and slammed him to the ground.

His grandfather's face bent low. "I have sacrificed for this! Your parents sacrificed for this!"

"My parents died for a mistake! For a mistake you're still making!" Malcolm shouted back.

"You will not be allowed to undo everything our family has—"

There was a blur of blue, and his grandfather's head suddenly rocked to the side. Both Malcolm and his grandfather turned their eyes to look at Aleid, who was now hanging in the air beside them.

"Aleid? What are you—"

She struck again, sheering away the lower half of his stony face with a flying punch, and then curved around and came in for a third strike. This one crumpled the silvery metal of his left cheekbone.

"Aleid!" Malcolm's grandfather roared.

"Felix!" Aleid shouted. "Do it now!"

And there was Felix, walking up beneath his sister. Tall, determined, dark eyes clear and focused on Malcolm's grandfather. The Felix Malcolm knew, not the sunken man he had seen at his grandfather's elbow moments before.

"Let the words I speak stir your memory!" he shouted. "Sandra! Heleen!"

Malcolm's grandfather moaned, closed his eyes and tipped sideways. As he fell, Malcolm felt the hand that held him against the ground coming apart, crumbling back to dust. By the time his grandfather hit the ground, he was just a man again, half-buried in the rubble that had formed his body. Aleid and Felix advanced on him. Malcolm saw him struggling, but he didn't rise.

"Is he...?" Malcolm began, coming to join them.

"I took nothing," Felix said. "But I sent him down a rabbit hole of memory that, I suspect, will swallow him for quite some time."

"You saved me," Malcolm said. "Thank y—"

"No," Aleid said. "Don't say that. We didn't save you. We almost let you die. We almost let everything..." Her words were for Malcolm, but when she raised her eyes from her father, her gaze went immediately to Felix. Their eyes locked and did not shift. "Do what needs to be done, Malcolm. Please finish this."

Malcolm nodded. He wanted to say more, but all around him he could hear the sounds of battle. Behind him,

Drew, Blair and Kaz fending off the aliens and klek. Beyond them, in the wider city, the booms and shouts of the others who had returned to reclaim their powers, to save their city. He located Drew at the edge of the melee, firing beams of white light at a cluster of aliens, and jumped in beside him.

"All done?" Drew asked. "Is it time?"

"Yeah."

Drew let the beam of light on his fingertips die and turned to run with Malcolm toward the Tower. Malcolm took a moment to check on Kaz and Blair, but they were clearly holding their own. Kaz was grinning from ear to ear and throwing the aliens back like they were toys. Blair was wielding one of her force fields like a cudgel, batting the aliens away as she shielded Kaz from attack.

Drew and Malcolm ran past Aleid and Felix, who were now digging their father out of the rubble, and clambered over the fractured concrete at the foot of the Tower. Down below, half-hidden in shadow, they saw the gate. Its silver filaments glimmered and shifted subtly.

"Okay," Drew said, tracing a line with his eyes from the gate to the sky. "I could maybe use a little more clearance. Think you can widen this hole?"

"On it," Malcolm said.

"Good. Then after that just keep everything off my back as long as you can."

Malcolm nodded and dug his hands into the rubble below him. He pulled at the foundations of the Tower and the street beyond, prying up huge slabs of concrete. He aimed a few at the aliens still sparring with Kaz and Blair, and was gratified to see at least one alien pinned beneath the slabs. He cleared a wide ramp down to the basement, digging deeper and deeper until he felt Drew's hand on his shoulder.

"Okay," Drew said. "Good enough."

Malcolm moved back as Drew raised his hands out to his sides. Malcolm couldn't help but blink hard as the world around him dimmed, his body telling him his eyes must be failing even when he knew they were fine. The sun above them seemed to waver as the light bent itself, answering Drew's call and flowing in around him. For a moment Drew glimmered as if he were under a spotlight, and brilliant motes of light danced around him. Then he brought his hands forward, and a river of golden light poured down onto the gate.

The reaction was instantaneous. In the street behind Drew the air shimmered, and then klek began to form as if out of nowhere. Their silver bodies gleamed in the now dusky light. Their clicking reverberated off the tall buildings, filling the street with a cacophony of sound. Malcolm leapt between them and Drew, and they came at him.

They swarmed him, but he didn't falter. He lashed out, grabbed the leg of the nearest klek and swung it in a wide arc, knocking the wave of robots back in a mass of thrashing silver legs. When they rushed him again, the little ones came first, clambering up his armor and trying to weigh him down. He leapt several yards in the air, thought *down* and landed flat on his stomach, the weight of his body crushing the klek beneath it. A split second later he was on his feet again, moving constantly, catching each klek that tried to reach Drew and sending it back into the crowd.

The fighting never flagged, the klek appearing as fast as he could smash them. He didn't have a moment to think. And yet he almost felt comfortable in the midst of it. This was what he had trained to do—what he had envisioned for himself—and here he was, doing it in service of his friends. This was what he'd thought it meant to be a Guardian before he had really become one.

When the klek stopped, he stumbled, momentarily disoriented. He spun, looking for more of them, but there was only glittering wreckage around him. He looked at Drew, who was still pouring light down on the gate. But the river had narrowed to a single beam.

"Drew?"

"I'm not getting enough light!" he shouted over his shoulder.

There was a grinding sound above them. Malcolm looked up and barely managed to leap away before a huge column of metal came down right where he had been.

He rolled over and looked up again. For a moment he thought he was looking at the leg of the largest klek he had ever seen. But then he noticed the seams running along it, the violet lights that ran up and down, pulsing like a heartbeat. He followed the leg to its origin.

"Malcolm? What's happening over there?" Drew said. "I'm gonna need that sun back."

"Um…" Malcolm stared at the place where the sun had been, now eclipsed by the alien ship that had left its perch atop the Tower. "I don't know if—"

"Just do what you can!" Drew shouted. "I need more light!"

"Uh, yeah. Okay," Malcolm said, getting onto his feet. The ship was directly over him now, standing on its five legs. Barbs and what looked like cannons were clicking into place along those legs, emerging from hidden hatches in the dark plating. Malcolm saw it towering above him, and the sight echoed another image in his memory. A grainy picture of a monstrous klek with one silver leg embedded in the opera hall. His grandmother, glowing with endless energy, more like a fire than a person, fist raised in defiance to the hulking creature. *Better to burn bright.*

Every nerve in his body was ringing, telling him to run. He could hardly think through the mental noise, the panic he felt racing through his veins. He felt like he was two again, everything around him too bright and confusing. Like he was sinking backward in time to the night of the giant klek attack, when he had lost half of his family.

And then he remembered his grandmother's face when she had come into the nursery, hugged him close. He'd felt so confused at the time. She hadn't looked brave. His unshakable grandmother had looked scared and sad. Hesitant.

And she'd gone out there anyway. Burned bright, and fought, and died. Malcolm took a few quick breaths, in and out forcefully. He looked back at Drew. *Some things are worth it.* And he leapt straight up.

TWENTY-SIX

One of the ship's legs bent inward to meet him. Malcolm's stomach dropped. The leg was as big as a skyscraper itself, and seeing it move toward him set off every warning light in his head. But instead of turning away, he aimed himself at the leg, focused on his momentum, and willed himself straight into it. His stomach lurched as his direction changed midair.

He hit the leg just below a cluster of barbs. Dark plating crumpled under his fists, violet energy sparked and crackled against his armor. And then he was through, tumbling into a hallway. He got to his feet.

All around him were walls that, sickeningly, looked like the bodies of the aliens—pink flesh interwoven with silver metal. The hallway spiraled away from him on either side, tilted upward to his right.

He wondered if he might be able to do more damage from inside. But even as that thought formed, he heard countless footsteps, coming from both directions—not the clicking of klek, but the solid pounding of alien feet.

I don't think this is where I want to be. He turned and faced the hole he had just made in the wall, sighted another one of the legs and leapt back out.

As he crossed the gap between legs, rising and then arcing down, he saw some of the cannons swiveling toward him. *Up,* he thought. *Up, up!* Three beams of green energy passed frighteningly close below him, carving lines into nearby buildings.

He reached the other leg and embedded his arms into the dark plating. Above him there was another cannon, already turning toward him. He reached up, gripped it and pulled it out of its housing, then leapt sideways.

By now more of the cannons were tracking him. He shifted his momentum as swiftly as he could, wavering through the air. Most of the blasts missed him, but a few found their mark and pinged off his armor. They didn't break it, but the hits threw his trajectory off enough that he landed directly on a cluster of barbs. When he hit them, two of the blades snapped off, but he heard his armor crack too. The remaining barbs started scrabbling at him, digging in and pulling him tight against the ship's hull, opening more rifts in his armor.

He struggled for a moment to turn himself so he might grab at the blades, but he couldn't. So he punched forward instead, tearing through the ship's outer hull. He found himself in another hallway, this time spilling out almost directly on top of an alien. It raised its legs to grab at him, but he bounced off it and scrambled farther down the spiral hallway. Once he had enough momentum, he threw himself back through the wall.

As he cracked through the outer hull, he reached out and grabbed on, swinging around and embedding his other fist in the ship's metal plates. He looked up, gauging distance, and jumped again. This time he aimed for the central body of the ship.

He collided with the bottom of it, and as he did, the cannon fire eased off. Malcolm gave himself a moment to breathe. But the underside of the ship came alive almost immediately, hatches whirring open as countless multi-jointed arms emerged, each tipped with a jagged blade. They grabbed at him, but Malcolm kicked them away, dangling by his arms and lashing out in all directions with his feet. Once he had cleared a space for himself, he swung his legs and kicked them into the ship, freeing his arms to tear a way inside.

But there was no inside. He punched in two feet deep and still found only the dark metal. He dug in five feet, six, until he had burrowed almost completely into the ship's main body, and nothing changed. *This isn't working.* He paused, breathing hard. *I need to think.*

As soon as he stopped, he felt panic. It had been there all along, but he'd held it back by keeping himself moving. Looking down from where he hung on the underside of the ship, he could see the damage he'd done to its legs. Those vast legs, each a skyscraper in itself. The holes he'd punched through them looked like nothing more than scuffs. Like he was trying to destroy a car by keying its paint. And his armor was already cracked. He couldn't beat it this way. He needed to think. Thinking meant panic. *My grandmother was the most powerful of the Gravenhursts, and it took everything she had to beat the giant klek. This thing is even bigger. How do I beat an entire alien spaceship?*

He looked down at Drew, visible from this height only by the thin ribbon of light he was still pouring down on the gate. The shadow of the ship still lay across him. And the aliens looked closer now. He could see the blue flashes of Blair's force fields out in front of them, but there were more aliens now, it looked like. He cast his eyes out across the fractured rooftops of the city. He could see the occasional flash of light from battles farther away, but there seemed to be fewer of them. And in the streets he could see aliens and klek hurrying back to protect their gate. His team didn't have long, and Malcolm couldn't move something this big with only brute force. But brute force was all he had.

He refocused on the ground. He could see the pile of rubble that had been his grandfather's body. His grandfather was gone, and so too were Aleid and Felix. But he stared at the rubble as a previous thought came back to him.

What was it Drew said to everyone? Don't try to beat the aliens. I don't need to beat the ship, I only need to move it. Use its weight against it.

He looked around, focusing through his panic. He checked the position of the five legs, figuring out which held the most weight, and started clambering along the bottom of the ship toward it, punching new hand- and footholds as he went, fighting his way through the bladed arms that emerged everywhere around him.

Finally he reached the leg and pulled himself up on top of the joint where it connected to the ship's body. A cannon emerged just in front of him, its mouth glowing green, but Malcolm kicked it off the hull. He spared himself one look down at his friends.

The aliens were almost on top of Drew now. And there was something else. One of the ship's other legs was moving, joints bending slowly as it lifted itself toward Drew. Cannons were pivoting.

"Oh crap."

Malcolm jumped up as hard as he could, willing himself higher. And then, at the crest of his jump, he shifted his thoughts. *Down.*

With a lurch he started hurtling downward. He stretched his arms out in front of him and pointed his legs skyward, turning himself into a spear, a missile, soaring like his invincible aunt Aleid. He put everything into the fall, hurtling down faster and faster. *Down. Down.*

When he hit, he sank deep into the metal of the joint, dark plating rippling out to form a crater around him. The entire ship shifted, leaning sideways into the skyscraper beside it, and the leg that had been moving toward Drew came back down to try to right the ship. The building the ship had fallen against cracked and began to crumble, but the ship stayed upright.

Malcolm pulled himself out of the metal. Violet energy crackled across the plating around him and pooled at the bottom of the crater like liquid. He'd torn deep into the joint, but it wasn't broken. And as he stood up he felt the armor across his arms and shoulders crumble. He took only a moment to process that before leaping again.

This time when he reached the height of his jump, he shifted his armor upward, leaving his legs completely unprotected. He layered everything over his head, his chest, his arms, and he curled both arms over his brow. He squinted between his forearms as he began his return trip down, spurring himself faster and faster, aiming and adjusting his momentum to hit at the exact epicenter of the crater he had made.

Faster, he thought. *Please.*

He struck, and everything vanished in a storm of violet sparks and dark metal shards. There was a deafening rending sound all around him, like the metal itself was screaming. And then he felt air on his face, and he pulled his arms away.

He was dangling from the bottom of the joint, staring down at the ground far, far below him. He reached to grab at the metal above him and noticed that his right arm was slow to respond—like it was half-asleep.

The joint was sheared through save for a narrow column of dark metal where Malcolm hung. The top of the leg, cracked and broken, dripped violet sparks into the air. He'd moved the ship, and he could see the sun halfway down the Tower now, still not quite reaching Drew. He sighed, took another look at the street below and focused himself.

He mustered his armor. There was barely any left—a thin sheen over his chest that he moved to his leg. Then he held on tight to the one remaining column—as tight as his tired arms could manage—and kicked. And kicked again.

The last column joining the leg to the ship's body snapped, and the ship lurched. The leg started to fall away as the ship stumbled after it, moving out and away from the Tower. And as it tilted, Malcolm lost his grip.

He was falling from almost a hundred stories up, with nothing to stop him, no armor left to protect him. No powers, no clever maneuvers.

I'm going to die.

It isn't such a bad way to go, he thought. At least he'd made a few friends before he died. Fought a fight he knew, at last, was worth it. He wondered if Drew, Blair and Kaz would mourn him. He hoped Drew wouldn't blame himself. Maybe Malcolm's sacrifice would spur them all to greater heroism. He could be their tragic backstory.

As he turned slowly in the air, he tried to catch sight of what was happening below. He could see the base of the Tower, bathed now in sunlight. He couldn't see Drew anymore, only a blinding stream of light, so bright it might have been a piece of the sun itself. Malcolm looked away, and through the streaks burned into his retinas he saw a small form arcing above a mass of aliens. It might have been Kaz or a rogue piece of rubble.

He looked out at Porthaven, trying to take everything in, but he was lower now and all he could see were the shattered skyscrapers around him. He would never look out from the Tower's ballroom again. Never see the glimmering curve of Lockheed River. Never eat another calzone from Sigmund's. Or eat anything, for that matter.

The ground was getting close now, and his thoughts felt like they were coming apart. His mind was split in two. Half of it was a blinding glare of fear and panic. The other half felt placid, disembodied. Like it was already dead.

When he felt hands under his shoulders, it took a long, long time for his mind to come back together, for things to become coherent enough for him to understand. He looked up and saw his aunt Aleid, teeth clenched as she gripped him tight and tried to slow his fall.

"Aleid?"

"No dying today," she said. "Not for you. Not because of me."

"Umm, okay." He still felt disembodied. It was hard to get his tongue to work. "We need to get to the ground though."

"I want to get you somewhere safe first," she said.

"Yeah," Malcolm replied. "But you're about to lose your powers."

As soon as he said the words, Aleid veered downward, making Malcolm's stomach lurch and snapping things back into focus. It was still a long way to the ground, and everywhere beneath them, as far as Malcolm could see, aliens and klek carpeted the streets. The excess light from Drew's beam cast them all in searing relief, shadows of spindly legs and thick bodies dancing across walls of the buildings around them. Malcolm glanced up. The ship was already righting itself on its four remaining legs, moving up toward the sky, the sun.

Aleid shifted suddenly, and Malcolm snapped his eyes back down. They were still at least ten stories in the air.

"Aleid? I think you're about to—"

"I felt it," she said, adjusting to a gentler angle. But she seemed to be slowing as they flew, struggling to maintain their altitude. They were five stories up. Four. Three.

Malcolm felt a sharp sensation on the side of his neck and brought his hand up. And then the same sensation repeated itself everywhere—tiny sparks, flashes of heat, crackling across his body, under his skin. He groaned.

Above him, his aunt screamed.

He could see something sloughing off her hands, glittering dust that left a visible trail in the air behind her.

The nanites, burning away. His aunt's scream stopped, and her hands went limp under Malcolm's arms.

"Aleid? Aunt Aleid!" Malcolm shouted as they both fell.

He landed hard on his back. The air left his lungs, and stars filled his vision. He felt himself slide farther down, coming to rest in what felt like a fissure in the road. Except it was warm. And, he realized with a jolt, it was moving.

He blinked hard, trying to clear his vision, and saw aliens on either side of him. He pushed futilely at their pink skin and silver metal plates. He couldn't move them. But after a moment he realized they weren't pushing back. They were barely moving at all, only vague shifts and twitches to show they weren't dead.

Slowly he pulled himself onto his feet. His legs didn't want to hold him, and his back screamed for him to lie down, but he climbed up and over the form of one of the aliens until he could see the street around him. There was Aleid a few feet away, tangled in the broken legs of a large klek. He pulled himself over to her. Her eyes were closed, but she was breathing. There was a gash across her shoulder, and for a moment the surreal sight of his invincible aunt's blood made him dizzy. But he took a steadying breath and turned away.

Ahead, in the street closer to the Tower, someone was moving. Blair was shouting something, pushing hard against the fractured wreckage of a klek. It shifted, and she was reaching down, and then there was Kaz, struggling to her feet. They embraced.

"Drew?" Malcolm tried to shout, but his voice wasn't up to the task. He couldn't see anyone at the base of the Tower.

He stumbled forward over the wreckage and the still forms of the aliens until he spilled down onto the pavement and dragged himself the last few yards to the mouth of the hole in the Tower's base. There was thick black smoke coming out of it—and from the broken windows above, he saw. Gravenhurst Tower was on fire.

He crawled across the fractured concrete, whispering Drew's name, until he heard someone coughing. He hurried forward and found Drew on his hands and knees, eyes squeezed shut against the smoke. Malcolm laughed in relief, but the lungful of smoke he got left him coughing too.

"Drew," Malcolm said once he could breathe again. "Are you okay?"

Drew didn't answer, but his hand reached out at the sound of Malcolm's voice. Malcolm gripped it, pulled Drew's arm across his shoulder and hauled them both to their feet. As he did, he caught sight of Drew's face. One of his cheeks was a mottled red and black—a burn worse than any Malcolm had seen outside of movies. Malcolm groaned and gripped his friend tighter as they stumbled out of the smoke and into the clear air of the street. They fell to the ground and rolled onto their backs.

Drew took ragged breaths, and his coughing finally slowed. "Did…did we…" he said, voice hoarse.

Malcolm surveyed the scene around them. The aliens were still unmoving, and the klek lay dead on the ground. Kaz and Blair were walking their way, hand in hand. Malcolm raised his arm and tried to put up his armor. Nothing happened. It was like trying to flex fingers that just weren't there anymore.

"Yeah. You did it, Drew." Malcolm let his hand fall again—it didn't feel any heavier than usual, but he was so tired that it might as well have weighed a ton. "Man, you should have seen yourself. Light pouring out of you like you were a star."

"Me? You moved the whole damn alien ship."

They both turned just enough to smile at each other. Then Malcolm grimaced. " 'Course, it's still got four legs. And we don't have powers anymore."

Drew nodded, and they both looked up. The ship was above them, standing tall once more, its hull alive with violet light. Malcolm watched its cannons, but they didn't swing their way. The ship simply stood there, stock-still, outlined against the sky.

"Think it's going to kill us now?" Kaz asked as she came up to them and sat down on the ground by their heads.

"Dunno," Drew said. "Looks like we gave it something to think about, at least."

"Should we get out of here?" Blair asked.

"Later," Drew replied. "Too tired."

"Okay," Blair said. "But I think the ship's still dangerous, and now Gravenhurst Tower is on fire, so maybe we sh—"

With a *clunk*, a large hatch came open at the base of one of the ship's legs. Malcolm forced himself to sit up, spurring another round of coughing. Kaz and Blair got to their feet, and Malcolm tried to follow suit, but he was driven back down to the ground as the ship started emitting some kind of signal. It wasn't so much a sound as a sensation. Malcolm felt it at the base of his skull, a painful, electric humming that made his muscles clench.

Out of the corner of his eye he saw something move. He struggled to turn his stiff neck and watched the aliens rise to their feet en masse.

"You've gotta be kidding me," Kaz said. She looked like she was struggling too, but she was still on her feet. She bent her knees and raised her fists, ready to fight.

But the aliens didn't come for them. Instead they all started toward the hatch—madly, desperately, crashing together, crawling over each other. Some limped while others scuttled faster than Malcolm had ever seen them move before. They thundered through the hatch by the hundreds, until none of them were left in the street. The hatch closed, and the sensation stopped, and Malcolm could stand again.

And then he realized they weren't alone in the street. Coming through the wreckage of fallen buildings and destroyed klek were the others, the seventy-six people who had been fighting all over Porthaven. They looked battered and exhausted, but they kept coming, wary eyes on the ship.

With a groan, the legs of the ship bent outward all at once, its body dipping down. Malcolm wondered if it would come low enough for those bladed arms to reach them— or maybe simply drop down and squish them flat. But it stopped a dozen stories above them. And suddenly the legs straightened themselves, throwing the ship into the sky. The violet lights on the hull flowed faster, shone brighter, and it was sailing up, up, past the shattered crown of Gravenhurst Tower, past the blue of the sky, until it wasn't even a dark blotch above them.

"Holy crap," Kaz said. "They left. We did it."

She whooped and leapt into the air, fist raised to the sky. All around them, in the street and beyond, they heard voices shouting, crying out in joy and relief. Malcolm would have cheered too, but just the thought made him feel tired. He settled for grinning madly at his friends and laughing when Kaz tried to bend Blair down in a dip and they both ended up on the ground.

"You know you're gonna have to talk to people now," Drew said, struggling to sit up next to Malcolm. "I know you don't think you're good at it, but people have got to hear what happened. What the Gravenhursts did. You'll have to tell them."

"Yeah," Malcolm said. "I know I will." Strange, he thought, that he could feel nervous about simply talking after everything they had faced. He shook off the thought and reached out a hand to clasp Drew's. Drew took it and then pulled Malcolm into an unexpected hug.

"Everything hurts. And I think I burned half my face off. But…that was awesome, Malcolm."

"Yeah," Malcolm said, returning the hug as best he could with his aching arms. It felt good, even as it hurt, and he let himself linger in it. Everything that came next might be huge and confusing, but this small moment felt good. "Thanks, Drew."

They released each other, still smiling, and turned to gaze at the city. It looked hollowed out—like it had been a ruin for years, not just days. Malcolm thought back to his birthday, the moment he had stood in the ballroom and looked out at Porthaven. His excitement. His love for it. His feelings now were a lot murkier. He didn't know if he was happy or heartbroken to see it in this state. He looked up to where the ballroom had been. It was gone now, crushed by the ship when it landed. And the rest of the building didn't look like it would last long, the way the fire was spreading.

"Dude, your grandfather is going to be so mad at you," Kaz said behind him.

Malcolm laughed. It ached all the way up his spine, but he couldn't stop himself. He laughed until it tingled in his fingers and his eyes watered.

TWENTY-SEVEN

Two Months Later

Malcolm nodded to the prison guard behind his plexiglass window. The guard pressed a button to buzz him through the locked door. Malcolm passed through into the visitors' area and heard the door lock behind him again.

He went straight across the room to the small table at the far end, under the row of opaque windows. His usual spot for his morning interview. The journalist was already there, of course—she always showed up early. Her name was Julia, though he couldn't remember which newspaper she worked for. Of all the reporters who had come to see him, she was the only one who had started right off with hard questions. *How could you not have known sooner? Why didn't you try harder to go public?* While he'd asked the guards not to let the rest back in, she kept her access. And she had been waiting here for him every morning for two weeks.

She didn't look up as he approached, instead setting her phone to record the conversation and digging pen and paper out of her bag. As she finished and placed the phone down on the table, she finally looked up at him and smiled.

"How are things today?" she asked.

Malcolm shrugged as he sat. "About the same as yesterday. Things don't change much around here. Which is kind of nice, actually."

Julia smiled wryly. "Can we start?"

"Me first," Malcolm said. "That was the deal. You said you'd bring me information today."

She sighed. "We've only got half an hour. They really don't give you newspapers in here?"

Malcolm shook his head.

"Okay, let's make this quick. They're still trying to figure out what to charge you with, since this situation is kind of… unique. Some are leaning toward fraud, some are trying to legislate something new, but—"

"That wasn't what I asked for," Malcolm said. "I didn't ask you for information about me."

She squinted across the table at him. "Okay. Just thought you'd be curious."

"Like you said, we only have half an hour."

"Yeah. Um, your grandfather saw his first trial yesterday. For insider trading. Pleaded not guilty."

Malcolm snorted, then nodded for her to continue.

"He's got himself a good lawyer, despite all your family's assets being frozen. But I don't think it will stand up to the paper trail that, um…" She flipped through her notes. "… Darla Gutiérrez has on him. She's not much of a witness, since her memory is pretty fuzzy. But she had the evidence all lined up before her powers went."

"Gutiérrez?" Malcolm said. "I never knew her last name. She wanted us to call her Gatekeeper."

"Oh, because of the…right. Colorful. Your aunt Aleid is backing her up. She's a cool customer, huh? Your grandfather started shouting at her in court and she just kept testifying like she couldn't even hear it."

"Yeah. That's Aleid. What about Felix?"

"Still refusing to talk to either side. Not saying anything at all, from what I could find out."

Malcolm nodded. He felt his stomach twist. He'd learned, in the past two months, how ludicrous guilt could be. He knew without any doubt that he was doing the right thing by laying his family's secrets bare. And yet he still felt guilty for it, knowing how much it was hurting his family.

"Melissa's in trouble alongside your grandfather for the business stuff. The investigators are still piecing together how much she knew and how much your grandfather kept from her, or…or had Felix erase."

Malcolm winced.

"Sorry, I know you don't like it when I bring that up," Julia said.

"No, no, it's okay. I mean, it makes me feel gross, but I don't want to pretend it didn't happen."

Julia nodded. "Speaking of which, more people have started recovering memories. I guess now that Felix's power is gone, its effect is fading. That means the prosecution has a lot more potential witnesses."

"That's good. That's really, really good. Um, what about Eric?"

"He seems to be doing okay. He was never involved in the business stuff, which leaves him in about the same situation you're in. Except he's not in jail, because they don't have anything to charge him with yet and, unlike you, he's not staying in custody voluntarily. But he hasn't fled the country or anything." She gripped her pen and sat forward. "Now can we—"

"What about my friends?"

"I thought they came to see you. Can't they answer your questions?"

"They did come by. It's been a while. I guess it's busy out there with everything. And…I like to hear about them. So please, just quick."

Julia shrugged. "They're mostly keeping private—I mean, as much as they can. Oh, the other day some people came forward claiming to be Kazue's parents. Don't know what's going to come of that yet. The media loves your friends, and the other people who fought the aliens can't stop talking about you all. Drew especially."

She squared her shoulders like she was bracing for something, and Malcolm sighed. He knew what was coming. "You know, if you put yourself out in the media a bit more, it could help when it comes time for your trial. I could arrange a camera—"

Malcolm shook his head. "No. If you want someone to be a public face for this, you'll have to convince Drew. Or Blair, or Kaz. Though you can pretty much assume Kaz'll say no. I just—this is enough. These interviews."

The journalist's shoulders sagged, but she bounced back quickly. "Okay. My editor would have killed me if

I didn't try at least one more time. Anyway, is that good for now? Can we start my questions?"

"Sure."

She flipped back one page in her notebook. "We got up to the last battle, right? After the aliens left. What happened after that? How did you guys get out of Porthaven?"

"Walked," Malcolm said. "I mean, everything in Porthaven was built around the alien tech, the nanites. And those were gone. We spent some time trying to find an old—I mean, sorry, *normal* gas car. Even tried to get one of the older trains running. But the tracks all ran on the ambient grid too. So we walked."

"Walked? Everything had been evacuated for a hundred miles around the city. I think the official reports said the police met up with you in…" She leafed through her notebook. "…Maddersville? That's a long way to go on foot."

"Yeah. It was a few days of just, like, walking along the road. We thought we'd meet up with cars sooner than that. Thought people would come running once the ship left."

"Everyone was too scared, and still waiting for the Gravenhursts to give the all clear. Must have felt pretty awful for you, traveling like that. I mean, I've seen footage of the way you used to jump. Practically flew."

"Honestly? I kind of loved it. It was just me and my friends, and nothing was trying to kill us. Not that I don't miss the powers or anything—I totally do. But walking wasn't so bad."

"You miss the powers?"

He nodded.

"Have any regrets about what you did? You've had some time to think now."

"No. Not regrets. Just missing them."

The questions continued for another twenty minutes, with her checking the clock on her phone intermittently. When they only had a couple of minutes left, she squared her shoulders again.

"There's something else I want to talk to you about. Think of it as friendly advice. You need to get yourself a lawyer." Malcolm was already shaking his head. "No, I get what you're trying to do, Malcolm, but you shouldn't be reckless about this. Throwing yourself on the mercy of the court when you don't even know what they're going to end up charging you with is...Look, you're not a fool. But you're doing a damn good impression of one right now."

"No," Malcolm said. "No, no, really. I know it might not go my way, I know that, but...my family took something that wasn't theirs. They—we kept a threat to the world secret because it made us powerful, rich, famous."

"But you didn't—"

"Even if I didn't make the decision, I definitely benefited from it. They screwed over everyone around them while I got the rewards, and it almost cost us *everything*. At this point I feel like the only moral thing I can do is throw away any power I have, as hard as I can. Make myself small, like I should have been from the beginning."

"I'm not saying plead not guilty, or try to find loopholes, just someone to advocate..." She trailed off as she watched Malcolm's face. "What do your friends say about all this?"

"Not much. I don't want the whole conversation to be about me when they're here."

Julia tightened her lips. "Well, I'm not them. But if I were, this wouldn't be what I want you to do. It's not about giving up your power, Malcolm. It's easy to play the sacrificial victim. The hard thing is to take what power you have and use it to make sure things change." She shrugged. "But I'm not them, and I'm not you. Up to you how you want to play this."

Malcolm looked up at the window. Nodded. "I guess I felt like I shouldn't have had any power to begin with, so..." He sighed. "I'll think about it. What you said."

She glanced at the clock. "Time's up anyway. I need to go home and compile all of this. If I have follow-ups, can I come back?"

"Sure, yeah. You know where I'll be."

They both stood and shook hands, and Malcolm lingered as she gathered her gear and made her way out through the visitors' exit. This room was one of the sunnier ones in the detention facility, so he liked to stay as long as they let him. But once the door closed behind Julia, he turned and walked to the inmates' door, where he waited behind the really tall kid who always came out to see his mom in the mornings. Once the door opened, they both stepped through, back into the bland interior. Back into the routine.

"Malcolm," said a voice. It was the guard behind the plexiglass. "Stay out there. You've got some people who were waiting for their turn."

"Huh? Oh. Okay." He turned around.

Drew and Kaz were just coming through the door on the other side of the room. Malcolm's breath caught, and he practically ran to them.

"Hey!" he said. "Hey! Um, wow, it's awesome to see you."

"Yeah, you too, man," Drew said. The bandages were finally off of his cheek, and Malcolm could see the burn scar their final battle had left behind. It was big. But somehow it only made Drew look more heroic. "I can't remember, are we allowed to give you a hug, or is there, like, a no-touching policy?"

"What? No, no, this place isn't too rigid."

Drew put his arms out and gave Malcolm a quick hug. Malcolm glanced at Kaz, but she shook her head.

"I have my own personal no-touching policy."

Malcolm smiled at that. "Is Blair okay? Is she coming?"

"Stayed home today," Kaz said. "She started to remember some things this week. Which is awesome, but it gives her headaches. She figured you would understand."

"Oh yeah, totally. That's so great, that she's starting to get her memories back! Should we sit down?"

"Sure. Is there somewhere we can be a bit, um, private?" Drew asked.

"Not exactly, but..." He led them back to the table where he and Julia had just been sitting. It was the farthest away from the doors, and a couple of tables away from other visitors.

"Okay," Drew said. "If this is all we got." The smile had dropped from his face, Malcolm noticed.

"Everything okay? I mean, are you guys doing okay? Kaz, I heard about some parent thi—"

"Nope, not talking about those bozos," she said. "But, I mean, generally we're doing fine. Blair's mom is letting me stay with them."

"Drew? What about your parents?"

"Might be the first time I actually have their attention," Drew said. "My dad's lawyering up, just in case there's some spillover from the Gravenhurst stuff. But in general things are pretty okay. All of this, what we did, is a distraction from them hating each other. So things are better for now. But that isn't why we came, actually."

"Oh?"

Drew glanced around at the other people in the room, but they were busy with their own conversations. He leaned forward and dropped his voice. "Blair's memory isn't the only thing that's started to come back. Have you noticed anything, like, weird?"

"Weird how?" Malcolm asked.

Kaz grunted. "That would be a no, then. You'll have to show him."

"Why me?" Drew said. "Why can't—"

"Because they don't usually like it when you break stuff in jails."

"I guess that's fair," Drew said.

"What are you guys talking about?" Malcolm said.

Drew pursed his lips and put his hand out flat on the table, palm up. "This."

The light from the windows above them flickered as if there were clouds passing by. But the light on Drew's hand grew brighter, illuminating the brown of his palm, until it coalesced and formed a tiny, almost invisible ring of golden light. It hovered over his hand for a few seconds, and then he shook it away.

"Whaaaaaaaaaaaat…" Malcolm said.

"Yeah. Exactly. And it's coming back with Blair and Kaz too. You haven't noticed anything?"

"No. But I haven't really tried." Malcolm shook his head. "It doesn't make any sense. The nanites are gone. We aren't even in Porthaven anymore. How would—"

"Just try it," Kaz said.

Malcolm nodded and sat forward in his chair. He reached for that missing part of himself. And at first nothing happened, but it felt unquestionably different. Like he had reached for that phantom limb and found flesh and bone there—not a lot, but a little. He concentrated harder, and slowly something unfolded from his skin, forming a pale, geodesic shape just large enough to cover three of his fingers, thin as paper.

He stared at it, then at Drew and Kaz. The same mixture of fear and excitement he felt was mirrored in their eyes.

"Um. What the hell does this mean?"

"We don't know," Drew said. "But maybe it's time you got out of here. We might need your help."

ACKNOWLEDGMENTS

This book was a journey for me. It took years, and countless drafts, and it would never have made it to this point without the help of a lot of wonderful people.

Thanks to everyone who kept me writing and spurred me on when I stumbled, especially Logan Lawrence, Amber Wiggins, and of course my wife, Alexis Arbuthnott.

Thanks to my mentor and friend Kathleen Wall, as always, for wise words, invaluable insight, and reminders that if you want to finish a novel, you had best take care of yourself along the way or you'll never make it.

Thanks to all the wonderful people at Orca for taking my words and polishing them to a shine. My editor, Tanya Trafford, who helped me see the parts of the story I had lost sight of; Vivian Sinclair, my copyeditor, who saved me from publishing a book that was half commas; Dahlia Yuen, the designer; and Ruth Linka and Andrew Woolridge, who make Orca a company that I'm proud to work with.

And thanks, last but not least, to anyone who reads this book. You're the ones who get to decide what the world will be next, and I can't wait to see it.

SHANE ARBUTHNOTT's debut novel, *Dominion*, was nominated for multiple awards, including the Kobo Emerging Writer Prize. That novel's sequel, *Terra Nova*, published in 2018, also received great critical acclaim. His short fiction has appeared in *On Spec* and *Open Spaces*. Shane grew up in Saskatoon, Saskatchewan, and now lives in Regina with his family.